AMANDA BOOLOODIAN

A.I.R.

STOLEN
SIGHT

BOOK THREE

Printed in the United States of America
Copyright © 2017 by Amanda Booloodian
Published by: Walton INK

ISBN-10:0-9973353-5-1
ISBN-13:978-0-9973353-5-4

Walton INK
www.Booloodian.com

Book cover designed by Deranged Doctor Design.

Dedicated to silver, even though...

CHAPTER 1

W HOSE IDEA WAS IT TO relocate a nymph into a sorority house?" I asked as we drove away from Zeta house.

"I'm pretty sure that was her own idea," Logan said. "Felicity has a good head on her shoulders, though. Nice girl. Which other Lost do we have on our list for the day?"

"That's it."

"We're not seeing the fairies?" He seemed bothered by the idea. As one of the Lost, a being from another dimension, Logan was particularly active in checking up on everyone he could.

"Usually the changelings take more time." I took out our tablet and looked through today's calendar. "Want to head back to the Farm?"

"Let's manage the paperwork from home. Washington is in town. I'd like to avoid the bureaucracy."

"We are the bureaucracy."

The Agency for Interdimensional Relocation, AIR, had changed in the past few months. At least the office had. Being more high-tech came with the price tag of extra visits from government committees.

"Who ever heard of a portal review?" Logan asked. "They either work or they don't."

"They're probably checking the logs. Who's visiting this world, who we're sending back, that sort of thing. I think it's good that someone is stopping by from time to time."

Logan didn't say anything. Last winter, our previous boss had put me on a hit list so he could maneuver illegal activities with less chance of being caught. That resulted in him being dragged into a dimension of demons and my soul being shattered into countless pieces.

For Logan, the less government involvement, the better. I still couldn't decide if he was overly paranoid. One of his sons seemed to be following in his footsteps. Maybe elves were just naturally like this.

Still, when I powered down our tablet, I put it into a case that blocked all transmissions in and out so that if our superiors wanted to jump on and listen to our conversations, they wouldn't be able to. It was a gift from Logan and I figured it was better to be on the safe side. A little paranoia could be healthy.

"Does Margaret need us to take care of anything while we're in town?" Logan asked.

"No, Gran's out with Dee Dee today. I think they're shopping."

"Want to head out to the Sanctuary and check in on the fairies anyway?"

"Hmm," I said, trying to buy some time. I looked at my partner who was smiling and humming under his breath while he waited for my answer. Elven smiles were practically a contagion. "Yeah, we can go there." He was using the fairies as an excuse to ride the horses. That was usually the case.

Logan started singing an old cowboy song under his breath and changed directions to the Sanctuary. I didn't have to hear the words to know that the song was about cowboys. It was always about cowboys.

My phone rang and Ethan's name popped up on my caller ID. I smiled but hesitated to take the call in front of Logan. Logan was on good terms with Ethan, but they weren't friends.

"Go ahead and take the call from your lawman," Logan said.

I grinned and hit the talk button.

"Hi, Cassie," his voice sounded strained.

My smile sank. "What's up?"

"Look, I, uh, know we don't talk about your job." He stopped, and I heard him cover the phone up and begin speaking to someone else. "Sorry about that," he said when he got back to me.

"What's going on?"

Logan stopped humming.

"I might have a case that I need your help with, or at least your opinion on." Ethan didn't sound happy about the prospect.

"Sure, where do you need us?" I asked.

He told me the address. "Sorry about this, Cassie."

"It's no problem."

"You might not say the same thing once you get here."

After we hung up, I typed the address into our GPS. "Do you mind if we swing around?" I asked Logan.

"We could do that. Seems awful strange for the local law to drag in outsiders," Logan said.

"It does."

The thought of working with Ethan wasn't a comfortable one. He didn't know who I worked for beyond the Department of Treasury. Our first meeting a few months ago hadn't started out well, but it ended with him asking me on a date. Technically, we hadn't worked a case together, which made it easier for the confidential information to stay out of our relationship.

"Does he know about you?" Logan asked, keeping his voice casual.

"My abilities? No way. I'll leave that out for as long as I can." My last serious boyfriend, fiancé really, tried to have me committed when I told him about my abilities. I'm not one of the Lost, but I'm not your ordinary human either. Everything leaves a trace as it moves through this world, and as a Reader, I see the trails that are left behind.

I was thankful that Logan let the subject drop.

"Lots of construction going up around here," Logan said.

"It seems like there's construction everywhere around town now," I said.

"Looks like we've found our address," Logan said, stopping on the side of the road.

Apartment buildings were being erected all around us. We couldn't go any further due to the sheer number of police vehicles. Since we were visiting Lost today, we were in a regular car instead of our usual SWAT-style truck.

We approached the crime scene tape and we were immediately stopped by an officer.

"This is a crime scene. Please return to your vehicle and leave the area." The scorn in his voice was palpable.

"We're federal agents. Lieutenant Ethan Parker contacted us," I said.

"You're an agent?" the man snorted. "Likely story. Move along."

Logan tensed beside me. People's first reaction to me was never a pleasant one, just one of the many side effects of a damaged soul. Once people got used to me, they got over it, but Logan always took those first reactions personally.

When I went to get my ID out of my back pocket, the officer put his hand on his gun. Moving much slower, I took out the ID and handed it over.

"This looks like it came from a cereal box," the guy said, tossing it back at me, "move along."

Sometimes, I hated being me. Usually, I could take the rudeness with a grain of salt. Having a shattered soul made me stronger than I had ever been in the past, so I let the downsides slide off, but being at my boyfriend's civilian crime scene had me anxious already.

"Listen here, you pompous—"

"Officer!" Ethan barked from beside a large piece of yellow construction equipment with the letters CAT on the side. "Stop screwing around and let them through!"

The officer looked surprised and stood aside. Logan lifted the tape and we walked onto the official crime scene.

Ethan appeared glum when we approached. "Agent Seale," Ethan said, shaking Logan's hand. He hesitated when he turned to me. "Agent Heidrich." He gave me a handshake too.

I guess that put us squarely in the professional category today. At least Ethan had the sense to appear uncomfortable using my last name. Still, I thought we were past the stage where he called me "agent."

"Lieutenant," Logan said, "what do you have for us today?"

Ethan took off his sunglasses and looked at us. "It's pretty muddy back here. I should have given you a heads up about that."

Behind him, a large sheet had been pinned down to the ground to keep from blowing away.

I frowned, knowing there was probably a body underneath. "We're good, lieutenant."

He flinched slightly when I said lieutenant, but he was right. At a crime scene, business is business. Maybe it's best to keep it professional.

"Right, we have one body. White male. He was found by a crewmember who arrived this morning."

"This morning?" Logan asked, raising an eyebrow.

"Yeah, we're getting ready to move him now. I wanted to hold off till you got here. We, uh, initially held off to find the rest of him."

"Pieces missing?" I asked, trying to keep myself from grimacing. Ethan nodded.

"We'd better take a look," Logan said. "Everything around the body been processed?"

"Yeah, you're good to go. Listen, Cassie, maybe you shouldn't—"

"Lieutenant," Logan interrupted, "we don't know each other well yet, but here's a friendly warning. It might be a good idea to drop that train of thought before it goes any further."

My face was already red. Ethan was going to suggest I stay away, not look, or something equally stupid. Lips pursed, I ignored both of them and stalked over to the cloth.

A year ago, I would have flipped the covering over to prove I had no issues. I was a month shy of completing my first year in the field. Seeing that this scene covered a wide patch of ground, I knew better than to charge in. Instead, I walked to the edge of the cloth, knelt down, and waited for Logan to join me. This gave me a moment to ready myself.

"Let's see what we've got," Logan said.

I lifted the cloth.

Red. There was a lot of red scattered over the ground. It wasn't the bright red that you'd see on TV or in the movies.

Instead, it was a ruddy color that covered the grass and soaked into the ground. The stench released from under the cloth made me swallow hard and use my jacket to cover my nose and mouth. It took me longer to identify pieces. My mind didn't want to focus. Closest to me, a pool of pale flesh puddled together. Skin and muscle littered the ground. Ragged strips of flesh looked torn and shapeless.

"We're not sure what exactly happened here," Ethan said, keeping his voice low, "but the ME has looked things over and we've scoured the area. Tentatively, we're calling it an animal attack."

Shaking my head, I lowered the cloth and as one, we moved away from the remains.

"You think that's what it was?" Logan asked.

"There's a lot of bone missing. What's left doesn't show any bite marks that we've seen yet, but I can't think of anything else that might be able to do this. In the case we worked together this spring... well, this seemed odd as well, so I thought you all may be able to give us more," Ethan said.

"What do you say, Cassie?" Logan asked.

"Weird is right up our alley," I mumbled. Louder, I added, "We can take a look, but I think we need Rider."

"I'll call him in." Logan tapped his head. "Wait for me before you get started."

He walked off to call our sometimes partner, Rider Wolfe. As a werewolf, he would be able to pick up smells that might help us identify things we might overlook. The head tap is the part that made me nervous. It was only natural that he would want me to read the Paths in the area. With a death that violent, I was afraid of what I might see.

Then there was Ethan. Using my power meant that he'd see me wandering around following trails invisible to anyone but me, and that's if I was strong enough to control all the forces inside me. With the added difficulty of pieces of souls from various Lost swirling around, it made things volatile and unpredictable at the best of times.

"Cassie, I'm sorry to drag you into this," Ethan said.

He had waited until Logan was out of normal earshot range. Ethan and I had never learned how to work together while seeing each other, and I had hoped we wouldn't have to. Ethan looked so worn, though, that I knew it would be worth it to help if we could.

Forcing a smile on my face, I said, "You're doing your job. If we can help, we will."

"Yeah, but it's a hell of a thing to invite someone you see personally into something like this."

"Rider's on his way," Logan said, returning, "and I called Hank to get us logged in." He turned to Ethan. "Hope you don't mind, but I also let your officer know that we'd be expecting company."

"That's good. Not sure what got into him earlier," Ethan said.

"Did you all find anything else on site?" I asked, steering away from the officer. I didn't want anyone to get into trouble.

"We're not too sure about that. Since we don't know what or who we're dealing with, it's hard to say," Ethan said.

"You found something?" I asked.

"Mostly the usual construction stuff, but there's something the work crew noticed. It's down this way."

Ethan led us to the end of the new street where we stood around a hole dug for a walkout basement. It appeared that people were getting ready to pour concrete.

"What are we looking at?" Logan asked.

"The crew put down some rebar yesterday," Ethan said. Seeing the confusion on my face, he added, "The metal poles. They strengthen the concrete. They poured piers, which help with stability. You can see where the concrete is coming up out of the ground."

"Sure." I nodded and let him continue.

"The rebar they laid over here looks the way it should," Ethan said, "but over there, it has been moved around. That wouldn't be a big deal, because it's easy to move, but there's also a hole that wasn't there before."

Logan's forehead wrinkled. "A hole?"

"Yeah, we can circle around if you want, but it looks like someone dug a hole." Ethan shrugged. "It's out of place, so I'm not discounting it. It has already been photographed. We're getting ready to see how deep it is."

"Let's go down and check it out," I said. It was better than going back to the body and it didn't add up. Why would Ethan think a hole was important?

My boots were coated in mud by the time we made our way around the building site.

"Any luck?" Ethan asked an officer nearby.

"No, sir, it looks like it drops a few feet then slants back. We're having a hard time getting pictures since there is an angle in the space."

"Thank you," Ethan said and turned to us. "Nothing much we can say. It could be nothing."

"Do you wanna take a look?" Logan asked me.

"Uh." I took a quick look at Ethan. "I can."

Logan nodded. "Ethan, could you do us a favor and meet our colleagues and bring them down here."

Ethan looked carefully at Logan, but nodded his head slowly. "We can do that. Officer," Ethan said without taking his eyes off Logan, "would you meet the feds and bring them this way?"

"Sure thing." The officer walked away.

Logan waited until the officer was out of hearing range. "You've got to tell him sometime."

"Do I?" I meant for that to sound sarcastic instead of an actual question. Logan hadn't left me much choice by saying that in front of Ethan.

Logan shrugged.

"You're right," I said. Apprehension dug into my stomach.

"You need backup?" Logan asked.

Ethan had his arms crossed. He didn't look upset, but alert.

"No," I said, "but we could use a few minutes."

CHAPTER 2

E THAN LOOKED AT ME EXPECTANTLY.
"I was really hoping to avoid this, or at least be somewhere," I gestured around at the construction site, "more private."

Still, Ethan didn't say anything.

I plunged in. "Right, you already know that my job can be out of the ordinary. What you don't know is that I am out of the ordinary."

He smiled and started to say something.

"No, that came out wrong," I said.

"Whatever it is," Ethan said, moving closer and putting an arm around my waist, "you can tell me. If you want to give me the short version here, we can pick it up somewhere private later."

I felt heat rush to my cheeks, but it was good to feel his arm around my waist. Comforting, even.

"First off, I'm not crazy." I looked at him and tentatively waited for a response.

"Not crazy. Got it." It looked like he understood the seriousness of the statement.

"But the thing is, I can see things that other humans can't. It's a skill that comes in handy with my job." I looked away from him and tried not to throw out the words as fast as I could. "I can see things that others can't see. Traces of where people or things were in the past, or what someone's feeling."

He was silent for a moment. "I'm not sure I understand."

"Everything leaves a Path in this world. I can follow those Paths and get information from them, even if what or who left the traces is no longer there."

"That sounds pretty useful."

I blinked at him, completely taken off guard by his reaction. "I see things that aren't there. Well, they are there, but no one else can see them."

"I'm not going to pretend I understand what it is you're saying, not completely, but I understand your sincerity, and I can see by those around you," Ethan nodded towards Logan, "that they know about this."

"They do," I said uncertainly.

"I don't know what your job entails, but it seems to me you wouldn't have gotten to where you are if your partner thought you were crazy. At least not in law enforcement of any type."

"That's true," I said. I wasn't sure how this turned into Ethan assuring me that I wasn't crazy, instead of me convincing him.

"It sounds like a useful tool."

"It can be," I looked away, worried about how much to tell him, "but things have happened in the past year that have made it unpredictable. That's why Logan thought it would be best for me to tell you. A year ago, I could probably have gone by completely unnoticed, but now it's hard to say."

He tugged me closer to him. "Maybe we can get together sometime soon and you can fill me in." It hadn't been a hug, but more than I thought I'd see on a job site with everyone around.

I looked up at him. "You're really not put off by this?"

Ethan chuckled. "I'm still not really sure what *this* is, but I believe you, if that's what you mean."

My tension started to fall away, and I smiled at him. "I'm really glad I said yes to that date a few months ago."

"So am I."

At that moment, I really wished we were alone. I wanted to wrap my arms around his neck and kiss him, but with the crime scene not too far away, it wasn't the best time.

"I guess we should get to work." Regret filled my voice.

Ethan moved his arm and gave my hand a reassuring squeeze, then stepped aside.

"We're ready, Logan." I didn't bother raising my voice. I knew Logan could hear everything we said. Elves had exceptional hearing, even when their ears were tucked away to look more human.

Logan joined us, grinning ear to ear. "You're a good man, Ethan." To me he added, "Feeling better now?"

"Yeah. I think that will make things easier," I admitted. "Still, do you have a dart?"

"You think it's a good idea for me to dart you here in front of your boyfriend?" Logan glanced from Ethan and back to me again, clearly unsure.

I shrugged and looked at Ethan. "It may seem odd, but know that whatever my partner does, he does it for a reason and I trust him."

Ethan looked more confused than ever, but nodded.

Thinking that this was a lot of effort for one crime scene, I walked over to the large hole in the ground. Logan and Ethan were close behind. Closing my eyes, I dredged up thoughts of the known world and stretched my mind beyond. There was a short mental struggle where my mind didn't want to move past what it truly knew to be real.

Usually, things were much simpler.

Much faster too.

Pushing myself further, I felt the familiar snap as my brain made the jump. I held back the raging flow of the Path before it became too much to handle and allowed only a trickle of the energy to come through. Blinking, I opened my eyes to a whole new world. Shimmering rivers of colors twisted through the landscape.

Lots of light blue tones gave the impression of crewmembers going about their work, but in a bored, monotonous way. I caught the pluming gold colors of Logan out of the corner of my eye. I avoided looking at Ethan altogether, afraid of what it might show me after our conversation.

Looking out over the site, I mostly saw what I expected, but there was a distinctive Path that stood out from the others. It was gray in color, but throughout it were fine threads weaving in and out, which were a multitude of vivid colors. Yellows danced outward and purple stretched. Each time they were engulfed once again by the larger gray Path. There was even a glimpse of a shining teal color, which I couldn't recall ever having seen before.

"I think something was here," I said. Looking into the hole, I could see the palest of gray leading inside. I stood up and scanned the area for evidence of what had made the marks. "But it doesn't make much sense."

"Is something buried down there?" Ethan asked.

I looked at the Path leading away from the hole, seeing that the gray grew darker. The sight of it made my stomach clench. Closing my eyes, I pressed the Path away. The shimmering colors melted away leaving the dullness of the real world behind.

"Um…" I looked at Logan, unsure of what to say in front of Ethan.

"Why are you standing in a graveyard?" Rider's voice came from close by.

I looked up, thankful for the distraction. My best friend and sometimes partner was standing well away, looking uncomfortable.

"It's a construction site," I said. "They could be digging holes for buildings."

"Ethan," Logan said, "I'd like you to meet our colleagues. You've met Rider, and that fella over there is Vincent."

Oh shit. That single thought filled my brain for a few moments before I plastered a smile on my face and moved toward the group. Vincent was the man that had wrecked my soul. It had been an accident, and he had only been doing his job. Now we partnered up together from time to time while he tried to figure out how to fix what he had broken.

Not that I held any of that against him. The *oh shit* sentiment had more to do with Ethan and Vincent meeting. Ethan had no idea that Vincent and I had almost dated. Vincent, however, knew about Ethan. To know was one thing, to see it may be altogether different.

Since Vincent was an agency-sanctioned assassin, I had been hoping to keep the two apart.

Vincent's eyes were tight when they were introduced, but when Ethan put out his hand to shake, Vincent didn't avoid it. The moment their hands touched, fury and misery slashed across the landscape. Even without opening the Path, the strength of the emotions felt suffocating.

Vincent and I almost became a couple, and it wasn't fair that he still felt this way. We resonated together like nothing I had experienced before, but before we came together, he had pushed me away and decided that we wouldn't see each other.

This was his choice.

Then Vincent took a step back from Ethan and watched me. I could see the concern lining his face and the feeling began to lift. He must have bottled up his feelings again.

Rider watched his partner carefully. Besides me, he was probably the only other person that noticed. As a werewolf, sometimes he could sniff out things like that.

Ethan looked from Vincent to me. Maybe Rider wasn't the only one that noticed.

"Let's saddle up and get this show on the road," Logan said. "Cassie, what do you have for us?"

I looked at Logan, confused for a moment as my worlds collided. "Right. There was definitely something in this area. No idea what it was. I'd have to follow it to see if it's related at all."

Logan raised his eyebrows at my succinct wrap-up. "Anything more specific?"

My partner wasn't going to let me skate by on this one.

"I've never seen anything like it. The Path leads away from the hole, but I don't see anything leading to it beyond the police, crewmen, and us. I'm hoping Rider can help us out further," I said.

Rider's nose flared. "There are workers, policemen, and objects. Workers for days, over and over again."

"Can you tell if there was anyone out here last night?" I asked.

Rider began to walk carefully over the area. His nose wrinkled by the hole. "Your smells are most recent. Several humans from earlier this morning. Yesterday, late day, there were people as well. In between, I can sense nothing else. There were objects only."

"Do we know when the victim died?" Logan asked.

Ethan shook his head. "We assume it was sometime last night. With the remains being the way they are, we can't know for sure at this time."

"Do we have anything that links this site to the death?" Logan asked.

I shook my head. "I can follow what I see here. I won't know until then."

"Then let's check out the crime scene we know we have so the lieutenant can get moving on this," Logan said. "Rider, we need you up there. Ethan and I can stay with Cassie."

"I'd like to, but I need to be at the crime scene since I brought you all in." Ethan didn't look happy saying no.

"Alright, Vincent, you're with Cassie," Logan said.

The fact that I needed a babysitter at all pissed me off to no end.

I gritted my teeth in frustration and walked back over to the scattered rebar. The faster I started, the faster I could get back to the real crime scene. I could hear the others walking away as I closed my eyes to reach for the Path.

Again, there was a struggle. I was used to the Path fighting me, but this was altogether different.

"You appear to be having more difficulty than usual," Vincent said, keeping his tone even.

"It's fine," I said, urging my mind to make the jump.

Finally, the Path locked into place. I let out a breath that I didn't realize I had been holding. My eyes opened to the scene similar to the one earlier. Vincent's released agitation marred the Path with black and red that seemed to resist the flow of the energy, but it was nothing that wouldn't smooth over with time.

"What are we looking at?" Vincent asked.

"I'm not really sure. Something came out of this hole. It may not even be related."

"An animal?"

"I don't think so. The Path starts out almost non-existent. It's like a gray puff of smoke, but with something else wrapped around inside."

"Starts that way?"

"Yeah." I began to follow next to the Path. "It starts to get darker as it moves away."

"What leaves a gray Path?" Vincent asked.

"Anything can leave gray. It's the stuff threaded throughout that is more interesting."

"How so?"

"All Paths left behind are distinct, but if I followed Rider's Path, it would shift and move as Rider does. With his moods and actions. This..." Finding the words to describe what I was seeing was a struggle. "This is something I haven't seen before. The colors look like they are actively covered up by the main Path."

Vincent was silent and I started to lose track of time. We followed the trail as it wove through clumps of trees. We continued to move through some of the buildings under construction.

"It's starting to turn almost black," I said, "and the lines of colors are more distinct."

I reached out to touch the Path, intrigued by the twists of color, but hesitated. I'm not sure I wanted that strong of a connection with what I was following.

"Tell me about the lines of color," Vincent said, keeping his voice light, almost soothing, as if we were meditating.

"It's like a cobweb of reflected color threaded throughout the center of this Path. At least, I think it's only the center. It twists and moves as if the gray is trying to drown the color."

"Here," I gestured to an area invisible to anyone but myself, "it's actually almost entirely black at this point." Once again, I reached out to the color, but paused short of making a connection.

"I think this is related to our crime scene," Vincent said.

"Is it?" I asked, watching the swirls of black glitter overtake a vivid string of teal engulfing it. That color was gone, but a brilliant blue made its move to break away, only to be absorbed again.

"We're almost to the others."

"It's like the other colors are trying to escape. Maybe if I put some more power into it—"

"No." The words came out like an order.

"Did you by some stretch of the imagination think that I was asking for permission in any way?" I asked. I was only half paying attention. The swirling river of the Path held too much interest.

"Cass, what's going on?" Vincent asked.

"That's what I'm trying to figure out." I moved on. I was starting to feel light-headed. Something inside of me wanted to call out to those little threads. I'm not sure if I wanted to join with them or take them away.

I started to feel like I was floating. Maybe flowing away on the river of the Path.

A hand clasped my shoulder. My shoulders dropped. Time to come back to earth.

Looking ahead, I could see a turbulent mass. "What's that?"

I started to move forward, but another Path moved in and blocked my way.

"Cass, time to come back."

Those swirls and curls of color stretched away from the inky cloud and became more vivid. They seemed to call to me.

"Cass?"

CHAPTER 3

RIGHT," I SAID, TRYING TO look away. There was almost a pulse to the cloud. I reached out again, but something blocked my hand. "Sure, coming back."

When I closed my eyes, the Path was almost as vivid as it was with them open. Still, it helped me concentrate. I could hear someone talking, but I shut it out. The Path fought. It wanted to be seen. Those little strips of color wanted recognition. The dam I built up to stop the flood of power strained. Emotions boiled up around me, making me feel smothered.

"Not helping," I muttered. Or at least I think I did.

Another hand settled on my arm. I looked up and Rider loomed next to me. No matter where I was in the Path, it seemed like he could follow me. His own Path shifted from instinctive animal to intelligent person, which was beautiful to see.

"You are taking your time," Rider said.

"Do you see it?" I asked him. I had never asked him what he saw when I was in the Path, but I know that it affected him in some way.

He shook his head. "Others are worried."

"I'm trying," I said, getting aggravated.

"Maybe we should move away," Rider suggested.

I glanced at the black mist. "Maybe," I said with reluctance.

He kept a firm grip of my arm as we walked away. The lure from the Path behind me caused me to look over my shoulder a few times.

"Is it easier now?" Rider asked.

When I took another step, my world lurched. Exhaustion poured over me like bags of sand. I wanted to close my eyes and sleep, right then and there, but other things started clamoring around my skull. Like unruly children, shards of souls rushed forward.

"Not now," I muttered, driving them back. The last thing I needed was to have the soul shard of a raging minotaur mucking up my day.

The Path, the soul shards, the exhaustion, everything. I shoved it down. I blinked in the dull light of the world and swayed.

Rider steadied me.

"I'll be good in a minute," I murmured, hoping that only Rider could hear. "This is embarrassing."

He looked puzzled. "You have done nothing wrong."

I shook my head. How could I explain? My own powers were betraying me. Even now, I wanted to see the swirling black mass. I'd had a hard time opening the Path, and had an even more difficult time forcing it away.

Looking back at Logan and the others, I found my partner trying to keep Ethan's attention. Vincent was nowhere in sight.

"I hope the others feel the same way you do," I said. "Where did Vincent go?"

"I think he was worried that he might have been making things more difficult."

"That may be my fault because I think I said something I shouldn't have. I don't think it was him, but he'll blame himself. Will you keep an eye on him for me? Make sure he's okay?"

Rider smiled. "He is my partner. I will look out for him."

"What did you all find?"

His smile died. "It is a horrible sight. Ethan is having it cleaned up now."

I nodded. "That's good. Did you get anything from the area?"

"I found nothing. The man was torn apart by nothing and then part of him left. Logan has called it in to Hank."

"What?"

"I smell no other person. No human, no Lost. Only objects."

"But you said the man left."

"Logan said that it might be because of the bones. His bones left."

I shivered at the thought.

"They are finishing their conversation. Should we join them?" Rider asked.

"I think so."

I began to lose balance after only a few steps. My body was worn.

"Do you need assistance?" Rider asked, looking worried.

"What? Oh." I hadn't noticed that I stopped moving. "No, I'm good. I was just thinking."

Rider didn't look convinced, but I straightened my back and kept walking. No way was I going to let Ethan see me any worse off than he already had.

Logan looked me over, but didn't say anything when we walked up. Ethan's expression appeared to be a mixture of worry and leery. Not a good combination. I couldn't say that I blamed him, though.

"You alright?" Ethan asked.

"Yeah, I'm good. Rider says you all didn't find anything," I said, changing the subject.

"Nothing we can use to help. Hank said we need something solid to dig deeper. How about you?" Logan asked.

"I'm not sure what it was." I gave them a quick recap of what I saw.

When I looked at Ethan, he looked uncomfortable, but he tried to cover it up. Swallowing hard, I concentrated on Logan as I finished filling them in.

Logan shook his head. "Sorry, Ethan, it looks like we wasted a bunch of your time. I'm not sure we can help further."

"Maybe," Ethan started, and then stopped. He cleared his throat and tried again. "You see movements that people make?"

"Yes," I said, wondering where he was going with this. My stomach started twisting in knots when he paused for a while before responding.

"Is there any way to see what carried parts of him away?" Ethan asked.

"I'm fairly certain it was whatever was heading towards him," I said carefully.

"Did you see anything in the trail leading away?" Ethan asked.

I shook my head. "I only saw the approach."

Gran was the psychic, not me. Still, I could see his question before it formed.

"Can you check for us?" Ethan asked.

"Sorry, she can't do that," Logan said flatly.

Ethan's eyes roved around the site. He looked as worn as I felt.

"Well, I appreciate your time on this," Ethan said. "Sorry to drag you out here on a wild goose chase."

I started to say something, but Logan beat me to it.

"I'm sorry we couldn't help further," Logan said.

"I guess I should get back to it then," Ethan said. "Thanks again."

Ethan went back to the group of people who were loading up coolers. I really didn't want to think about the coolers.

I watched him go and felt wretched about not being able to help further.

"Let's mosey on out of here," Logan said. He smiled at me, but I could tell it was forced. It looked wrong for an elf to fake a smile.

"Yeah," I said to Ethan's retreating back, "we should go."

I made it to the car without assistance. Once I sat down, I stopped moving altogether. Sleep took me before Logan drove away.

When I woke up, it was almost dark outside and I was in my own room. I moaned and tugged the blankets over my head. Maybe it hadn't been as bad as I thought it was, although remembering Ethan's retreating back wasn't helping that argument.

It hadn't been all bad. Sure, I had left without actually being able to help him. After wasting so much time staring at one Path, I had exhausted myself to the point I couldn't check the departure trail, but Ethan had believed me. That was an outcome that I hadn't expected.

As a bonus, I was wearing my clothes. Either Rider was over his boundary issues or someone else brought me to my room. Since Rider was still terminally confused as to why friends don't see each other naked, I was betting Logan brought me home.

How embarrassing is it that my partner had to carry me to my room?

Voices carried up the stairs. At least I could thank Logan for bringing me back. I tossed the covers off and went downstairs to the kitchen.

Seeing Ethan at the table with Gran, I froze.

"There she is," Gran said. Her southern accent dialed up to eleven because of company. "I told you she'd be along shortly. I'll just scooch on out of here so you two can have some privacy. Coffee's ready if you want some."

Gran was out the door before I could protest.

"Hi. Um, I wasn't expecting to see you," I said awkwardly.

"I came to apologize in person. When you didn't return my calls... well, I wasn't sure you'd see me in person either."

I poured myself some coffee to look busy. "I guess I didn't hear the phone." I took my time adding cream and sugar before sitting down opposite of Ethan.

"Are you okay?" Ethan asked.

"Only tired. I'll be good as new after a good night's sleep and plenty of caffeine," I said.

Ethan frowned.

"I'm glad you called, though," I added. "I would have called you back later tonight or tomorrow."

He shook his head. "I'm not going to pretend I know how any of this works."

I slumped back in my chair. It was going to be one of those kinds of talk.

"But," he continued, "I'm feeling out of my depth here."

That was no surprise. "Don't worry about it."

"Asking you to the crime scene was one thing. Then, I mean, I could tell there was something wrong and that you were tired, but I asked you to do more."

"It's no big deal," I said.

"I felt like an ass then for asking and then I walked away, back to work."

27

"You were doing your job," I said while fiddling with my coffee cup to avoid looking at him.

"I should have taken the time to see what was happening."

"We were both at work," I said. "You did your job, and I did mine. End of story."

Ethan shook his head. "Do you know what time it is?"

I looked around for the clock. "It can't be too late. The sun isn't all the way down yet."

"You mean up," Ethan said.

The clock read 6:04. Frowning, I glanced out the window.

Shoot. The sun was coming up, not down.

Ethan was quiet for a few moments. "I'm sorry I pushed," he said at last.

"You didn't know."

"And I'm pretty sure your partner doesn't think much of me now."

"Like I said, you didn't know. Logan will get over it."

"I'd like to know more," Ethan said. "Maybe then I'll know when I've asked too much."

"You may want to think that through," I said. "We haven't been seeing each other that long."

"I thought it through last night."

I shook my head. "There are things you're not going to like. You've only caught a glimpse."

Ethan chuckled. "I'm sure there are things about me that you're not going to like. Look, I'm not saying that we have to learn everything there is to know about each other overnight, but I'm hoping that we can continue to learn more about each other. Say, tomorrow night? Dinner?"

He looked sincere. Would it be nicer of me to let him go now?

No, that's what Vincent had done. Turned me away without listening. Without giving us a shot. I wouldn't do that to Ethan.

"What time do you want to pick me up?" I asked.

He smiled. "Anytime you'll let me."

"Six-thirty?"

"I'll be here."

"While you're here, do you want some breakfast?"

"I should probably go. I didn't want to intrude, but I wanted to catch you before you went to work. I think your grandmother might be expecting someone."

"What makes you say that?"

"I hadn't even rang the doorbell yet and she let me in."

"You've never been properly introduced to my grandmother, have you?"

"I introduced myself this mornin'," Gran said, sweeping back into the room. "But a proper introduction to the man who's courtin' my granddaughter would be appreciated."

"Ethan, this is my grandmother, Margaret." I smiled when he stood to be introduced. He really was a great guy. "Gran, this is Ethan."

"It's a pleasure to meet you, Ethan. Let me freshen your coffee," Gran said.

"I don't want to put you to any trouble," Ethan said.

"It's no trouble at all. I'd get you breakfast, but you'll be called away before you can enjoy it. I'll fix you up some toast. Cassie, do you want to get Logan's coffee?"

Ethan sat back down looking mildly confused. I winked at him and got up to get coffee, adding liberal amounts of chocolate syrup and sugar.

When I reached the table, I leaned over to whisper to Ethan. "I'm not the only one in the family with a unique set of skills."

I sat the cup down across from Ethan and Logan walked in through the back door. Ethan sat up a little straighter and I grinned, but hid it by drinking more coffee.

"Howdy," Logan said with his usual drawl. He sat down across from Ethan.

"Mornin'," Gran responded, "I've got sugar cookies for the kids. Susan will be by later to pick them up."

Gran set a stack of toast down in front of Ethan. I got out butter and jelly.

"Thank you, Margaret," Ethan said. "You really didn't need to do that."

"It's my pleasure. Eat up while you can," Gran said.

"I'm surprised to see you this morning, Ethan," Logan said.

"I owed Cassie an apology for yesterday. You, too, for that matter." Ethan looked at me. "And I'm sorry I didn't understand."

Logan nodded. "How did things go yesterday after we left?"

At hearing the question, Ethan looked tired. "We got the site cleaned. The construction company is trying to get us to open things up, but we can hold it for a while longer to see if we can find anything else of use on site."

Ethan's phone rang and he looked at the readout. "Will you excuse me for a minute, I need to take this."

"No problem," I said.

"How are you doing today, partner?" Logan asked as Ethan left the room.

"With a bit more caffeine and a shower, I'll make it through the day. Thanks for getting me home yesterday," I said.

"We should probably discuss what exactly happened yesterday."

I glanced nervously into the living room. "Now?"

"It can hold till later. What do we have on the agenda for the day?" Logan asked.

"I haven't checked yet, but I imagine it involves paperwork for yesterday."

Gran was filling a to-go tumbler of coffee. I stood and stretched. Ethan walked in frowning. "I'm sorry, I need to go."

"What's going on?" I asked.

His smile was strained. "Another day on the job."

"Here you go, young man," Gran said, giving Ethan the coffee.

"Thank you, Margaret," he said. "You really didn't have to do that."

"I'll see you out," I said.

In the living room, Ethan glanced back at the kitchen then whispered. "Why do I get the feeling I'm a step behind Margaret?"

I laughed. "That's because you are. Don't worry, you'll get used to it."

He smiled and took my hand as we reached the door. "Does that mean you'll let me hang around long enough to get used to it?"

My heart thudded with the warmth of his hand. Pixies and butterflies started wrestling in my stomach.

"We'll have to wait and see how tomorrow night goes," I said, teasing.

"I'll be on my best behavior."

I opened the door and stepped out into the dawning of a new day.

"It was nice to meet your grandmother. It was good to see Rider and Logan again, and to meet your, uh, other partner, Vincent?"

"I really didn't mean to throw all that on you yesterday. I thought we could help," I said.

Ethan nodded. "I'm glad I got to see you in action. Until tomorrow night then?"

"I'll be here," I said.

Ethan looked awkward, but the moment only lasted a few seconds. Then he kissed me. My stomach tightened and my mind went blank of everything except for his warm lips on mine.

When he drew away it felt reluctant, but that may only have been a projection of my own feelings.

"I'll see you tomorrow."

I watched him leave. Once he got into the car, I could tell that his thoughts were already on work. Still, he paused and took a moment to wave before driving off.

CHAPTER 4

I T FELT LIKE I WAS walking on air when I went back to the kitchen.

"He seems like a very nice young man," Gran said.

"He's a good cop, too," Logan said. "Nice of him to stop by and check on you."

"It was," I agreed, unable to keep the smile from my face.

"Oh dear," Gran said. She stared at nothing and frowned.

"What's up, Gran?" I asked.

"You better get cleaned up," Gran said.

"Work?" I asked.

"Your mother," Gran said.

I groaned. "It's a Thursday. I'm surprised she'd bother missing work."

My mother and I didn't see eye to eye on anything. Okay, somewhere in the back of my mind I knew we might agree on something; the sky is blue, for instance. But to the forefront of my thoughts, there was nothing.

"That's my cue to get out of Dodge," Logan said.

He had met my mother over Christmas. Although he smiled and said all the right things, my mom still disapproved.

My mother disapproved of everything to do with my job.

"Tell Anala I say howdy," Logan said. "I'm going to head out to the Sanctuary this morning. Want me to swing by and pick you up?"

It was a tricky choice. Meet with my mother or deal with a thousand pounds of horse ready to throw me off.

"I think pick me up after the Sanctuary." I asked. "I'll catch up on our reports this morning."

"Will do." Logan tipped an imaginary hat and left through the back door.

I think Logan had assumed my mother would be a bit more like Gran. Gran rescued a cat, gave a fairy a home in the backyard, and made sure he and his kids never went long without sugar.

My mother was the opposite. The cat would probably be pedigree, she would pretend not to see the fairy because such things don't exist, and I'm pretty sure she doesn't know any of her neighbors. She also suppresses her psychic gifts.

After trudging upstairs, I took a shower and got ready for the day. I was looking longingly at my bed and thinking about taking a nap when the doorbell rang. Mom lived an hour away, so she must have started out early. She only worked about thirty minutes away, so hopefully it would be a short visit.

Gran was ushering Mom into the kitchen when I went downstairs.

"Morning, Mom." I poured myself more coffee and sat down at the table with her.

"I'm sorry to stop in unannounced," Mom said.

"Don't you go worryin' about it," Gran said. She handed her daughter a cup of coffee and joined us at the table.

We sat quietly for a few moments before I broke the silence. "How's work?"

"Work is going well," Mom said. "The firm is hiring a few new accountants if you're interested. It's entry-level work, but you've been out of the game for a while. I'm sure you could move your way up in no time."

Shoving down the string of passive-aggressive, and some overtly aggressive, comments was difficult, but I managed. "Thank you, but my job is going well."

"Hmm, yes. Well, let me know if you change your mind. It's a shame to see that degree go to waste."

"What brings you by today?" Gran asked before I could reply.

"Well, Bob and I were thinking about going out of town. It's very last minute. We'd be leaving tomorrow morning. I told him that I shouldn't be taking off work on that short of notice, but he thinks it would be good for us to get away."

Mom was twisting the wedding ring on her finger in an absent-minded way.

Warning bells clanged around in my head. "Is everything alright?" I asked.

"Of course," Mom said. "It's only a little vacation. I think he's getting a bit overworked, to be honest."

I didn't even think my mother knew it was possible to be overworked.

"I thought I'd see if Cassie would be free to watch the house over the weekend," Mom said.

"Cassie has a date tomorrow night, but I could come over and watch the house," Gran said.

"A date?" Mom perked up over the word.

"Yes," I said, unable to stop the smile that crept up.

"Who is the lucky guy?" Mom asked.

"His name is Ethan. We've only been seeing each other for a little while," I said.

"He is a very pleasant young man," Gran added.

"I'm so glad to see you dating again, Cassie," Mom said. "After that horrible man, Zander, I've been worried about you. Tell me about Ethan."

"Uh…" This left me nearly speechless. It took me mind a moment to soak in that my mother approved of something I was doing. "He's a nice guy. He used to live here when he was a kid. He moved while he was in elementary school."

"What does Ethan do now?" Mom asked.

"He's a Lieutenant on the local police force," I said.

Mom's lips pursed. "Are you two getting serious?" she asked.

This was an issue I had with Mom. No matter how old I was, I didn't know if she meant serious as in, 'are wedding bells sounding' or 'are you sleeping with him.' The fact that the answer to the first was no and the second was yes made it difficult to answer.

34

"We've only been seeing each other a month or so," I said, keeping it safe.

"No reason to rush these things," Mom said.

I could tell she didn't approve, but for her to keep silent on the issue was something I never expected from her.

Shocked, I looked at Gran, who had also raised her eyebrows. This new, milder Mom was starting to freak me out.

Gran cupped a hand over her daughter's hand. "I can come over and stay as long as you'd like."

"Thanks, Mom," Mom said. "Can I pick you up tonight?"

"I'll be ready," Gran said.

"Well, I need to get to work. I need to get ahead of my work so I'm not behind when I get back." Turning to me she added, "Shouldn't you be off to work soon?"

"I'm working from home this morning," I said.

"Hmm," Mom said. "Let me know if you want more information about our openings."

I gritted my teeth. "Thanks, Mom."

Gran walked her daughter out while I gathered my phone and tablet, ready to start my day. While the tablet made a connection to the office, I listened to my messages. Ethan had left two yesterday, and one this morning letting me know he was going to stop by. Vincent had also called, but didn't leave a message.

My fingers drummed a beat against the table as I contemplated if I should call him back or not.

"Do you think your mother and Bob are fighting?" Gran asked when she returned to the kitchen.

"Maybe Or maybe he really needs a break. I know if I had worked insurance for as long as him, I'd be stir crazy."

"Hmm, maybe. They've been married for what, ten years now?"

My dad passed away when I was around four. I don't remember much, only that one day he was there, and the next he was gone. I had been almost sixteen when Mom remarried. Bob and I got along for the most part.

"A little longer," I said.

"Time flies, I guess. I'm gonna go pack for the weekend."

"Need any help?"

"No, I'm fine. You make your call and do your work."

I waited till Gran was in her room before calling Vincent.

"Hey," I said, "I'm returning your call. What are you all up to today?"

"It's good that you called. Rider said you didn't look well when you left yesterday."

I attached the keyboard to my tablet and started opening up work forms. "I'm fine. Tired, but that's all."

"We should talk about what happened."

"Hmm, which part?"

That seemed to catch him off guard. It took him some time to answer. "You had a worse response than normal. Even after I left."

"What happened had nothing to do with you. You shouldn't have left."

"You're right, I shouldn't have. Rider said you had trouble even with him there doing... whatever it is he does."

"It all worked out in the end," I said, trying to steer away from too serious of a discussion. That probably wouldn't lead to good places.

"I think we should start meditation again," Vincent said.

"It was only one time," I hesitated, "but, well, do you think it would help?"

"We need to do something. At the very least it may give you more control."

My soul had sucked up pieces of other souls that had been stolen from the Lost. "It would help if the soul shards from the Lost were out of my system. If you could—"

"No. It's too risky."

"Riskier than me losing my grip, going into a rage, and hurting someone?" The memory of a Lost tied to a fragment inside me could spring forward and take over, which made me unpredictable. I had to encourage my partners to carry around tranquilizer darts in case a minotaur, or something worse, decided it wanted to rage out of control.

"Yes." His tone was even, but I sensed the intensity behind the words.

"Fine," I said, exacerbated. "Control. We can work on that."

He was a Walker with the power to take souls. To me, it seemed like an obvious fix to my issues.

"Rider and I are in Lynn County today," Vincent said. "I'm not sure when we'll be back."

"We can play it by ear. Tell Rider hi from me."

"Be safe."

He hung up before I could respond.

The paperwork didn't take as long as I expected. It never did when I actually got started. As I was wrapping up and considering a nap, Gran called me into her room.

The second I walked in, her cat hissed at me and ran into the hallway.

"One of these days he'll get used to you," Gran said.

"He likes Vincent and Logan and loves Rider. But it's me he can't stand."

"Maybe you feeding him for the next few days will help."

"Maybe. Need help packing?"

"Not with the packing, no, but I do need something done while I'm gone. Dee Dee was going to take me tonight, but I don't think I'll get the chance."

"Sure," I said, "what do you need?"

"There's somethin' I was supposed to deliver this evenin'," Gran said, handing me a small red box with a black ribbon tied around it. "Here's the address. Make sure you get there before dark."

"Sure, I'll drop it off today."

"Before dark," Gran emphasized.

"Before dark," I repeated.

"Thank you," Gran said. "Logan's going to be here any minute."

"Anything for us?" I asked.

Gran stared into space for a few moments. "Nothin' clear. You take care of yourself while I'm gone. And don't forget, before dark." She eyed the package and nodded to herself.

"You've got it, Gran. Take care. Call me if you need anything."

I packed my bag for work. Computer, phone, stun gun, real gun, pepper spray, cuffs, and any other odds and ends that I could throw in. When Logan arrived, I was ready to go.

"That didn't take you as long as I thought," I said, hauling myself into the truck. The large SWAT-style truck was conspicuous, but ideal for relocating Lost.

"We got a call," Logan said. "Someone broke into the Palmer's house this morning. We're going to take a look."

"Was anyone hurt?" I asked.

"No one was home. Mr. Palmer returned for an early lunch, and found the place wrecked up."

"What happens with something like this? Do we handle the breaking and entering, or did they call the police?"

"They pass for humans, so they called the cops. We're only there to provide support and see what we can see. Are you up for this?"

It was a loaded question. "Yeah, I'm tired after yesterday, but I'll live."

Logan nodded. "You wanna tell me what you saw?"

I frowned. "I told you yesterday."

"You told me about a gray trail that turned black, but you ain't fooling me, partner. I saw the look in your eyes. For a few minutes, I wasn't even sure it was you we were dealing with."

"It was the Path. All those colors shifting around and reaching out. It was beautiful. But yeah, I almost lost control at the end."

"We need to come up with a better plan than me carrying around a dart dosed to knock you out."

"Vincent thinks we should start meditating again."

"Do you think that'll help keep things under control? I'd hate to have to dart you in front of your fella."

"Hopefully, it won't come to that. Still, better that than I hurt someone. It would be easier if Vincent would just take the soul fragments out of me."

"Not sure that's the wisest decision," Logan said.

"Yeah, he basically said the same thing."

"We'll figure something out. Till then, meditation sounds like a good start. Looks like the Palmers aren't the only ones with trouble today."

A few streets away from the Palmers' house were several cop cars and an ambulance blocking the road.

"Better call it into Hank," Logan said. "See if it might be something related to the Palmers."

I took out my cell phone and speed dialed the office.

"What do you have for me?" Hank asked.

I told him where we were and what we saw.

"Let me bring it up. I'll call you back." He hung up.

"Let's go ahead to the Palmers," I said, "and see how we can help them."

There was one police cruiser when we stopped at a ranch-style house and Logan led the way. Mr. Palmer met us at the door.

"Thanks for stopping by, Logan, Cassie."

"Sorry to see you under these circumstances, Bill," Logan said.

"They came in some time after we left. I'm thankful Clair wasn't home. To think someone might have forced their way in with her here. I can't stop thinking about it."

I'm sure he was worried about his wife, but I couldn't help but believe that it was lucky for the robber she wasn't there. The older a changling is the faster they can change. At Clair's age, it would probably take her less than a minute to turn into a monster. The robber wouldn't stand a chance.

It was sweet that he worried, though.

The house was a disaster. It looks like whoever did this, was doing it out of spite. Everything had been tossed out of cabinets and pushed off shelves. The TV and electronics were broken. Drawers had been emptied.

"What did they take?" I asked, looking around. The TV didn't look expensive, but why smash it instead of stealing it?

"Nothing that I've noticed so far," Bill said.

An officer walked into the living room. He eyed me up and down, but addressed Bill.

Thankfully, the phone rang, so I went outside to take the call.

"The issue a few blocks away doesn't appear to be connected, but we'll keep an eye on things. How are the Palmers?"

"The place is trashed, but it doesn't look like anything has been stolen. We should know more in a while. Got us logged?"

"You're good."

Inside the house, an officer was talking to Bill and Logan. Another uniformed man stepped out of the hallway, saw me, and then charged over.

"Ma'am, I'm going to have to ask you to leave." He held out a hand and put his other on his belt.

Crap. I plastered on the most innocent smile I could come up with. Under the circumstances, it wasn't great.

"Everything good there, Ron?" the officer that had been talking with Bill and Logan was watching us.

"It's okay officer, I'm a federal agent," I said.

Logan didn't look happy. "She's my partner. She's supposed to be here."

Ron didn't drop his hand.

"I'll show you my ID," I said. I reached slowly for my back pocket, doing my damnedest to look non-threatening.

When my hand moved, he pulled his gun.

CHAPTER 5

MY EYES WIDENED.
"Ron!" his partner yelled.
I reached for the Path, ready to tear into its full power.
It didn't come.

Panic welled up and my skin went cold. Adrenaline burst through my system.

"Ron!" his partner said, circling into Ron's vision.

Pushing once more, I strained to reach the Path. Something else broke free and rose out of me. A soul shard belonging to one of the Lost surged forward, using my situation to get a foothold over me.

"Logan?" It was the quiver and fear in my voice that got Logan's attention.

He must have thought I had the Path open, ready to act.

Logan's face began to contort, become more angular, and he moved forward.

The soul of the Lost overcame me and time slowed almost to a stop.

My heart beat faster in my chest and I put my hand over it, trying to press it into place. I had no idea what was taking over, but it didn't seem like it wanted to attack anyone, so things could have been so much worse. More importantly, it was leaving me in charge of my own thoughts and actions, even though it appeared to be affecting the environment drastically.

Not knowing how long I had, I moved beside Ron. He was nearly frozen in time, along with everyone else. I twisted the gun in his hands, prying his fingers off and then I knocked the weapon to the side. The fall of the gun slowed to a stop, appearing to hang in mid-air. Then I moved back to where I was before. I'm not sure if time was delayed or if I was moving quickly. Either way, it was using a lot of energy and draining me fast.

Dammit. How do I get things back to normal?

My heart thudded in my chest, much too fast for a human. I put my hands up ready to knock Ron's away. Hopefully, everyone would think I knocked the gun out of his hands. That was the plan anyway. Now I only had to get that tiny fragment of soul to let go.

Easier said than done. Vincent said that maybe meditation would work to take back some control. Closing my eyes, I concentrated on my breathing. Inhale. Exhale. Inhale. Exhale. It took some time, but my heartbeat began to slow. Then I felt the tiny piece of soul in the back of mind. It wiggled, trying to stay in pace. As my heartbeat slowed, it became easier to coerce it away.

My eyes flew open the moment the fragment lost its hold.

The world sped up. I lashed out, hitting Ron's hands away as hard as I could and the gun finished its fall and clattered to the floor.

Ron looked shocked. Something must have looked off to his partner as well. He looked at the weapon on the ground, and then at Ron, before springing into action. He shoved Ron into the wall.

That was lucky. It gave Logan a few seconds to pull himself together. I wasn't sure if he had an idea about what happened, but at that point, I didn't care. I stepped out of the house and into the front yard.

My eyes began to sting and I was shaking from head to toe. I really hated it when people pointed guns at me.

I'd love to say that I recovered at this point and went inside to give Ron a piece of my mind. But things rarely work the way I want them to.

The Path had abandoned me.

The essence of a Lost took over.

Two of my nightmares rolled together in one. Added on top of that, there had been a cop that wanted to shoot me.

My eyes stopped burning as the last dregs of adrenaline were used up.

That officer, Ron, or whoever he was, had to be severely stupid, or some major stuff was going on his life for him to have reacted that badly to my soul.

He was ready to kill me and my powers failed.

How is this my life?

Thinking about what had happened only made it worse, so I thrust the events into a dark corner in my mind. A plan of action, that's what I needed.

The Path wasn't always accessible. That much had become clearer over the past few months. I needed something else to rely on to get myself out of dangerous situations. Something that would be there all the time.

The answer was clear. I'd been putting off taking self-defense classes for a few months now. Maybe if I had some practice, I would be able to react better to situations like the one inside.

Today, I would find a local class.

Once I made the decision to learn, the shaking began to die away. If I knew I could defend myself, I would become a better asset to my partner as well, instead of a hazard, which seems to be what I have become.

The raised voices from inside the house had died away. Still, I was in no hurry to poke my head back inside. Ron appeared to be a powder keg ready to go off. I didn't want to be the match.

So I waited.

Logan came out of the house and he looked oddly calm, considering he had almost elfed out in front of civilians less than five minutes ago.

"You doing okay out here?" Logan asked.

"About as well as can be expected, I guess," I said. "Listen, I'm sorry about what happened."

"You've been hanging out with Vincent too much. Seems to me that you're the one that almost got shot."

A chill ran down my spine. "You know what I mean, though."

"Yeah. I know. Still, I didn't see Kevin, the other officer, more than glance at you. It was Ron that couldn't hold his shit together."

I blinked. It was rare to hear Logan curse.

"What's going to happen now?" I asked.

"Well, if it were up to me he'd be hung before sundown. He should count himself lucky his partner reached him before I did."

I didn't even want to imagine what Logan could do to a person if he tried. Elves are relatively slight in build, but they're exceptionally strong. Logan could probably toss Ron around like a rag doll if he chose to do so.

"That would have been a hell of a lot of paperwork," I said, trying to lighten the mood.

"Yeah, that might take some of the satisfaction out of things." Logan looked back at the house and crossed his arms. "Kevin would like to have a few words with us."

"While Ron is...doing what?"

"He's cuffed," Logan said.

"He's arresting his partner?" I couldn't even imagine a situation where I could arrest Logan.

"Cassie, the man pointed a gun at you. He almost fired. Would have fired if you hadn't taken the gun out of his hands."

"You know he wouldn't have done that if I were normal," I said.

"Officers have gotta face a lot of stuff in the line of duty."

I knew Logan was right, but I still felt like crap that the officer had run into me.

"Anyway, I wanted to check on you before Kevin brought Ron out, or before anyone else arrives."

"Ugh. Crap. Let's get this over with."

Logan nodded and let out a sharp, piercing whistle.

Ron appeared bleary-eyed and confused when Kevin brought him out. He didn't glance around but looked straight forward. Kevin was grim. Ron slid into the back of the police cruiser. Kevin said a few words and then shut the door. He looked at his partner for a moment through the glass before coming over to us.

"Agent Heidrich," Kevin said, "I want to apologize on behalf of myself and my partner. He's...well, I'm not sure what happened in there."

"I appreciate your help." I had no idea what to say, and he looked like he was in the same boat.

"We need to know how you'd like to proceed here," Kevin said.

"What?" I asked.

"Ron drew a gun on an unarmed federal agent. It's a bad week to be a government official, I guess."

"Why's that?" I asked, confused.

Kevin looked at us. "As I understand it, you two were at the crime scene yesterday."

There was no need for him to say which crime scene. "Yes," I said.

"Turns out, the victim was a state government employee. A clerk of some sort. This morning, there was another incident with someone in social services. Now this."

"It sounds like a bad week to be an officer," I said, looking at the police cruiser.

"Well, I think I made my viewpoint clear," Logan said.

Kevin nodded. There was something profoundly sad about the look he had. I wondered what exactly Logan had said to him.

"But, I've talked to my partner," Logan continued, "and I think she'd rather see this handled quietly."

I nodded in agreement. "If that's possible."

"Are you sure that's how you want things taken care of?" Kevin asked.

"Yes, but," I looked at Logan, "we're going to have to call this in, aren't we?"

Logan nodded. "I'll talk to Hank. I'm pretty sure he can manage to leave this low key. The boys from DC are leaving, it'll help that they won't be around."

I heard a car and looked down the street. Shoot, I knew who would be behind the wheel.

"Did you call Ethan?" I hissed at Logan.

Kevin shook his head. "I called Lieutenant Parker. I'm afraid this is above my pay grade, and since it involves a government official, it firmly resides in his ball court now. Besides, I can't bring my own partner in."

"Shit. This isn't going to help keep things low key, is it?" I asked.

"I'm sure Lieutenant Parker will be fair," Kevin said.

I took a moment to smooth out my hair as the car came to a stop. Then I realized what I was doing and put my hand down. Still, if this screwed up my date, I was prepared to get pretty pissed off at Ron *and* Kevin.

Ethan's brow was furrowed when he got out of the car. He walked up, looked at Ron in the back of the car, and shook his head.

"I was told there was an incident involving a federal agent," Ethan said, crossing his arms. The lines of his jaw were rigid.

"You could say that," Logan said.

Turning to Kevin, Ethan asked, "What happened here?"

Kevin told him. Ethan paled and became more tense the longer Kevin talked. Luckily, Kevin kept it brief.

"Is that how it happened?" Ethan asked me.

I nodded. "Yes, but I'd like to not make a big deal over this. The guy is obviously under a lot of pressure or something."

Ethan looked at Ron and back to us.

"Logan, do you have anything to add?" Ethan asked.

"I had a few words with Kevin and Ron. This is your rodeo now," Logan said.

I'm not sure if I wanted to know what Logan said or not.

"Agent Heidrich, can I have a word with you?" Ethan said.

I shrugged and walked back to Ethan's car with him. There was no way Kevin could hear anything from that distance unless we yelled. Logan would be able to hear it all, but Ethan didn't know that.

Ethan looked over my shoulder at Kevin and Logan. "Are you injured?" His voice was almost as hard as his expression.

"I'm all right," I said, crossing my arms. "I knocked the gun out of his hands. Nothing happened."

"He could have killed you."

"Like I said, he's obviously under some sort of strain."

"What are you even doing here?"

"Excuse me?" I asked, feeling my blood pressure rise.

"You. Here. At this crime scene. Why are you here?"

"I'm working," I snapped.

"Sorry. It's just... dammit, Cassie, he's a cop. For his own partner to cuff him? This isn't good."

"How is this my fault?"

"It's not. God, no. I didn't mean for it to come out like that. It's just... I don't know what to do here. Half of me wants to smooth this over, the other half wants me to turn him over to Logan."

I cringed. "That wouldn't be a good idea."

I turned around to look at my partner. He was talking with Kevin, but I could tell from the pleased look on his face that he was listening.

Shaking my head, I turned back to Ethan. "You need to smooth this over. He came out of the back room and saw a strange woman entering a crime scene. People were talking to him, and then yelling."

"He pulled a gun," Ethan said. "Of course they were going to yell."

"Was it an overreaction? Yes. One hundred percent agree with you. Maybe some therapy, administrative leave or something is in order. Take his gun away, yes, but I don't think he should be arrested."

"What happens isn't up to me. You know that, right?"

"I know, but if it comes from you, it's going to be better than coming from his partner," I said.

"Are your people going to go along with this?"

"I'm not saying all of them will be happy about it, but with the extenuating circumstances, they'll want to make sure this doesn't become a big issue."

"Want to describe some of those circumstances?" Ethan asked.

CHAPTER 6

I GLANCED AT LOGAN AND SHOOK my head. "There's nothing I can tell you. Nothing that makes any sense anyway."

"Right," Ethan said. "Anything we need to know about the crime scene?"

"Not that I am aware of. We haven't been here that long."

"But why are you here, today, at this house?" Ethan asked.

"You know I can't answer that," I said, not looking at him.

"Fair enough, but you're sure you don't want to press charges?" Ethan asked. "This isn't something you're doing just because it would work best for the agency."

"Positive."

"Right." Ethan looked around, appearing to take in the scene again. "We'll do what we can."

Ethan called Kevin over and I left to join Logan.

After his conversation with Ethan, Kevin looked like a weight had been lifted.

"Would you ever arrest me?" I asked Logan.

"I've cuffed you before, but arrest? Depends on what fool thing you were doing and your reason for doing it," Logan said.

"And if you didn't know the reason?"

"I could ask you the same question," Logan said.

"Me arrest you?" I had to hide my chuckle as Ethan let Ron out of the back of the police cruiser. "I don't ever see that happening. I'd trust that you had a reason for what you were doing. Unless you weren't yourself, of course. I guess that's possible in our line of work."

"It is at that," Logan said. "Let's get inside and see if we can help Mr. Palmer."

"Sure thing," I said, glad to have the whole mess behind me.

In the house we started picking up the mess in the front room. It wasn't long before Ethan knocked on the still open door.

"Cassie, can I see you for a few minutes?" Ethan asked, not entering the residence.

"Sure," I said, setting a framed picture back on a shelf.

Ethan walked into the front yard, well away from the front door, and I followed. It was a relief to see that the other officers were already gone.

"Is everything…"

Ethan cut me off by wrapping his arms around me and squeezing me in a tight hug. After a moment of surprise passed, I returned the gesture. Time ticked by, but he didn't seem inclined to talk yet and I was enjoying the closeness.

He had been at another crime scene earlier in the morning, and then he walked into this one. It hadn't been a great day for him.

Ethen let out a breath and loosened his hold on me. "Sorry, I needed to get that out of the way before I went back inside."

"You didn't hear me complaining," I said. After having a gun pointed at me, I'm sure I needed the reassurance as much as he did. "You're going back inside?"

"Kevin was about to wrap things up, but I want to make sure nothing was overlooked. He also mentioned that you all aren't taking the case."

I could hear the question in his voice. "Yep, it's yours. We're here to help clean-up."

"Well, I wanted to check in with you before I spoke with Mr. Palmer, but I need to get back to the station."

"I appreciate that." I clutched him closer for a moment before stepping away.

Ethan spoke to Mr. Palmer for a few minutes before leaving.

Logan and I helped Mr. Palmer get the house back in order. Vast improvements had been made by the time Mrs. Palmer got back, but there was still a long way to go. We ordered food for everyone, but after six o'clock, I think the Palmer's were ready to be done for the day. At least done with us.

We drove out to my house to call everything in to Hank. It had taken us a while to decide whether to provide a report, or phone in the details. Turns out, we ended up doing both. I called and started with the update on the Palmers, then went over the details. Hank was agitated that we hadn't spoken to him earlier, but he had to admit in the end that nothing had actually happened. The fact that the Path didn't open and that the soul shard took over, I kept to myself. After Logan's concern earlier in the day, I didn't even tell him that the Path didn't open.

Logan went home and I finished the write-up on the day. Then I left to run Gran's errand. The sun was starting to set, so I high-tailed it over to the address. She had insisted I get there before dark. There was still light in the sky when I drove up, so I guess that counted.

It was a cute white house. When I walked up the front steps, I noticed two rocking chairs on the gray painted front porch. There was a cheerful wreath of flowers on the door.

When I knocked on the door and there was no answer, I started having doubts. Maybe they had left for the night already. I should have gotten a more specific time from Gran.

After knocking again, I heard a rattling noise inside. It looked like I hadn't missed them after all. The rocking chair on the front porch creaked as it started to rock. I got a chill that worked against the warm weather.

The noise inside stopped. Feeling creeped out, I thought about leaving the present at the front door, or maybe sliding it into the mailbox. Then I realized I was being paranoid. It was a friend of Gran's, not someone ready to pounce on me.

Still, I hesitated before I knocked again. The second my knuckles hit the wood of the door, it opened. The creaking of the rocking chair stopped as well.

"Can I help you?" The man was a little taller than I was and a good many years older. He was dressed up as if he were going out for the evening.

"I'm sorry to stop by so late. I'm here to drop something off to you?" I didn't mean for it to sound like a question, but the man's eyes were a piercing blue and he didn't appear to blink.

Looking at the package, a grin broke out over his face. The hairs on the back of my neck stood up. The smile seemed too wide for his face.

"Did Margaret send you?" he asked.

"She did." I held out the wrapped box.

"Please, you must come in," the man said.

Gooseflesh broke out over my arms. No way was that going to happen.

"Sorry, I need to be somewhere," I said, gesturing with the package for him to take it.

His cold fingers wrapped around my wrist while his other hand covered the box I was holding. He didn't hold me tightly, but when I tried to step back, the grip was solid.

"Are you sure I can't offer you a drink or something for your trouble?"

"Um, no. I have a friend waiting for me."

Warning bells were going off in my head. I felt almost the same sense of fear I had experienced earlier in the day when the gun was pointed at me.

The deathly-cold hands were still on mine, but the apprehension died away. It was Gran's friend. Sure, he was creepy, but in the dim evening light, anyone can look scary.

The man's grin faded slightly, which was a relief. He looked almost normal this way.

"If you're sure," he said and let go, taking the package.

"It was nice meeting you," I said, trying to be polite, but his eyes were glued to the box. He drew back inside and shut the door.

I stood there for a moment. When the rocking chair creaked and started moving again, I jumped. Telling myself over and over that an old man and a breeze didn't freak me out, wasn't doing the trick. It felt like hairs were rising on the back of my neck so I took the porch steps two at a time and hurried to my car. When I had driven a block away the feeling of being watched began to die away.

It was starting to get late, so I didn't call Gran on the way home. I'm not sure what my mother's sleeping schedule was, but while I was growing up she had always been very upset with any calls late in the evening.

Company, in the form of Vincent, met me when I parked in the driveway.

"Hi," I said while getting out of the car, "everything okay?"

He had been leaning against the wall by our front door.

"I thought we should talk," Vincent said.

Inwardly, I groaned. I was beginning to hate that phrase.

"If this is about today, I'd really rather not," I said.

Vincent looked confused. "What happened today?"

"Huh, come on in." I unlocked the door and went inside. Gran's cat took one look at me before he hissed and fled the room.

"Where's Margaret tonight?" Vincent asked.

"She's staying at my mom's house for a few days while my mother is on vacation." I led Vincent into the kitchen. "Have you had dinner?" I flipped on the lights and headed straight for the fridge.

"I'm good," Vincent said.

The doorbell rang. I frowned and looked at Vincent. "Is Rider stopping by?"

Vincent shook his head. "Want me to get it?"

"No, I will. I'll be right back." The unusual events of the day flooded through my mind in a rush, but I worked hard to push them back.

I peered out the front window and saw Ethan's car in the driveway. My heart fluttered, and I grinned before opening the door.

"Hi," I said. "Come on in."

"I wanted to stop by and check in on you after today," Ethan said, stepping inside.

"You didn't have to do that," I said. I don't think you could have pried the smile off my face. "Thank you, though. Have you had dinner?"

"I couldn't eat anything after today," Ethan said.

"Something to drink then?"

"Sure," he said, with the first hint of a smile.

"Did everything get smoothed over?" I asked on the way through the living room.

"Yeah, how about on your end?"

"They were a little miffed we didn't report it right away, but everything is good."

As I entered the kitchen, I could feel the tension from Vincent.

"How's Logan taking it?" Ethan asked, and then stopped when he saw Vincent.

I looked back, "Uh, Ethan, you remember Vincent from yesterday."

Ethan stiffened. "I'm sorry. I didn't know you had company."

"It's no problem, have a seat," I said.

Then two men looked at each other and awkwardness circulated through the room.

"Um, something to drink?" I asked.

"I should go," Vincent said.

"Uh, if you want. I'll see you out. Ethan, I'll only be a moment."

I walked Vincent to the door. He looked like he was struggling to say something. Or maybe to keep from saying something.

"You don't have to go," I said.

"It's much better if I do. But Cass, what happened today?"

"Oh, it was nothing. A little mix up over at the Palmers."

"You know you're a bad liar," Vincent said. The corners of his lips turned up slightly. "Everything okay though?"

"Yep." The moment the word left my mouth I regretted it. To my own ears, it sounded like I was trying too hard.

"Right." Vincent shook his head and looked across the living room as though he could see Ethan through the walls.

The air stirred between us as though charged. It was either his mood or mine. Vincent looked down at me, searching my eyes for something.

Maybe he was searching for himself. That little piece of his soul he had left inside me when he returned my own. Well, he gave back as much as he could.

Vincent tore his eyes away. "I'll call you tomorrow."

"Sure," I said softly.

He left without another word.

I stared for a moment before locking the door and returning to the kitchen.

"Sorry if I interrupted something," Ethan said.

"You didn't," I said, trying to reassure him.

"We never talked about... I mean, I never asked..." Ethan trailed off.

"What?" I asked.

"Are you seeing anyone else?"

I sucked at these conversations. "I'm not seeing anyone else." I tried to give him a smile. Now that he said the words, I wondered if he was seeing someone besides me.

My heart felt like it was being squeezed waiting for him to say something more.

He smiled, but it wasn't a strong one. "Does that mean we're still on for tomorrow?"

"I hope so," I said. "What do you have planned for us?"

"There's an art exhibition in the park by the University. I thought you might be interested. Although, I do have several backup alternatives."

"That sounds great," I said. Growing up in this area, I was somewhat familiar with the event and knew it would be fun. There were even a few Lost that attended. It would be nice to see their work.

Still, in the back of my mind, I wondered why he didn't say if he was seeing anyone else, but I wasn't able to bring myself to ask.

"Do, you want that drink?" I asked.

"Rain check." There was a tightness in the corner of his eyes.

"Are you sure?" I asked.

"It's been a busy week."

I nodded. "I heard about the other victim today. Are the cases related?"

"Too early to tell. Between you and me, it looks like they're connected."

"Do you want to talk about it?" I asked.

"No, I really wanted to check on you, though." He moved closer to me and took one of my hands. "I still can't believe someone almost shot you today." He put his hand on my cheek.

The warmth and feel of his hands made my insides turn to goo. I could see the concern in his eyes and wanted to find a way to relieve his stress.

"I'm fine," I said. "If you always think about things that might have happened, you'll drive yourself crazy."

He grinned and wrapped his arms around me, tugged me into a kiss. I breathed the outdoorsy scent of Ethan deeply. There was a cedar smell along with an enticing scent that I couldn't quite place. Too soon, he pulled his lips away. I looked up into his eyes and saw a spark there.

Then he was kissing me again. Harder this time. I dragged him as close to me as possible. Soon our bodies were crushed tightly together, which gave me a good feel for what was on Ethan's mind. My heart beat faster and his breathing increased. Then I could sense his hesitation.

His grip loosened and I let mine relax with it, but with reluctance. He drew his head back a fraction of an inch, then closed his eyes and pressed his forehead to mine.

We stood quietly while our racing hearts slowed.

"I should go," he murmured.

I bit my lip. "You don't have to."

"What would your grandmother say?" Ethan asked.

"Oh, she's gone for a few days. House sitting."

Ethan grinned, and for the first time all evening, it reached his eyes.

"What?" I asked, not being able to stop smiling back at him.

"I just thought that it's not all bad to think of things that could happen." He kissed me again.

When we broke apart, I said, "You're right, I can see where it's not all bad."

"I forgot to mention this earlier since I had other things on my mind, but you should know that I'm not seeing anyone else. And I don't plan to."

"That's good to hear," I said. Something inside me felt like it became untangled.

CHAPTER 7

E THAN DIDN'T SPEND THE NIGHT, but he didn't rush home either. Our days hadn't been great, but we had the chance to end the night on a happier note, and we took it.

Despite feeling content after I let Ethan out and went to bed, nightmares wove in and out of my dreams. I chalked it up to job related unease. At least it got me out of bed early. By the time I was up and moving, I heard someone downstairs. It sounded like Logan was ready for an early start to the day as well.

Caffeine was a necessity, so I headed straight to the kitchen. When I walked in, I stopped dead in my tracks. The chairs in the kitchen were back away from the table. Far away.

"Logan?" I called.

No answer.

"Gran?" I listened to the silence. "Anyone?"

Crap. My eyes darted around everywhere, and I stepped back out of the room. The living room appeared to be empty. The only noise I heard was my heart thumping wildly in my chest and my blood rushing through my skull.

Picking up my gun first thing in the morning wasn't second nature. Half the time on the job, I didn't even use it. Most of our assignments only called for tranquilizer darts. Luckily though, picking up my phone was second nature. I took it out and called Logan.

"Howdy," Logan answered.

"Have you been to the house today? Or last night?"

"No," Logan replied. He dropped the cowboy twang in a hurry.

"The kids?"

"No. What's going on?"

I turned and dashed up the stairs, intent on getting to my gun. "I'm not sure, what—"

Halfway up, a force slammed into me, throwing me backward down the stairs. Grabbing the banister on the way down broke my fall some, but not enough. Pain radiated from my side, hips, and butt, all of which hit hard at some point on the way down.

Fear pulsed through my system and I ripped into the Path. I had expected resistance. When it opened easily, the crushing deluge broke over me.

From the ground, I looked up the stairs. Like water pouring over the landscape, colors rippled over everything. My own Path was invisible to me, so the colors on the stairs were muted traces from the past that had mostly been wiped away.

There was something there, though. A shock of purple and blue wrapped in dark red.

It was energy. Released energy, but no sign of what had left it behind. I couldn't see any traces of a person. Only the burst of energy. Turning my head, I could see into the kitchen. Similar bursts of energy had been released there as well.

The rush of the Path was starting to buffet me around. I began to see ghostly traces of last night's visitors, Vincent and Ethan. It was getting hard for me to shift back into the present, but that's where I needed to be, so I fought hard to keep myself there.

Something was here. It had to be. The power didn't gather there on its own.

Somewhere from the floor, I heard my phone ring. Then the back door crashed open. Was it there? I tried to scramble to my feet, but stopped when Logan ran into the room. With the full onslaught of the Path, Logan's hidden explosion of gold was visible, and right now, it had ruby tinges. I could also see the dense black spot that Logan kept buried deep. Anytime I saw it, it filled me with dread.

Logan had his gun drawn and his ears were unfurled to their points. He looked like he was trying to look every direction at once.

"Where are they?" Logan asked, keeping his voice low.

"I only see spots. No traces of movement." I kept my voice low as well so Logan could hear over me.

He was on the balls of his feet and appeared to be concentrating on the sounds in the house. I heard Gran's cat hiss. Logan ran into Gran's bedroom as the cat ran out. It charged straight at me and jumped.

I was expecting claws and teeth. Instead, the cat shook and tried to hide its head in the crook of my arm. My heart broke seeing the little guy so scared. There was a crash in Gran's bedroom. The cat ran off. I sprang to my feet, my body protesting, and dashed to the room. Logan was jumping to his feet. I rushed over, but stopped when I saw the explosion of power that had knocked him over.

Like what I had seen on the stairs, the bright spot that marred the Path was purple and blue wrapped with red. I expected to sense emotion from such directed energy.

"What are you doing?" hissed Logan, who was listening intently and trying to find a target.

Hand outstretched, I walked to the fragment of Path that had caused Logan to be thrown backward. It hovered in the middle of the room. The Path flowed around it, but hadn't yet started to sweep the remains away.

"It's inert," I whispered. "I mean, I feel nothing from it. No anger, hate, malice, not even joy. Only energy."

"I'm not sure what that means," Logan said.

"Me neither." My hand hovered a breath away from the eruption. It may have been reckless, but I'm good at reckless. "I'm not sure what this will do, but here goes nothing." I stuck my hand in the Path.

"Don't—"

The moment my skin brushed the mark, the red wrapping to the color exploded outwards. The energy rushed over me. It threatened once again to knock me off my feet. However, as a Reader in the raging depths of the Path, I was able to bend the effects around my partner and me. Even with that, there was pressure.

The crimson flared, expanded, and then winked out. The pressure around us released.

Still, there was no emotion. Only passive power left dangling in the air.

The blue and purples started to flow away in the Path. I grasped it before it was able to flee. A buzzing tingle ran up my arm and down my spine. With strength and control of the Path that I hadn't felt in what seemed like ages, I struggled to move into the Past.

Unless the Path was willing, moving back against its flow, or rushing ahead, was a battle. The Path never seemed sentient enough to have a sense of purpose or plan. There were times however, that I was thrown back to watch past Paths emerge.

This was not one of those times. Even with power, control, and the remnants of the event in hand, I couldn't shove my way back. That Path remained in the present.

"I don't hear anyone," Logan said. If anything, this only appeared to make him warier.

His voice snapped me back to the present, which was probably a good thing, as I was already starting to feel run down.

"There may be nothing to hear," I said, watching the colors swirl together and disappear in a shimmering rush.

"Whoa now, partner, I'm not sure I follow," Logan said. His cowboy slang and tone were back. A sure sign that his tension was draining away.

"I don't understand it myself. With the power displayed there should be traces of the person that left it. I'd expect to see signs of it for days, or even weeks." I wandered out of the room, watching the flows. On the stairs, the marks remained.

"You're saying there's no Path?"

"There's a Path, but it's..." Slowly I started up the stairs. "It sits there, protected by something. As soon as that something is used up, everything flows away."

"Be careful," Logan said, his gun still drawn, "we don't know what we're facing here."

This time I studied the energy. "When I touched the thing in Gran's bedroom, it released its remaining power. When I made contact again, it used itself up and immediately started to wither away."

"What is it and where's it gone to?" Logan asked.

"I don't see anything that may have left it here. No one walked up here and dropped it off. It didn't arrive from anywhere that I can tell."

"You're saying whatever this is, it appeared out of nowhere?"

"It's starting to die away on its own now too," I said, ignoring the question. "Brace yourself." Before the red marks unraveled, I plunged my hand in. Redirecting the flow was easier this time. The same buzz ran through me. Almost like a small jolt of electricity.

When it was gone, I started to sway. I'd burned through too much power too fast.

"Time to come back," Logan said. There was a strain in his voice.

Biting my lip, I took one last look around. "Wait! There's something else here." In the living room, the Path was weaving around a spot.

"There's no waiting this morning," Logan said. "You're already spent."

"Okay, but remember this spot," I said and wobbled down the stairs towards the bend in the Path.

"Cassie, Rider's not around if you can't get yourself out of the Path." There was real worry in his voice.

"Right here," I said, pointing at the bundle. "Don't touch it, and remember where it is."

"Got it," Logan said.

I took a few steps and gripped the side of the couch. Closing my eyes, I began to drive the Path away. Again, I had expected a struggle, like at the construction site. I won't say it was easy, but I was able to shove back the roaring flow.

When I opened my eyes, I staggered. The world looked almost colorless. Even worse, I hurt like mad. The Path had kept the pain at bay, but it was now back with a vengeance.

"You're sure there's nothing else in the house?" Logan asked.

"There may be more of these," I said, motioning to empty air. "But I didn't see any traces of anything living moving around."

"And you're sure you would have seen something?"

"Even a bread knife that hasn't been used in years would leave a Path that would last a day or more. I don't see anything."

Logan relaxed a bit more. "I'm going to call in Rider to see if he can find anything. It wouldn't be bad to have Vincent here as well. Things appearing out of nowhere seems like something a Walker may have experience with."

"You think a Walker might be able to do something like this?" The thought was unsettling.

"I'm not sure, but Vincent should know. He might even know if we've woken up the wrong passenger." Logan must have seen the confusion on my face. "We may have ticked off the Walkers. They might want retaliation for what we did this past spring."

I cringed. A few months ago, we had trapped a Walker inside a stone statue, which was now hidden in my sock drawer. He was a terrible man, responsible for the deaths of many Lost and the shredded remains of their souls, which now resided in me.

"Let's get some coffee in you and see if we can't perk you up." Logan started heading to the kitchen.

"Wait! What if there are more of those things around?"

Logan froze.

"If this," I motioned to the air, "is one of those things, maybe I should check the Path for more."

"After yesterday, we shouldn't risk it. I didn't think we were going to get you back."

It was a valid concern. Other Readers have followed the Path straight into death. They may not have even noticed it happening. "Do we have any other options?"

Logan studied me. "You were laying on the ground when I came in. On the phone, it sounded like it threw you back like it did me in the other room."

"Yeah, down the stairs," I said.

"When you touched it again, it should have thrown us both back again, but didn't."

"I bent the Path around us."

Logan nodded. "We can try another way. Call the others in." He hesitated, then walked into the kitchen and picked up the closest chair. He waved the chair through the air as though it weighed nothing, and started moving around the room.

Some of my anxiety faded as I watched the display. Logan swept his makeshift weapon under the table and triggered the remains of what had moved the chairs. It knocked his chair away, but he kept hold. Then he made his way over to the coffee maker and started it up. He was every bit a lion tamer without a lion.

While watching Logan clear the rest of the kitchen, I called Rider.

"Good morning," Rider said with far too much enthusiasm. Like Logan, he was a morning person.

"Hey, are you all headed to work yet?" I thought I managed kept my voice even, but Rider must have sensed something.

"What is wrong?" he asked.

"I had a little trouble at the house this morning. I was hoping that you and Vincent would stop by."

"We are already on the way. Vincent said we needed to be there."

Of course he did. I wonder how much he still feels through the piece of my soul inside him.

"Thank you," I said. "I'll see you all soon."

What I needed was coffee and lots of it. Typically, I drank it with sugar, but to get back my strength quickly, I kept it black, not wanting to spend the time doctoring it up.

Gran's cat came over and wrapped himself around my leg. Feeling shocked by the change in affections, I petted the cat carefully and made sure he had food and water.

Logan stood at the wide opening between the kitchen and the living room. His ears were still stretched to their points.

"Do you hear anything?" I asked.

"Nothing," Logan said.

Some of my tension had already died. I was fairly sure now that there was no one in the house.

"It's a good thing Margaret wasn't here," Logan said.

Picturing Gran flying through the air was awful. Fear and the remaining anxiety bled away leaving anger in its wake.

"That could have killed her." Knowing he had taken a hit, I added, "Are you alright?"

"Only a tumble. You?"

I shrugged. "That could have really hurt Gran."

Logan nodded. "I'm going to check the rest of the house."

"Leave the spot in the living room alone."

CHAPTER 8

L OGAN AUDIBLY MADE HIS WAY through the house. Twice I heard a crash. Each time, I jumped up to bolt out of the room, but Logan would announce he was fine before I made it far.

I worked steadily through several cups of coffee in my quest to feel human again. reading the Path when it was that energetic used way too much power.

When the doorbell rang, Logan called that he'd get it. Soon after, Rider and Vincent made their way to the kitchen, followed closely by Logan.

"I found two more. Left the one in the living room. They were all on the ground level, except the one on the stairs," Logan said.

"What's going on?" Vincent asked.

I shook my head. "First, I want to see if Rider can tell if someone was in the house."

"Someone came in without permission?" Rider asked. He sounded confused and angry.

I hesitated and looked at Logan. "Um, we're not exactly sure yet. There's a spot in the living room to avoid, but maybe you or Vincent might sense something."

"Me?" Vincent asked. His eyebrows raised ever so slightly. "I'm not sure there is anything I would be able to sense."

His confusion was evident. Logan and Rider had both mentioned Vincent's expressionless face in the past. For me, his face usually gave him away.

"We have a few questions to that end," Logan said. "If a

Walker went from the space between dimensions, could he, or she I guess, come out anywhere?"

Vincent's expression grew dark. "You think a Walker was here?" Even without the Path open, I could feel his anger start to build.

"Maybe not," I said quickly, "but, if they did, would you be able to sense it?"

Vincent's eyes turned black. I had never seen them change color so fast. The emotion hit me, and I sucked in a deep breath, attempting to maintain control and trying not to be thrown into the Path.

"Rider, we need to check the house now." Vincent stalked out of the room.

"Wait a minute," I called.

Rider paused, but Vincent continued.

"Dammit," I muttered, jumping up and running to the living room. Vincent was half-way up the stairs.

"Logan, do you remember where the spot was?" I asked.

He showed me.

"Rider, do you mind looking around? Avoid this spot and don't step near it." I stood next to the invisible bundle of energy, ensuring my friends didn't walk into it.

He nodded and set to work, making his way around the first floor. When he started up the stairs, he stopped. From where he stood, I could tell it was about where I had run into whatever was on the stairs.

"What is it, Rider?" I asked.

"What is what?" he asked.

"You stopped. I wanted to know what you found," I said.

"Only an odd smell. It does not belong to anything and is very faint." Rider's nostrils flared. "Old...but also new." He shrugged his shoulders and continued upstairs.

"Why don't you let me keep an eye on these two? Maybe get yourself another cup of coffee," Logan said.

It was on the tip of my tongue to say I didn't mind, but when I looked at him, I could tell he was worried. "Sure," I said. I took a last look up the stairs before retreating to the kitchen.

After pouring myself the remaining liquid happiness, I started a new pot. Waiting patiently wasn't my strong suit.

Rider didn't take too much longer to go through the house. When I heard him and Logan talking in the living room, I joined them.

"Did you find anything?" I asked. I wasn't sure what I wanted to hear. Either way, it wouldn't be good news.

"I found nothing I would not expect to find. The one odd smell was in a few different areas. This world can be full of strange smells," Rider said.

Vincent joined us from Gran's bedroom. His eyes were no longer flat black, but he still radiated fury.

"I didn't find any traces," Vincent said.

That made me feel lighter. "That's a relief."

He shook his head. "I would not necessarily find traces. It's a matter of skill with the Walker."

The relief was short lived. If it was a Walker, it was a skilled one.

"Could a Walker send something through to this dimension without crossing over?" Logan asked.

Vincent appeared to think that over. "In theory, it should be possible, though I've never tried. Was something left behind?"

Logan and I gave him a quick rundown of what had happened.

"What made you call Logan in the first place?" Vincent asked.

"The chairs in the kitchen had all been moved," I said.

"The one here in the living room is still around?" Vincent asked.

"Let's find out," I said. Logan started to say something, but I cut him off. "I should only need to open a small part of the Path to see."

Closing my eyes, I imagined a dam holding back the torrential Path. When I mentally stretched into the Path, the world shimmered once again, but the flowing overlay moved gently. The smoothness was similar to how the Path looked last year before my soul had been broken and my power went out of control.

Rider shivered as the Path opened around him. Somehow as a werewolf, he could sense the Path when I opened myself to it.

Logan's Path was hidden now, but Rider's was visible. My soul sometimes acted strangely when I looked at Vincent's present Path, so I avoided it. Instead, I focused on the burning form hanging in mid-air.

"It's still here," I pointed, moving my finger as close to it as I could without touching it, "but it's starting to bulge."

"What do you mean?" Logan asked.

"It's like the red twined energy is holding the other back, but it's losing its grip."

"Perhaps you should move away from it," Vincent said.

"If you two don't sense anything, maybe we should set it off?" I suggested.

"No," Vincent said.

"Hold your horses," Logan said. "Cassie has a good point. Maybe you could find something if it's in motion."

Logan was generally our lead when we work together. Vincent and Rider must have come to some sort of silent agreement while I watched our target.

"Do you think you can spread the effect like last time, Cassie?" Logan asked.

"Sure, let me know when you all are ready," I said. There was really nothing they had to do, but I needed the few seconds to open the Path entirely.

A gradual change would have been nice. Imagining the mental dam opening up and letting the Path through sounded great in theory. In practice, the moment I put a chink in that wall, it came crashing down. The torrent rolled over me.

"Go for it when you're ready," Logan said.

I sensed Logan and Rider tense. Vincent shifted closer. Focusing my strength as a Reader firmly on the present, I touched the red-striped energy.

Raw power exploded out. It took more effort to make the Path curve around multiple people, while still assuring they received some effect. Once the power had extended itself, I was tempted to try to follow its Path back to when it was created. It may have been my last chance, but I knew I was pushing my limits already. I did a quick scan of the room before forcing the crushing tide away.

When the world turned listless, I went straight for the coffee, grateful that I had another pot already waiting.

"Did either of you sense anything?" Logan asked as they followed me into the kitchen.

"Nothing," Vincent said, "but if it was a Walker, once again, I may not notice."

"Think there's someone upset about this spring?" Logan asked.

Vincent shrugged. "If they had some knowledge about the events, it's possible."

"Have you heard anything from other Walkers? Has anyone mentioned it?" Logan asked.

"I've been out of touch," Vincent said. He looked ill at ease with the way the conversation was going.

"Are there—"

"What about Rider?" I said, interrupting Logan. "Did you sense anything?" I thought I saw Vincent give me a small look of gratitude, but he looked away too quickly for me to tell for sure.

Rider was concentrating hard on his own coffee and had been quiet since we entered the kitchen.

"Rider?" I asked.

He looked like he was about to say something, then stopped. After a few moments, he tried again. "There is a similarity to something that I am familiar with."

"From your world?" I asked.

"It did not originate in my world. I am not sure where it originated."

We gave him space to continue, but when he didn't seem interested in going further, Logan asked, "What is this similar to?"

"Magic," Rider said.

I frowned, not quite following.

"Similar, but not the same?" Logan asked.

"I have not experienced it in this dimension. I am not sure if it would be the same," Rider said.

"You're saying this might be magic?" I asked. "As in witchcraft or Harry Houdini?"

69

Rider shook his head. "I do not know Houdini, and to my knowledge, I have never met a witch. This was similar to a warlock."

"Warlock?" Vincent said. I think even Logan and Rider heard his skepticism.

"I haven't seen any in this world," Logan said. "AIR doesn't have any mention of them."

"You've checked the AIR records?" I asked. "For a warlock?"

"They're nasty pieces of work," Logan said. "One warlock could do a hell of a lot of damage."

Logan and Rider fell silent. I looked at Vincent. My eyebrow raised mirroring his own disbelief.

"You two are saying that warlocks exist. That magic exists," I said.

"Lots of dimensions use magic," Logan said dismissively. "It's the warlock part that concerns me."

"How could I have been in this job for this long and not know that magic exists?" I asked.

"It's not something a Lost is going to stand up and announce," Logan said.

"What do we do?" Vincent asked.

"Do? I'm not sure there's anything we can do," Logan said.

"Move?" Rider suggested.

He didn't look like he was joking. "What? I'm not moving!"

"I don't think there's reason to get out Dodge," Logan said.

That helped me relax a bit.

"A warlock would find her anyway," Logan said.

Great, I shouldn't move because it would do no good.

"Still, if this is a warlock, what happened this morning was little stuff." Logan looked apprehensive as he continued. "More of a hello, than an attack."

Rider looked mournfully at the table.

"But it might not be a warlock?" I asked. The way they were acting was unnerving.

"If not, it is something similar," Rider said.

"What do warlocks do?" Vincent asked. "What can we do to prevent them from becoming more aggressive?"

"They do whatever they want," Logan said. "The ones that I've had the displeasure of meeting have been sadistic bastards. What I want to know is how you managed to get on the wrong side of one?"

"Me?" Shocked at the question, I wasn't sure what Logan thought I was hiding. "I didn't do anything!"

"Could it be a part of the case?" Vincent asked.

"Then why would it come after me? Ethan is..." The thought stuck in my throat. Could this have happened to him, too? Could it have been worse?

I snatched up the landline and left the kitchen. My hands were shaking as I dialed his number.

"Couldn't wait until tonight to see me?" Ethan asked when he picked up the phone.

I could hear the smile in his voice and blew out a sigh of relief. "Something like that," I said, trying to sound coy rather than nervous. "I forgot to ask if we were having dinner at the park." It was a good pretext to call.

"There's a nice spot a few blocks away. I thought we could stop by there."

"That sounds great. Everything going well this morning?"

"So far so good," Ethan said.

"That's good to hear. I'll see you tonight?"

"You certainly will."

My fear died. The guys were talking when I returned to hang up the phone in the kitchen. I poured more coffee, before sitting down at the table.

"I'm going to make a few discreet calls to see if anyone knows anything about a warlock locally," Logan said. "It may be best, at least for the time being, that we keep this away from work."

Vincent and Rider nodded.

I shrugged. "As far as I can tell, it's not work related."

"Ethan's okay then?" Logan asked.

"Yeah. It might have nothing to do with his case," I said.

"It's too soon to rule that out," Vincent said.

"If a warlock caused the damage to yesterday's victim, we would have no way of knowing," Rider said. "I smelled objects only at the graveyard and around the victim. It is possible for a warlock to mask the scent."

"That was a construction site. Not a graveyard," I reminded Rider.

Starting at Rider's head, a shiver rolled down him, straight to his feet. "I do not understand why humans would build on top of the dead. Is it a monument of some sort?"

We all looked at Rider. His primary partner spoke up first.

"What do you mean the building is being built on top of the dead?" Vincent asked.

"The bodies underground. It appears to be very old, but it is an uncomfortable thought in my world to build over the dead," Rider said.

"What makes you think there are bodies under the ground?" I asked.

Rider looked confused. "There is not much that will mask the decay of the dead, depending on how deep they are buried. With more than a few together, the smell will remain until the bones are dust. Even then, there is a smell, but you may not recognize it as a person or animal. These are very close to the surface."

I was horrified by the thought.

Rider looked at our faces. "You did not know the dead rested there?"

"We did not," Vincent said, keeping his voice level.

"Something was hauled out of the ground there," I said.

"Or crawled out." Vincent's eyes held traces of fear.

"No, no, no, I'm not sold on warlocks yet. There's no way you're telling me zombies are possible." There was a squeak to my voice that I wished wasn't there.

Vincent shook his head. "No idea."

I looked at Logan and Rider.

"Rumors only," Logan said. "Rider would have noticed the smell if something dead came out of the ground."

"Unless the scent was masked by something, like a warlock," Rider said.

"We need to get back out to that site," Logan said, standing up. "I'm going to run home, get ready, and call Hank on the way. We need to get construction halted." Logan looked me over. "Rider, can you run out and get us some breakfast? There's a donut store on the edge of town. I should be ready by the time you get back."

Rider nodded and left.

"We'll need some coffee to go," Logan added.

"I'll make it," I said.

"I'll be back in thirty." Logan left through the back door.

This left Vincent and me in the kitchen alone, together.

CHAPTER 9

T HE SILENCE STRETCHED OUT, ALTHOUGH I'm not sure it could be described as awkward. Vincent and I were usually pretty comfortable with each other when our situation wasn't strained.

"Would you like some more coffee?" I asked. "It sounds like it's going to be a long day."

"Thank you. I'd like that."

He was the only one of my partners that took his coffee black. For me, it wasn't by choice. This time around, I added plenty of sugar to mine.

"I'm glad to hear that nothing's wrong with Ethan," Vincent said.

"Are you?" I asked, taken aback by the statement.

Vincent nodded. "He appears to make you happy. I wouldn't want that taken away."

"Thank you. We're doing pretty well."

"It's been a rough morning."

"You mean after learning about warlocks and zombies?" I asked.

A flicker of a smile appeared on Vincent's otherwise impassive face. "I meant your fall down the stairs."

"Oh, yeah. A few bruises, but I'm sure I'll be fine. Um, Rider said you two were already on your way?"

Vincent nodded, but didn't say anything.

"So, you knew something was wrong?" I asked, prying a little deeper.

"I did."

"Is that..." I stopped trying to think of a way to phrase my concerns about him knowing what was happening to me. My face started to turn red and I couldn't ask, so I switched gears. "How come you know something is wrong with me, but I never know anything about you?"

He frowned. "You seem to know precisely how I'm feeling."

"When we're apart, I mean."

"I go through a great deal of effort to hide my thoughts and emotions. The fact that you know them when we're together is disturbing enough."

"Why do you do that?"

"It's...complicated."

I rolled my eyes. "I'm sure I couldn't possibly understand."

Vincent sighed and slumped back in his chair.

There have been rare occasions when I have seen Vincent like this, exposed to the world. Each time I felt like I was intruding on a private moment. One where he let his guard down.

I wondered if he had moments like that when he was alone.

"You are infuriating," Vincent said.

"That sounds about right," I said.

He didn't look at me, but he smiled. A genuine smile. It softened his face and made my heart beat faster. The expression slipped away, but his face remained softened, and his mask of indifference didn't return.

"Walkers don't tend to get many questions from those around them. What people already know about us causes them to be leery. You make things...difficult."

Right, of course I do. I felt a cloak of depression sink over my shoulders. "Don't worry about it. I need to go get ready."

"Wait." Vincent reached out and grabbed my hand as I started to stand up. "That came out wrong."

My hand tingled and warmth spread up my arm. I closed my eyes and let that connection, that closeness we shared, fill me. I'm not sure what he felt. I wasn't even sure I wanted to know.

What I did know was that he was still holding on. When I looked at him, he had his eyes closed. It would be nice to think that this connection would have been there even if we didn't each have a small part of the other's soul.

But people didn't work like that, did they?

When he opened his eyes he looked at me, and I could feel the sadness and regret well up, causing my own to deepen. My eyes started to burn. Vincent slowly took his hand away and I could see him retreating into himself.

I forced a smile and left the room before any tears decided to arrive. It didn't help that I felt stupid. Why did I have to get so worked up around him? I seriously needed to get a handle on myself. Vincent wasn't the only one that could bottle up his emotions.

Since I had already prepared for work, there wasn't much for me to do. Focusing on something was always key, so I did a quick internet search for self-defense classes, and then stuffed my gear bag with some exercise clothes. In the bathroom, I checked myself out for bruises and took some ibuprofen to dull the ache that had been caused by my fall.

I heard voices below, but I didn't hurry. When the doorbell rang, I knew Rider was back. With the gang all together, I took my bag and went downstairs. From here on out, Vincent was another partner. Nothing more.

There may even have been a small part of me that believed it.

Vincent appeared to be taking the route of ignoring what happened. The strained look in the corners of his eyes was the only indication that something had passed between us.

That worked for me. Ignoring things was my specialty.

"Hank is working to get a temporary stop to construction. We need to head to the Farm for some equipment. Cassie, can you reach out to Ethan and let him know we're checking out a lead at the construction site?" Logan asked.

I glanced at my phone for the time. "I'll get in contact with him. Do you all need me at the office?" Mentally, I was crossing my fingers. Fitting self-defense classes into my crazy schedule wasn't going to be easy, but there was one this morning I could make if I hurried.

Logan looked surprised. "No, we can get the equipment. You want to catch up to us at the job site later?"

"Yeah, give me a call when you're on your way," I said.

"Will do, we can take the truck," Logan said, leading the others out.

As soon as they left, I jumped in my car and headed to the gym. I called them on the way, to make sure there was room in the class. They were friendly on the phone, which was a good sign. It didn't hurt that the first class was free.

Out of the fifteen people in class, only two of us were women. The next hour was hell, and here I thought I was in reasonably good shape. At first, I was able to blame it on being tired after a rough morning, but after the first twenty minutes, I wondered if I had ever exercised before. After thirty, I was trying to figure out why anyone would put themselves through this torment. We did a few drills, which I thought might slow things down, but that wasn't the case. If anything, the people in the class worked harder. Even after the brief cool down, I was still panting and covered in sweat.

Oddly, though, I felt good, as if I had accomplished something. After class, I signed up for a full month.

It was on the way home that I realized I had forgotten to call Ethan. Since I was feeling exceptionally gross, I waited until after a quick shower to give him a call.

"Two calls in one morning? To what do I owe this pleasure?" Ethan asked.

Two calls in one morning. Crap. He was going to start thinking I was the clingy type if this kept up.

"Um, this one is work related," I said. "We, uh, found out some information about the work site."

"What did you find?"

I should have thought this through. Explaining that Rider 'smelled' dead bodies in the ground was out of the question.

"It's a theory at this point, but we're getting construction stopped," I said.

"We haven't released the crime scene yet. You should be good there. I'll head in that direction, though."

"It's actually the secondary site we're interested in today. Although, I'm not sure how far that will widen."

"That site was released the first day. Any evidence is probably long gone."

My phone beeped, signaling a call waiting.

"Logan's getting some stuff, and we're meeting at the site. That's him on the other line. I've gotta run."

"See you soon," Ethan said.

I wasn't sure if Ethan was supposed to be at the site or not, but I guess it was too late now. I switched over to Logan's call.

"We'll be at the site in fifteen minutes, give or take. I'm not sure who Hank has lined up to meet us, but we can't get construction stopped until we give them facts to back up our suspicions."

"How are we going to do that?" I asked.

"Ground penetrating radar. Meet us out there?"

"Yeah, I'm about twenty minutes away," I lied. "Ethan's on his way as well."

"Should make for an interesting afternoon. See you out there."

Drying my hair was agonizingly slow, so I left it damp. I threw on clothes and rushed back to town. Morning classes weren't going to work. On the way to the job site, fatigue became more pronounced, I started to notice muscle aches and I was starving.

When I arrived on site, vehicles from the construction crew were everywhere, but I drove up as close to the area as I could get. My partners and Ethan were standing around doing pretty much nothing. Ethan was there chatting with another officer, but there were also workers. A man in a yellow hard hat looked like he was giving out orders to the crew. When I got within earshot, I could tell he wasn't happy about how the day was turning out.

At least it was Friday.

Ethan nodded in my direction as I walked up. I gave him a small wave, but headed straight to Logan.

"What's going on?" I asked.

"Difference in opinion," Logan said.

I watched the man in the hard hat. "Which opinion is ours?"

"We," Logan gestured to the three of them, "think we'd like to take our equipment down to the site and get this taken care of. That guy over there," he pointed to the guy talking with the workers, "thinks we shouldn't be allowed on the property."

"Oh joy, what did Ethan say?" I asked.

"He thinks we should wait for the city inspector to show up," Logan said.

"Sounds reasonable." I stifled a yawn.

"The general contractor is short tempered. How are you feeling?" Logan asked.

"I'm fine, why?" I asked.

"We may need you to calm the situation down a bit," Logan said.

"I'll do what I can."

The construction crew was getting smaller as guys broke apart to move to other buildings. Eight apartment buildings were going up, each of them in various stages, so there was plenty for them to do.

The next twenty minutes seemed like some sort of standoff. The general contractor stayed in his corner, Ethan and the other officer stayed off to one side, talking, and then there were the four of us. Logan was humming to himself, I've never seen Rider look so bored before, Vincent was silently keeping an eye on everyone in the vicinity, and I felt ready to eat my own fist, which was starting to make me cranky.

Ethan and the officer broke rank first and joined us.

"We got word that the building inspector is on his way," Ethan said. "What are you all planning on doing out here?"

"We're going to take a deeper look at the site," Logan said.

"I am interested to see what the machine we brought tells us," Rider said.

A small white truck parked behind my car. A balding man in glasses got out, put on a hard hat, and then picked up a clipboard. The general contractor crossed his arms and watched the man approach us.

"Good morning, officers, I'm Simon, chief inspector for the city." Simon shook everyone's hand as we introduced ourselves. "I understand that some environmental controls need to be checked on this site."

"You could say that," Logan said.

"The environmental report was signed off on about seven months ago. An independent lab found nothing on the site that would cause an environmental issue," Simon said.

"They would have to be very specific in the area and depth they checked in order to spot our concern," Vincent said.

"You have the proper testing equipment?" Simon asked, looking around the area.

"In the truck. Mr. Davidson asked us to wait until you arrived," Logan said.

"Well, let's get this done so these men can get back to work," Simon said.

Logan and Rider went to the back of the truck to get out the equipment. Elves are curiously strong for their build. It was a mark of his irritation that Logan didn't try to hide that fact when he swung the equipment down off the truck.

"That looks like an over-sized push mower," Ethan said.

"Ground penetrating radar," Logan said.

"Do you plan on going over the whole lot with this?" Simon asked.

"We have a pretty good idea of where we need to look," Logan said. "Rider, get the flags. Mark everywhere we should be checking."

Rider looked somber, but grabbed a bag, and headed around the hole that was waiting to be filled with a building. The walk out basement still didn't have concrete down, so that was working in our favor.

When Simon and the police followed Rider, Mr. Davidson sprang into action.

"This is a load of bull, Simon, and criminal. How am I going to explain a whole day lost on this site?" Mr. Davidson asked.

"We'll be as quick as we can be, Mr. Davidson," Simon said.

Up close, Mr. Davidson was a lot bigger than he looked from a distance. He wasn't too much taller than I was, but you could tell he worked construction. His arms bulged and the veins in his neck were standing out.

This morning, the Path had come to me quickly. Out here, I struggled again.

Vincent kept one eye on me and one eye on the hulking contractor.

"We've got our permits." Mr. Davidson's face started to turn red as his voice raised, and his emotions started running through the atmosphere. They weren't as strong as Vincent's, or some of the Lost that I've worked with, but the fact that I felt it without the Path open was saying a lot.

"I understand that, Mr. Davidson. And the sooner we get this over with, the better for everyone," Simon said. It didn't seem like the contractor phased him in the least.

Ethan, on the other hand, was keeping a close eye on the frustrated man.

I tried to tune them all out by turning away from the others and closing my eyes. Mr. Davidson's increased volume wasn't making my struggle to read the Path any easier. Concentrating hard, I let my mind flow to the edges of its knowledge. After a few tries, the sides fell away, and my mind made the jump.

Breathing a sigh of relief, I turned to the others. Simon had walked away, joining Logan and Rider. Rider had put two flags up already.

Ethan was trying to calm down Mr. Davidson. Nothing works better than a Reader to calm a situation down. Choosing a serene memory, I embraced the emotion and let it fill me up before allowing it to pour into the Path. With some coaxing, the feeling wound around Mr. Davidson.

It was working on Ethan, and the officer with him. Vincent had made himself virtually immune to my antics, so it didn't affect him, but Mr. Davidson was having a hard time. He looked torn between holding on to his anger or letting it go.

"I think we're good here. Let's go check on Logan and Rider," Vincent said.

"Sure," I said. Worried about leaving Ethan behind with a ticked-off general contractor, I added a bit more emotion and tied it off to Mr. Davidson.

Ethan gave me a warm smile as I walked past him. I looked back a few times, worried that I had pressed things a bit too far.

"I think I may have overdone it. Do you think they're okay?" I whispered to Vincent.

He didn't glance back, but I noticed that Logan looked up.

"I'm sure they're fine," Vincent said.

I wasn't convinced, but we were starting to get close to the gray Path. Enamored with the thought of all those colors twisting around, I moved towards it to see if they were still visible. The gray was muted, as before, but as I followed the Path it turned darker, and I started to see the threads wiggling under the gloom.

"Cass?" Vincent said.

"Hmm," I replied, reaching out to touch the bits of color.

Vincent moved in front of me, blocking my way.

I put my hands on my hips and frowned.

"I think we're getting off track," Vincent said.

Looking around, I saw that I had walked past everyone as I followed the older Path.

"Oh. Sorry." Why was I even over here? I mean, it's interesting, but nothing new to be discovered. "I got distracted."

Lines of worry were worn onto the edges of Vincent's eyes. "Let's get back to the others."

"Yeah." I tried to stop reading the Path, but it acted like rubber. Trying to use force only caused it to bounce back harder. Keeping it open was easier, so I dammed it up until I was left with a small trickle of power. Even Rider's Path was barely visible.

"We're getting ready to start," Logan called.

When we came over, Logan handed Vincent a laptop. "You and Simon keep an eye on this," Logan said. "Rider, go get the shovels."

Rider looked all too happy to move away from the site.

Logan plucked up the first flag, turned on the machine, and drove it slowly over the area.

Over Vincent's shoulder, I watched the screen. Wavy lines spread across the monitor, black, green, yellow, and red.

"You've got it, Logan," Vincent said.

"What are we looking at?" Simon asked.

Logan swung around and ran the machine over another swath of ground.

"Once more," Vincent said.

The wavy lines became straighter on the second and third strips Logan went over.

"Let's hit the other side," Logan suggested.

Vincent frowned. "I think we have to start and keep moving in one direction."

"Maybe we should start again," Logan said.

"We've got what we need for now," Vincent said.

"Looks like we're about to have company anyway," I said, noticing Mr. Davidson approaching. "He looks calmer at least."

"Nice job on that," Logan said.

Rider had given Ethan a shovel to carry. I'm not sure why Rider thought we needed six shovels, but he appeared to be carrying another five.

"I'm still not sure what we're looking at here," Simon said.

I stepped away when Logan came over and Mr. Davidson joined them.

"See these smooth lines? Those are the natural ground. Then here, the ground starts to get disturbed. And where the flag was, that's a body."

Looking around, I saw another dozen or so flags. My stomach was growling, but I wasn't hungry anymore.

"A body?" Simon asked.

CHAPTER 10

Y ES," VINCENT SAID.

Mr. Davidson nodded and looked around. "All these are bodies?"

"Yes," Vincent said.

"If that's true, we'll have to stop construction," Simon said, "but how do you know these are bodies and not animal carcasses or something?"

"The environmental survey checked for old cemeteries on record. There are none here," Mr. Davidson said.

Simon shook his head. "We're going to need more proof than some wavy lines."

"That's where the shovels come in." Logan beckoned Rider and Ethan over. "Let's get started. I'll take this spot. Ethan, you're going to want to oversee this. You and Simon. There are shovels if you want to help dig."

Mr. Davidson was still looking around at all the flags. "There's no way you're going to let us build here."

I'm not sure if he was talking to Simon, or us, but if those were bodies, he probably wasn't wrong. At least for the next few weeks, there wouldn't be construction in this area.

Having no interest in seeing what they would unearth, I went over to where the gray trail exited the ground. With the Path so closed off, I couldn't see anything useful. It was tempting to take a deeper look again, but I resisted the urge.

Mr. Davidson came over and started picking up pieces of rebar. He would lift a metal bar and drop it again. When he finally found a smaller piece, he swung it a few times and started humming. Then he turned back to the group huddled around an ever-expanding hole in the ground.

"Mr. Davidson," I said.

He continued humming. I ran after him, moving in front of him before he reached the group.

"Mr. Davidson, I'm going to have to ask you to stop right there," I said.

He kept moving forward. When he got close, he started to raise the rebar.

"Stop!" I yelled.

The Path surged around me and I welcomed its strength. As Mr. Davidson swung the rebar down on me, I lifted my arm in defense, creating a solid wall of Path at the same time.

Like a wall of air, it was invisible, but strong enough to stop the rebar. Davidson jerked the metal back and swung down again. Again, he struck air. His grin was becoming manic, and I was starting to falter. The Path dragged at me. It pushed, shoved, and turned me around. Something came between Mr. Davidson and me, which came as a great relief.

When the Path surged, I fell on my back and was trapped in its flow. The sun rose and fell countless times. The grass grew, it was cut, and then it grew again. When dirt was poured over me, I started to panic. If this was the past or future, I couldn't tell. Whichever it was, the ground where I laid was covered with something. When I moved my arms to try to thrust it away, nothing happened.

Suffocation. I was being buried alive and suffocating. Trying to tell myself it wasn't real was no use. I couldn't touch it, but I could see it. The air tasted like dirt. I coughed and choked on the flavor.

There was a sharp tug on my chest. The feeling of hurtling forward stopped. Then the ground fell away. I felt heavier, but the air was fresh. Looking around, I saw that there was some sort of monument. It was broken and covered with dirt, but there had once been something there. Or maybe there would be?

It started to move away. The farther I got from it, the more sense things began to make. Strong arms were wrapped around me. There were noises. Real and tangible sounds that I could latch onto.

The air around me began to shimmer. When Rider appeared, apparently carrying me, I breathed a sigh of relief. He looked tense and had his eyes focused forward.

I reached up and touched his face, and he looked down.

"There you are," he said.

"Here I am."

"I could not find you."

"I think you're carrying me," I said.

Rider smiled. "It is time for you to come back."

Nodding, I closed my eyes and tried to press the Path away. It was a struggle. When I opened my eyes, the present was shaped around me, but the Path was still there.

"I think we need to move farther away," I said.

Rider nodded and kept walking. I closed my eyes and concentrated. When I felt the world lurch, my mind snapped back. I opened my eyes to the dull hues of the natural world.

"I don't think I've ever been as happy to see the real world as I am right now," I said.

"You are back," said Rider, beaming down at me.

"Thank you," I said. "I'm not sure where I would be if you weren't here."

"You would have found your way, but it might have taken longer."

His optimism amazed me. I shook my head and looked around.

"Where is everyone?" I asked.

Rider turned around. Ethan was at a squad car, arms folded, and in a serious discussion with Vincent.

"Shoot. Rider, do you mind setting me down?" I asked.

He put me on my feet, but kept a hand on my arm, trying to keep me steady. I saw that Logan was talking with Simon. Logan looked like he was trying to keep an eye on everyone at once, while having the creepiest smile plastered on his face.

Elves shouldn't be allowed to fake a smile. It never worked the way they thought it did.

"Who thought it was a good idea to let Vincent and Ethan talk?" I mumbled.

"Vincent said he is smoothing things over. I am not sure what that means. Is something wrinkled?"

"I think the situation is wrinkled."

"That may be true."

"What the hell happened?"

"You stopped Mr. Davidson from hurting Simon. Although Ethan thought that you were injured. Ethan has arrested Mr. Davidson. He made the officer do the actual arrest part. Logan is working with Simon now that he is assured there are bodies in the ground, and Vincent helped me find you. I did not know that was possible."

"How did he help?"

"He..." Rider's brow furrowed. "He tugged on a part of you and stopped you. Then he had me take you away. Like we moved you away yesterday."

"Hmm, away from the Path I followed," I said softly. I watched Vincent and Ethan. They didn't look happy, but it didn't seem like they were yelling at each other. "That was a smart move. Any ideas on what we should do now?"

"I think that will depend."

"On?"

"On if you are able to walk unassisted."

Exhaustion leaked through my pores. "I can walk."

"Are you sure?"

I took in a deep breath and let it go, giving myself a moment to think. "I'm sure I don't want to look any weirder in front of Ethan."

"He likes you," Rider said. "Once you two become friends, it will not matter."

For werewolves, friendships didn't come easy, but once you were their friend, it was for life. You each held up your own end of the relationship.

"I'm afraid it doesn't always work that way with humans," I said. "It can, but only if they really understand. Ethan and I don't yet have that type of connection."

"He appears to be receptive. Have you tried?"

That didn't take much thought, which was sad. "Not hard enough."

"It can take a great deal of time."

"Unfortunately, that time isn't now. I feel dead on my feet."

"Logan would like to know if you are able to drive," Rider said.

I looked down the hill at Logan. Simon was walking back to his truck, and Logan was watching us. Rider and Logan could hear at considerable distances.

"I can drive."

"Logan says that you did good today. Go home, wrangle up some grub, and kick back." Rider looked confused. "Grubs are bugs."

I grinned, and then I had to stifle a yawn. "In this case, I'm pretty sure he means grub as in food."

"You are eating the grubs?"

Logan looked like he was laughing. Even from a distance, the elf's smile was catching.

"I'm not eating them. Grub is an old slang word that means food," I said.

"So many words mean the same thing," Rider said.

"That's true, but you know the language so well, no one would know that you came from another dimension."

Logan and his family were the same way. Most Lost have to know the language at least passably well before they can be integrated into the community.

"I did originate from here. Before my mother passed away. I think that helps."

I patted Rider's hand in sympathy.

"Ethan appears to be waiting for you," Rider said.

Sure enough, Vincent was walking over to Logan and Ethan was leaning on his car. His arms were still crossed and he didn't look happy.

"I'll go talk to him, and then go home," I said before another yawn came.

Rider frowned. "What if there is more magic at your house?"

"Logan thought it might have been more of a greeting than anything else. I'm sure things will be normal at home."

He nodded slowly. "That is possible."

"I guess I'll see you tomorrow sometime, now that we seem to have a case."

"I will come over in the morning."

Remembering my date, which I hoped was still on, I said, "Not too early."

Each step towards Ethan seemed to weigh me down. Still, I fabricated a positive attitude and tried to hide my fatigue.

The approach was awkward and made even more so when Ethan didn't say anything as I walked up.

"Hey," I said before things got too uncomfortable.

"You doing okay?" Ethan asked.

"I'm good. I got a little shook up, but I'm all right." I should have asked Rider what Vincent had told Ethan.

"Shook up?" Ethan finally uncrossed his arms and stood up. "What were you thinking jumping in front of that guy?"

My mind was sludgy, so I hoped I had misunderstood him. "What do you mean?"

"Cassie, he could have killed you."

"But he didn't, I'm fine." I was tired, mentally and physically. Despite that, I could read between the lines. It boiled down to the fact that I was a girl and shouldn't have gotten in the way. Keeping my cool was difficult. Why did Ethan have to try to pull this macho stuff now? Still, I managed to bite my tongue.

"How you're not injured is beyond me. But that's not the point."

"What exactly is the point?" I asked. Immediately, I wished I could take the question back. No answer could come out of his mouth that I'd be happy with.

"The point is that it was reckless."

His concern and frustration were battling it out. I could feel each strike, even with the Path closed.

"I was doing my job," I said, dropping all pretense of positivity.

"There were others there that could have done that job, and what the hell was wrong with your partners? Rider didn't look like he planned to help at all until after the second strike. Logan seemed madder at Vincent than anything else, and Vincent was the only one that acted like he gave a damn."

"Are you kidding me with this?" I asked, lowering my voice. "This is my job and how dare you judge my partners. Rider knows I can handle myself and I knew he would help when I needed it. If Logan was mad at Vincent, you could bet Vincent was doing something out of line."

"It's not—"

"Shut up," I snapped. "Like it or not this is my job, and believe it or not, a woman can take care of herself. Don't ever, ever expect me to stand out of the way and let someone else get hurt. It's not going to happen."

"Cass," Vincent said behind me.

"What?" I asked, turning my frustration in his direction.

"I need to talk with you. Let me walk you to your car."

I rolled my eyes. "Fine."

It felt like my aggravation was the only thing keeping me on my feet as I stalked off to my car.

Vincent walked with me, but didn't say anything until we were far enough away that Ethan couldn't overhear.

"Are you alright?" Vincent asked.

"Don't you start too."

"I think you need to give him a break."

"What?" The words tempered my frustration with confusion. I never thought I'd hear something like that from Vincent.

"He was scared. That's all."

"You didn't hear what he said," I mumbled.

"I didn't have to. I've been there. He was scared and upset with himself for letting it happen."

"Letting it happen?"

"You know what I mean. Not reacting fast enough. Not being able to help."

"Is that what he said?" I asked.

"He didn't have to."

"Why are you taking his side?"

"We're not teenagers, Cass. There are no sides here. I'm sure he said something stupid, but from the way he talked, this was the second time in two days he could have been seeing you dead on the ground."

That took the wind from my sails and I slumped against my car.

"You didn't tell me about yesterday," Vincent said.

"It was a non-event."

"I'm pretty sure he doesn't see it that way."

"How do you know so much about what he's thinking?"

Vincent shook his head. "He wasn't the only one thinking them."

"That's not my fault." I crossed my arms, but couldn't muster up a glare.

"It's not," Vincent agreed. "I'm only suggesting that you take a step back and look at things from his point of view."

"The way he talks, his point of view is that I can't take care of myself."

"It's not that you can't take care of yourself. It's that you shouldn't be pushed into situations where you have to defend yourself. None of us should. But when you watch someone close to you being put through those things, you don't always have the best reactions."

"Why are you making so much sense? And why are you sticking up for Ethan."

There was the slightest tightening to Vincent's eyes. "The only person I'm looking out for here is you."

CHAPTER 11

AFTER VINCENT WALKED OFF, I momentarily thought of apologizing to Ethan. My mind was too muddled from fatigue to make that decision. There was more than a little chance that I wouldn't make it that far without falling anyway. With knots in my stomach, I looked over the site before I steered the car towards home. It was barely past noon and I was already planning on going to bed. After getting food that is. The faster the better.

Sometimes being a Reader sucked. Luckily, Logan had Vincent and Rider to help him out.

By the time I reached the driveway, I had already eaten my drive-thru lunch. When I entered the house, I had a twinge of uncertainty. After this morning, being home alone, not knowing what may be invisible and waiting for me, made me uncomfortable. Still, my bed called. The slow trek upstairs yielded no surprises. The only conscious decision I made was to turn on my alarm to ensure I had enough time to get ready for my date. Assuming I still had one.

When I woke up, I had fading memories of nightmares of being trapped underground. Even with the dreams, though, I felt renewed. Nothing like a little rest to fix all the woes of being too active at reading.

The enormity of this morning's workout had settled in. Before taking a shower, I had to take some more ibuprofen to soothe the muscles that had tightened considerably. When I was in the shower, I finally noticed a tapestry of bruises. I had it in mind to wear a dress, since I only rarely had the occasion to put one on.

The thought of explaining the bruises to Ethan, especially after our earlier conversation, made me decide on slacks.

Once I got dressed, I made a large pot of coffee and waited. I watched the clock tick through the minutes, my stomach twisting a little tighter as each moment fled by.

As I sat there, I second guessed my outfit, my hair, and whether or not to pack my gun. Since this was a date, I decided to forgo the gun, and I checked the bathroom mirror twice more. When six-thirty came and went, I considered calling, but I decided to wait it out. At six-forty, my fingers tapped on the table and my twisting insides started to sink while I stared at the clock. At six-forty-five, I got up, dumped out my coffee, and grabbed my tablet, ready to throw myself back into work.

The doorbell rang before the tablet booted up.

I blew out a sigh, not sure if it was relief or anxiety, and I answered the door.

Ethan stood there, looking almost as nervous as I felt.

"Hi, um, I wasn't sure if I should..." Ethan stammered.

I smiled. "I'm glad you're here."

"Sorry I'm late. I got held up. We can still make dinner and the park, though."

I snatched up my purse and we went into town.

"How are you feeling?" Ethan asked.

"Better than this afternoon," I admitted. "I'm sorry for... well, everything."

He shook his head. "I'm sorry too. I shouldn't have said what I did. I wasn't thinking."

"You were worried. I get that."

Ethan's hands tightened around the steering wheel. "Your partner didn't look too happy with me after you left."

"Vincent?"

"Yeah."

"Hm, I'm pretty sure that was aimed at me. He told me not to get upset with you."

"Vincent said that?"

"Yeah."

"I wouldn't have expected that."

"I reacted badly," I said.

"You looked...I mean, until you walked over, I thought..."

I shifted, uncomfortable with the direction the conversation was taking. "I'm okay."

"The way that guy came after you. I thought...well, I'm glad you weren't hurt."

He didn't actually come after me so much as I got in his way, but I wanted the subject to end. "I'm good. So, where are we going for dinner?"

It wasn't subtle, but it got the subject changed.

We weren't particularly talkative during dinner, but once we joined the crowds at University Park, we began to loosen up. At least I did.

"My mom talked about this when I was younger. I've always liked the idea of this festival," I said.

Lights were strung up all around the park. Christmas tree lights, lights focused on the artwork, lights under tents, and scattered here and there throughout the front side of the park. The scene looked like it should have been on a postcard.

"I don't remember if this event was around when I was a kid. Once I moved away, we didn't have anything like it. Not for art anyway. The three small towns in the area where I lived probably had less than a thousand people. We had carnivals and county fairs. Veterans Day was a big deal. The whole town would get together, and flags were set up all around. One year, families bought flags for each of the veterans in their family. The city bought them for those that didn't make it back home. We had well over a hundred flags flying."

"That would have been something to see," I said, imagining all those flags for such a small community.

"It really was. I love to see this, though. I have a friend who's an artist."

The sun started to fall below the horizon. Kids were running around, vendors were set up, selling drinks, cotton candy, and popcorn. While holding hands Ethan and I strolled down alleys of artwork that crisscrossed through the park. We'd stop and look at pieces that caught our eye. The artists were on hand to talk about their work.

We were going to walk to another area of the park where more work was set up, but Ethan wanted to go back and talk to one of the artists again. I told him I was going to get a drink and we parted ways, planning to meet back before going to the next group of artists.

After buying my drink, I stood and enjoyed people watching. Everyone from well-dressed politicians to stoned-looking college students were here. The artwork always drew a crowd.

The noise of the people began to fade. Frowning, I looked around. There seemed to be the same amount of people, maybe fewer kids since it was after nine, but the sound was muted, as though everything was moving farther away. It wasn't until the people began to slow that I started to worry.

It wasn't my hearing. Or if it was, it was my sight as well. My heart raced. This kind of thing happened when a piece of soul took over. Well, when a particular fragment took over. But in those instances it was me moving faster, not everyone else moving slower.

Panicking, I looked around, trying to find Ethan through the ever-slowing crowd. I was me. I'm sure I was me. Still, I probed around inside of my mind in an attempt to reassure myself that my soul was in charge.

"You are very much you," the voice sang out over the silent masses.

I jumped and spun around. My heart beat furiously. Dread fell over me when I saw an old man move through the people.

A blur appeared to the left, but when I glanced over, there was nothing. The man was much closer when I looked back. My hands started to shake and I backed up a few steps. I kept the man in sight while I tried to look around. Flickers of shadows moved through the still crowd. The people were almost at a standstill, but other vaguely human shapes flashed, moving too quickly for me to make out what they were.

Each time my eyes strayed away, the old man seemed to jump forward, coming closer to me than he should have been able to travel. I stopped focusing on the shadows and concentrated on him.

"Who are you?" I asked, trying to keep the fear out of my voice. I'd like to say I was successful, but that would have been too big of a lie.

"I am very much me." The old man chuckled, and I felt the hair raise on the back of my neck.

It wasn't the first time I had heard those words from someone. "You're not the same man that I met this spring in the woods," I said.

"No, no. That is him."

He was close enough to see the deep wrinkles in his skin and the texture of his long, white, wispy hair. It was his eyes that drew the most attention. They were the clearest blue I had ever seen, and despite his apparent age, they appeared sharp. It was hard to imagine that they would miss anything.

Without closing my eyes or looking away from the man, I drew open the Path, stretching my mind to plunge into the flow. Brilliant, pure white light blinded me and the Path snapped away. Pain slashed through my head leaving the feeling that I had been stabbed by an ice pick.

Clutching my head, my eyes scrunched up against the pain.

When I opened them, the man was practically nose-to-nose with me.

"Ah." My short, sharp scream was involuntary, and I stumbled back, somehow managing to stay on my feet.

The old man wheezed out what sounded like a laugh. "He is not me." He paused to catch his breath and laugh some more. "But there is still no peeking."

My heart beat so fast that I could hear my blood pumping through my head. Out of the corners of my eyes, I could see the flit of unknown beings moving closer.

"Who are you? What do you want?"

"What we want is also what you want." He cocked his head this way and that while peering at me with unblinking eyes. "At least for now."

"Who's we?"

"Tsk, tsk, tsk. Wrong questions."

The fear was starting to lean towards anger. Anger I could work with.

"Fine. An awful lot is going on right now. What is it that 'we' want?" I added as much snark to the question as I could manage.

He chuckled and began to pace back and forth in front of me. "Something is here. It should not be."

"That's not narrowing it down much," I said, crossing my arms. "Do you mean one of the Lost?"

"Lost? The Lost are not lost. They belong. The thing that is here was made. It does not belong."

"Made?" I'm not sure if I was really confused, or if the fear and anger were clouding my thinking.

"Yes, and you will remove it."

"Me? Why don't you all remove it? You've stopped time—"

The man let out a cackle of laughter.

It did nothing for my temper. "You, and whoever the rest of you are, can take care of it."

"Perhaps yes, perhaps no," he wheezed, trying to catch his breath. "First, we will see if you can take care of it. It will...relate to you."

"And if I don't take care of it?"

The man stopped pacing and glared at me. Any trace of humor died from his face. Pressure built in the area, the hair on my arms stood up, and I took a step back.

Then the man shrugged and the pressure died away. "Others will die. It will relate to you, so if you do not act, you will die as well."

Although the pain in my head was fading, I was having a hard time following what the man said. "Others will die? No one is killing the Lost."

"They are not the target. Not for death."

Thoughts of the man with his bones ripped out at the construction site lurched forward. I had to bury them or risk losing my dinner.

"What is it?" I asked.

"It is made. And it is here." The old man gave another gesture.

I turned and saw the path that wound away from the festival. "It's—"

The noise rushed back. It's funny how I didn't notice the deafening silence until the roaring of the festival returned full force.

People were moving as if nothing had happened. Frantically, I looked around for signs of the man, the shadows, or something that might be coming or going from the park where the old man had gestured. I almost tripped over my own feet trying to look everywhere at once.

"Would you like for me to call someone for you?"

I whirled around to see Zander standing behind me.

"Good Lord," I muttered. Could my day get any worse? "What do you want?"

"I'm concerned," he said.

I gave him my best, 'what the hell are you talking about' look and started scanning the crowds again.

"You're obviously in distress. I think I should call someone for you," Zander said.

A woman was standing not too far away, glaring at either Zander or me. Possibly both of us.

"What are you talking about, Zander?" I asked.

"Cassie, you went from looking entirely peaceful one moment to upset the next, without anything in between. I—"

"Why are you watching me?" I snapped, turning my full attention to him.

"I wasn't...I was only..." He very calmly stopped when his voice became edgy. When he spoke again, it was in a calm, controlled way. "I'm going—"

"I'm busy, Zander. Take your concern along with your psych degree and turn it towards your date."

"I don't think you should be around this many people when you are upset."

"What does that mean?" I asked, taking a step towards Zander.

He held up his hands in a placating gesture.

I rolled my eyes and crossed my arms.

"Just call the police," the woman behind Zander snapped.

"We just need to let her know that there are people who care," Zander said in his mellow voice.

That voice pissed me off. "You can take your 'I care' crap and—"

"Is there a problem here?" Ethan asked frowning at Zander.

Mortified by the fact that Ethan might have overheard, I could feel my face turn red.

"No," the woman behind Zander snapped. "Call the police and let's go, Zander. She's not our problem." The woman tugged on Zander's arm.

Ethan crossed his arms and looked at the two with a puzzled expression. "What are you accusing her of?"

"Existing," I said, trying to tune them out and look around some more.

"Being crazy," the woman countered.

Zander held up his hands again. "We aren't accusing her of anything. We only want to ensure that she gets help."

"You look familiar," Ethan said to Zander.

Zander put on a pompous little smile. "I get that a lot. I'm a psychologist here in town."

"That's right. You were harassing her at the station a few months ago." Ethan started to look agitated.

The hair on my arms stood on end and the pressure built once more in the area.

Zander's date glared at him and his smile fell away. "I was not harassing her."

There was no sign of the old man, but when I looked at the path he had indicated, someone moved out of sight.

"By the way, I'm Lieutenant Ethan Parker." Ethan's eyes bored into Zander's.

Zander appeared unfazed.

"Ethan," I said urgently, keeping my eyes on the sidewalk the old man had indicated. "I think we might have a more urgent situation." I didn't bother giving any other explanation, and walked off.

"You shouldn't support her delusions," Zander said. He sounded sad, which only ticked me off more.

While I took out my phone to call Logan, I heard Ethan say, "Take my word for it, continued harassment won't be tolerated."

CHAPTER 12

LOGAN PICKED UP ON THE first ring. "Howdy."
"Ethan and I are at University Park, moving towards the campus."

I heard Ethan behind me as I rounded a corner and disappeared from view of the festival. With lights shining yards away, the trees and bushes cast dark shadows across the walkway.

"What are we looking at?" Logan asked.

"I'm not sure yet. Uh...let's just say I have a tip. It could be nothing, but we're checking it out."

"Lost?"

"Unknown at this time."

"And you have Ethan with you?"

"Yep." I couldn't keep the tension out of my voice.

A couple walked by, laughing. Not five minutes ago, that could have been Ethan and me.

"This really could be nothing," I said again.

"Doesn't hurt to check it out. Want me to swing by?"

"Uh...yes." Having my partner show up on my date wasn't ideal, but neither was dragging my date into possible agency business. "I'll leave the line open, and if it turns out to be nothing, I'll let you know."

I slid the phone into my pocket, making sure not to break the connection, and started moving faster. Not knowing if I was following an actual trail or not made things difficult.

"You received a tip?" Behind me, Ethan sounded agitated, but he was keeping up.

"Yeah. Listen, sorry about Zander." Even now I could feel my face red with embarrassment over the situation. Zander really needed to stop showing up and making me out to be a crazy person.

It didn't help that he still managed to make me doubt myself. Maybe I shouldn't have told Ethan about what I could do. Letting civilians into my world never ended well.

"He was at the station this spring."

"Yep." I stopped and closed my eyes, intent on reaching out to the Path. My power may as well have been fairy dust. There was nothing to grab hold of.

"He was bothering you then as well."

Trying again achieved the same results. It was almost as if the Path didn't exist.

"He was." Opening my eyes, I started moving at a brisker pace.

"Does he do that often?" Ethan asked.

"Only when I see him."

"You might want to file a restraining order."

"Against Zander? He's harmless. Somehow, he thinks he's helping, or trying to anyway."

"You know him better than I do, but let me know if he bothers you again."

"Sure." I wasn't paying too much attention to Ethan. The concrete walkway spilled us out onto the campus. "We're on the quad." I hoped I said it loud enough for Logan to hear.

The quad was huge. Night had fully arrived, but there were people, probably students, in the large empty field of grass that was flanked by buildings.

I started to jog and look around for anyone moving quickly, or who looked like they didn't belong. "Not knowing what we're looking for makes this much more challenging," I said.

"What can I do to help?" Ethan asked, moving up beside me.

We passed a gap between buildings, and I slowed to look for movement in the shadows before venturing forward again.

"I'm not really sure. Do you see anything that doesn't belong?" I asked.

To his credit, Ethan didn't answer right away. He took his time to look around. "Nothing is jumping out at me."

At the next gap between buildings, I heard a noise and stopped. I struggled towards the Path again, but had no luck.

"Did you hear something?" I asked, keeping my voice quiet.

We listened intently. There was nothing visible between buildings, but then I heard it again.

"Sounds like scuffling," Ethan said, keeping his voice low. "From behind the building?"

"Maybe."

As quietly as possible, we moved between the large, white, stone buildings. When we approached the back parking lot, we heard a muffled yell.

Ethan and I glanced at each other before rushing forward.

The area was well lit and we didn't see any movement. The strangled shrieks were more insistent. It didn't take us long to cross the parking light and plunge into a more dimly-lit area of greenery.

"Stop!" Ethan yelled.

I jumped. Ethan had his weapon in hand and had spotted what we were looking for. Following his gaze, I saw a man holding someone else by the neck with another hand cupped around the person's mouth.

The man looked up, seemingly unconcerned. His face was so pale that it seemed to glow in the shadows. It looked as though he whispered something into the person's ear while keeping an eye on Ethan.

I grasped blindly towards the Path. "He said stop!"

The man jerked his attention to me and stopped moving.

"Logan, we're behind the professors' parking lot behind the business offices." I bit my lip and started walking away from Ethan.

The man's eyes bored into me. Whatever this thing was, it didn't seem to care about Ethan. Maybe for once, I could use the fact that people wanted to kill me to our advantage. I took a few more steps away and started to take a wide circle around the man. His eyes never left me.

"This is the police!" Ethan yelled. "Put your hands up and step away."

The words had no effect.

The pale man started to move in a circle, keeping track of me. His prisoner whimpered when moved.

Ethan started to move in the direction opposite me.

"Drop him," I said, keeping my voice level.

"Step away," Ethan repeated, "or I will shoot."

You are Einar.

"I don't know what that is," I said.

The man cocked his head.

I am Einar. You are Einar.

"My name is Cassie," I said. Then I stopped and stared at the man. "Ethan, did you hear him?" It hadn't registered right away that he hadn't spoken, but I could still understand him.

"He hasn't said anything," Ethan said, his voice agitated.

Repulsed, my skin started to crawl. This thing had somehow gotten into my head. That couldn't be a good sign.

Ethan had moved almost directly behind the man.

"Your name is Einar?" I asked, trying to keep the thing busy.

I am Einar.

Ethan started to move forward slowly.

"What do you want Einar?" I asked.

Ethan held the gun to Einar's back. "Put your hands up!"

Einar dropped one hand that had been holding the person, then slammed his hand, palm first, into Ethan's chest. There's no way Einar should have been able rotate his arm to hit Ethan like that without turning.

Ethan was lifted off his feet by the blow and landed on his back a few yards away.

Then, with a casual gesture, Einar snapped the hostige's neck.

The sickening crack made my stomach want to revolt. I covered my mouth and took a step back as the person fell to the ground at Einar's feet.

You are Einar, but it should not be so.

With a hand still over my mouth, I shook my head.

Einar took a step towards me.

BANG. Ethan shot into Einar's back.

A high-pitch scream encompassed my mind. I wasn't sure if it was my brain trying to blank out what was happening around me, or if the sound came from Einar.

You should not be. You shall soon be at rest.

I took another step back and shook my head. "I'm not who you think I am." My heart was racing. I groped blindly for the Path, but it may as well not have existed. It was gone.

Ethan fired two more shots.

Einar turned quickly while making a hissing noise in my mind.

"No!" I shouted, drawing Einar's attention.

He turned back to me and stepped forward.

Each step forward he took, I took one step back. My brain was screaming to run, but I was too afraid to turn my back to the creature.

Swallowing hard, I tried a new tactic. "Are you a Lost?" My eyes started to burn, and my muscles had been tense for so long that they were starting to get fatigued.

We are all lost.

We? There had been something on the edge of the words. Something that almost sounded like a voice under the voice. My eyes opened wide.

"What are you?" I asked.

Ethan, still on the ground, emptied the rest of his clip into Einar. When the screams filled my head, I tried to distinguish if it was one or more, but it was no use. It was only a scream.

The sound died away. *I am Einar.*

Einar rushed forward, and I tried to retreat backward. My muscles were screaming, my mind was a solid ball of fear, and the Path was nowhere to be found.

He seized me by the neck and started to drag me away.

"Let go!" I screamed.

Punching out behind me, I struck Einar in the face. It felt like I was hitting a rock.

They made you soft, Einar said, his voice somber. *Your pain will end soon.*

"You're the one causing my pain!" I started lashing out any way that I could. Using Einar's hold as leverage, I tried hitting, kicking, and clawing at anything I could reach. I went for vitals, but where most people would have had some sort of reaction, this guy had none.

"Cassie!" I heard Ethan yell.

We were already out of sight. Terror gripped me. There had to be a way to the Path, it was my only hope here. Fumbling through my mind didn't help.

"Cassie!" This time it was Logan's voice.

I felt a momentary wave of relief. The old elf could handle anything that was thrown at him. But then, Einar had withstood bullets. There wasn't even any blood that I could see. His skin was warm stone, like a rock that had been baking in the sun all day. Could an elf handle a beast like this?

"Why are you doing this?" I cried.

Leaders of this nation should not have created another Einar. They will pay, but your suffering shall end.

"No one made me!" My struggles were useless.

I knew Logan would be on his way. Thrusting my terror aside, I gripped a fury buried deep inside me. With that rage came the soul fragment of a minotaur. It roared forward, and for once, I didn't attempt to move it away. The minotaur was in charge.

The bellow that leaped from me was a noise that I have never heard any human make. I let myself fade into the background giving the rage free rein.

When I gripped my capturer's hand and twisted it away, I could feel my muscles strain. My blood boiled through me, strength surged, and I shoved Einar away.

He fell back, a look of shock on his glowing features. The sane thing to do would be to flee, putting distance between us, but sanity had left when I let go of my control. Instead, I surged forward and crashed into Einar, bringing us both to the ground.

Logan came out of the darkness. My gaze turned to him for a moment. Logan's face had stretched and become more angular. His ears were at their points, and he was on the balls of his feet, ready to attack.

My quarry was on the ground. In a storm of violence, I lashed out at Einar. The fact that he didn't fight back wasn't a deterrent. The fact that he was completely unharmed by anything I did was disturbing. When my fist smashed into him, there was no give. When my knee hammered into his groin and stomach, there was no reaction. The ferocity of the minotaur didn't leave space to speak.

I do not understand. Einar's words reached my mind, but the physical assault was all that mattered in my fervor.

Einar put one hand out, planting it in the middle of my chest. The feeling of flying through the air was unmistakable. Some part of me braced for pain, but it didn't register. I slammed into a tree and fell to the ground.

My body protested in my attempt to rise, but the spirit inside me wasn't ready to give up.

Logan had taken up my fight with Einar, but he wasn't getting any further than I had.

He is one of the Others. Einar stood and looked at me while effortlessly fending off Logan's strikes. *I shall come for you another day.*

It wasn't menacing, or threatening. It was a cheerless statement of fact.

Einar turned and ran. Logan sprinted after him. The minotaur inside me let out another bellow and urged me to my feet, ready to give chase. The essence that had taken charge wouldn't back down, but the feeling of wear and tear on my body was starting to become prominent.

Stumbling forward a few feet, I leaned against a tree. My veins felt seared, and my body pulsed with the need to fight my way forward.

Logan came back into view. His alien appearance was starting to meld with the more contoured face I was used to.

I struggled to pressure my soul back on top and take control, but the minotaur was resilient, and I had let it take charge.

With Einar gone, I surged towards the next target. My body tried to revolt, but strong will overrode everything else.

"You're going to hurt yourself," Logan said.

I swiped out, but Logan easily sidestepped the feeble attack.

"He's gone. That man is fast."

I swiped again. Logan pivoted away with the fluidity that I've only seen in an elf.

Logan shook his head slightly. "I really don't want to do this."

Under the hostility, the part that was me wanted him to get on with it.

"But you really will hurt yourself. If you haven't already."

He dodged again. This time he twisted and slid in behind me.

"Sorry, partner," Logan said.

Through the raving, I felt nothing. When I turned and lashed out, Logan was already out of reach. When I stumbled forward again, my body grew heavy. When I reached out, the ground started rushing towards my face. There was grass and dirt followed by dark oblivion.

CHAPTER 13

ONE THING ABOUT A MINOTAUR that I found amazing is the speed at which it metabolized. Whatever hormones that had pumped through my system quickly ate through the tranquilizer that Logan had given me.

Unfortunately, it left me cold, tired, and ravenously hungry. My mind was cloudy and I felt sluggish. When I opened my eyes, I didn't move, but listened to the indistinguishable sounds around me.

Trying to figure out my predicament, I concentrated on myself. The minotaur was gone. That was easy to tell because the blind rage had fled. After some probing, I decided that I was indeed myself again. Nothing else had filled the void between the shard of minotaur soul and me. Dull aches wrapped themselves around me like a blanket. It was hard for me to determine if I was injured.

My mind started to come into focus and I could make out voices, but I couldn't understand what they were saying. Wiggling my fingers and toes assured me that I wasn't too bad off. My hands felt wrong, though. I moved my fingers and wrists and found them cuffed behind my back.

Panic surged, and I scrambled into the Path. In my drug-addled state, it wasn't much use, but I didn't leave it. The Path had left me before and I was too afraid to give it up now.

With the Path open, I felt confident enough to raise my head and look around. The room was dark, but the Path held plenty of light for me to see my living room. I had been left on the couch of my living room. I twisted my wrists again.

Handcuffed, on the couch, in my living room.

Relieved, I closed my eyes for a moment and sagged against the cushions.

The voices stopped and Logan appeared from the kitchen.

"Good to see you up, little lady. Are you you?" Logan asked.

"I'm me," I said, depressed that the question needed to be asked.

Logan squatted down next to the couch on the balls of his feet. "Not sure how we'd tell if that's true or not. I think your man in there would have my ears if I had to knock you out again."

"Ethan's here?" I tried to sit up. "Is he alright?"

"Yep, you seem to be you. Hold still and I'll uncuff you."

"But he's not hurt?" I asked.

"He's got more black and blue on his skin than any one man should have, and he wouldn't go to the hospital, but he's on his feet." Logan took off my handcuffs.

"Why wouldn't he go to the hospital?" I sat up too quickly. My head swam, and I had to steady myself.

"Because I told him you wouldn't be joining him. He didn't like that much."

The doorbell rang.

Logan bounded up to his feet. "That'll be the doc."

"Dr. Yelton is here?"

He paused on his way to the door. "I wasn't too sure about calling in Dr. Yelton. I wasn't sure if he was familiar with your condition."

I rubbed my hands over my face and tried to kick my brain into gear. "Who then?"

"Dr. Taylor."

I nodded. It made sense after all. Maybe I had been asleep longer than I thought.

Logan led Taylor in and then he flipped on the light.

"Cassie, it's good to see you again. Even if it is under these circumstances," Taylor said.

The doctor's Path was interesting. Everything about him said he was human. His features were almost perfect, from his smooth light brown skin to brown eyes shaped like tear drops. It was his Path that sold him out. It was a secret that he'd rather not have revealed. I never asked him about his race. It really wasn't my business, and I've never told anyone his secret.

"It's good to see you again," I said. "Thank you for coming."

He sat a bag down on the coffee table in front of me and opened it.

"No, you need to see to Ethan first," I said.

Feeling lightheaded, I let the Path fall away. The fact that it came and went while at home, but not other places was troubling. I'm pretty sure a Reader's ability couldn't become agoraphobic.

Taylor looked up at Logan. "I didn't realize I had two patients tonight." He didn't look upset, but the question he wasn't asking was obvious.

"When I called you, I had every intention of sending him to the hospital. Things didn't quite work as planned," Logan said.

"I'm not deaf," Ethan said.

I heard him before I saw him. He exited the kitchen, walking gingerly.

"Are you okay?" I asked. "Do you need to go to the hospital?"

"When you have a doctor that makes house calls?" Ethan asked. "Once I know you're alright I'll... no, that's a lie. Once I know you're okay, and I get some answers, I'll listen to the doctor's suggestions."

"Ethan, this is Dr. Wes Taylor. Dr. Taylor, Ethan," I said, wanting to get things moving.

"Nice to meet you, Dr. Taylor," Ethan said.

"Call me Taylor," he said.

Ethan and Taylor shook hands.

"Who's in worse shape?" Taylor asked.

Ethan and I both indicated the other at the same time.

Once again, Taylor looked to Logan.

"Look," I said, trying not to get aggravated, "I still have tranqs running through me. I'm not even sure I could tell you what hurts yet."

"Is there a room I can use?" Taylor asked.

"Gran's out for the weekend. She won't mind us using her room for this." I made a mental note to call her. It seemed like she had been gone for a month and it had been barely over a day. Then again, this day felt like it had lasted a month.

Taylor took Ethan into Gran's room.

As soon as they were out of sight, I turned to Logan. "We've got to talk."

"We do at that." Logan sat down in a chair across from me. "I've been around here a good deal of years and been to a handful of different dimensions. I haven't seen anything like what I saw tonight. Ethan said he shot it?"

"Several times, but that's only half the story. We didn't bump into Einar on our own."

"Einar?"

I hesitated. "Did you hear him say anything?"

"He didn't speak a word."

"Right," I said. Puzzling over that was going to drive me crazy. Should I tell Logan everything? When it came down to it, he was my partner. If I'd learned anything in the past year, it was that I needed to keep him informed.

I gave Logan a rundown of the important events of the evening. While talking, the last dregs of tranquilizers started to wear off. The dull pains I had been feeling became more concerning and increasingly uncomfortable.

To Logan's credit, he listened without interruption. Once I mentioned the old man and time stopping, he got up and started to pace, while I tried to find a position that didn't hurt like crazy. I didn't bother mentioning Zander. He was a non-issue compared to the rest of the events and didn't have anything to do with the case at hand.

By the time I started talking about Einar dragging me into the woods, my speech had become more muted and broken as the pain began to hammer itself into the forefront of my mind.

Logan stopped pacing. "Need me to call for Taylor?"

"No. I don't think anything's broken. But my muscles feel like they're on fire, and the bruises aren't helping matters any."

He looked at me hard for a few moments before starting to pace again. "Whatever piece inside you that jumped out, I reckon it was trying to use muscles it possessed instead of the ones you have. What happened next?"

There wasn't much left to the story.

"You've had an eventful evening," Logan said while trying to wear holes through my carpet. "Let's start from the beginning. The old man thought the creature would relate to you."

"Yes."

"He wasn't wrong there. The thing talked to you, somehow, and no one else. It even called you by its own name."

I shrugged and immediately regretted it when pain lanced across my shoulders. I gritted my teeth. "Maybe it wasn't its name, but its race or something?"

"Possible," Logan said.

"Can we look it up at the office?"

Logan hesitated. He watched me and slowly walked over to the chair to sit back down. "Do you think we should look it up at the office? On the work computers?"

Even through the pain it was obvious what he was asking. "You think we shouldn't take this to AIR?" I didn't have the mental capacity to be subtle at the moment.

"I think we should be careful about the decision."

The door to Gran's bedroom opened which cut Logan off mid-sentence. Ethan and Taylor emerged.

"You're up next, Cassie," Taylor said.

"How are you?" I asked Ethan. I tried not to wince too hard when I drew myself to my feet.

"Been better, but nothing permanent. It sounds like I can avoid the hospital." Ethan gave Taylor a hard look, which Taylor appeared not to notice.

Instead of going to Gran's room, I went to Ethan and took his hand. His smile seemed forced, and I could tell he was uncomfortable. My attempt at a reassuring look was foiled when I winced at a muscle spasm. I dropped his hand and went to Gran's room before I made things worse.

"Logan?" Taylor got Logan's attention, tapped his ear twice, and shook his head no.

"Gotcha, Doc," Logan said. "Ethan, let's go make some coffee."

"Thanks. I wouldn't even think of asking him not to listen in," I said when Taylor shut the door behind us.

"Logan means well, and I know he worries."

"Ethan's really alright?" I asked.

Taylor frowned. "You can ask him when we're wrapped up here. It's the whole doctor-patient thing."

It was my turn to frown. "You've given us reports on the Lost before."

"As an AIR agent, you have certain authority granted when it comes from people from other dimensions. In this case, it doesn't extend to humans."

"I guess that makes sense," I said with reluctance.

"Let's start with where you hurt the most."

"In the body area," I said.

He gave a hint of a smile. "Let's get to it then. Undress and tell me, step-by-step, each thing that may have caused damage."

Some people may think that having someone as gorgeous as Taylor telling them to undress would be a fantasy come true. When Taylor was in doctor mode, the thought would never cross my mind. He was a consummate professional. As I undressed, I told him everything that happened. Using Gran's bed as an examining table, he went over everything from a possible concussion to cracked ribs. For each event, from Einar grabbing me around the neck, to me lashing out, he asked for more specific details. It was exhausting.

"I'm making it sound much worse than it was," I said.

Taylor raised his eyebrow, but didn't look at me. "I'm pretty sure the contusions and muscle damage tells a different story. Where did these bruises come from?" Taylor was examining my knees and legs. "Nothing you've said so far would lead to this type of bruising."

"I kicked and kneed him a bunch of times."

"Which account for these," Taylor said, pointing to marks on top of my knees, "but not the ones on the bottom of your knees."

My mind felt muddled when I tried to think back. I hated to admit how long it took me to remember how those bruises may have come about.

"Oh. Those may have come from earlier in the day."

When I left it at that, Taylor crossed his arms and waited for me to continue.

"Ugh. Fine, but promise you won't tell anyone?" I said. "Maybe file it under doctor-patient confidentiality?"

"I'd rather not agree to something like that. If someone did this..."

I rolled my eyes. "Someone did. I took a self-defense class."

It looked like it took Taylor a moment before that sunk in. "You're taking classes?"

"I took *a* class," I stressed.

"What type of class?"

"Krav Maga."

"You can get dressed now. I think Krav is an excellent idea." Taylor looked pleased by the notion. "Why is it a secret?"

"Any number of reasons. Not the least of which is the fact that I should have started ages ago."

"Are you worried about what your partners will think?"

I shrugged, and then winced, before putting on my shirt. "I don't want them to think I'm worried about the job."

Taylor nodded. "I'm fairly sure Logan wouldn't think that, but I can't say the same for your other partners since I don't know them as well. Logan, however, might think that he could help train you, which may end badly."

While I continued to dress, the confusion must have been plain on my face.

"Elves think a bit differently about fighting. Their instincts and reactions don't always mesh well with what your natural reactions might be. That, and when they teach fighting, they do it by fighting at nearly full strength from the start."

"Last fall I saw him start to train Jonathan. I never really thought about it before, but it was, well...more enthusiastic than I would have expected."

Taylor laughed. "It's a shame we don't live closer. We could train together."

"You know Krav?"

"Hold out your arm. I'm going to wrap both of them. Keep the bandaging tight. Compression is necessary." After I nodded Taylor continued. "Krav uses a mixture of martial arts for real life situations. I've practiced similar methodologies and even trained a few people in my time."

He made it sound like he'd been alive longer than he appeared. Every now and again, I got the feeling that he was much older than the thirty or so he looked.

"Maybe when I'm around the city, you could give me some pointers," I said.

"I'd like that." He sounded sincere. "In fact, it would be my pleasure. For now, though, you are going to need to take a few days off from training."

"It wasn't the first thing on my list of stuff to do after tonight," I admitted.

"In your line of work, I would suggest sometimes going in even when bruised or sore from work. That's what you'll be facing in the line of duty. It's not ideal for your first week, though."

"What's the verdict?" I asked, picking up my shoes instead of putting them back on.

"Before you go to sleep, take this. It's for the pain. It might even help you sleep through the night, but your bruises aren't going to make that easy."

I stowed the pill in my pocket while Taylor continued. "I would love nothing more than to tell you to spend the next two to three days in bed. But I know you well enough to assume that you wouldn't listen to that advice."

"Door number two?" I asked.

"I'm going to give you a muscle relaxer. It will probably make you tired, so no driving until you know how it'll affect you. Take one before you go to sleep for the next few days and tomorrow morning. You have several strained muscles, but none that appear to be torn. It's still going to take some time to heal."

"Sure," I agreed.

"Tomorrow, however..."

I groaned realizing I wasn't going to get off that lucky.

"And tonight," Taylor continued, "you're going to need to rest and ice the muscles in your arms."

"You know I can't take a day off in the middle of something like this."

"I'm not saying take the day off, but a day of research may be in order."

"About that..." Logan's hesitancy to research through AIR was bouncing around my head. "AIR still doesn't know about the souls of the Lost inside me. They don't even know about my powers being different from what they were a year ago."

"I thought that might be the case when Logan asked me to come here tonight."

"Well, this thing. We don't know what it is, but it seemed to...I don't know. Take an interest in me beyond the usual, 'I want to kill you' reactions I usually get."

Taylor frowned. "You're still getting those?"

Thoughts of the cop that tried to shoot me surfaced. "Yeah. Still there."

"You and Logan are worried about what might come out if this person turns out to be a Reader," Taylor said.

I hadn't really thought of that. "It would look bad for me," I admitted.

Taylor started packing up his things. "Still have the laptop Neil gave you?"

"Yes."

"Use that. It'll give you access to MyTH research."

"Thanks. How is Neil doing?" I asked as we left the room.

"You were actually a good influence on him. He stayed clean for a while. After a week, though, he couldn't take it." Taylor shook his head. "It's all or nothing with that kid. I've barely seen him around."

"I should have kept in touch."

"Well, he wasn't the best influence on you I'm afraid."

I felt so sorry for Neil. There had to be a balance for him somewhere between extreme genius and frying himself on drugs.

"He'll come around," Taylor said. "He won't be this young forever. Insufferable forever, yes, but this stupid? He'll outgrow it."

"Let me know if there's ever anything I can do."

"It'll be good for him to hear from you."

"I'll call tomorrow," I said as we entered the kitchen.

"Better wait until the late afternoon. Usually that's the best chance to reach him."

"Everything good?" Logan asked.

"I'll be good as new in no time," I said.

Logan cocked his head and waited for more.

"I need to take it easy tomorrow. Research, that sort of thing. Taylor's going to let us run our research through MyTH," I said.

"That's mighty nice of ya, Doc," Logan said.

"I know it's late," Taylor said, "but if Jonathan's around, I thought we'd go over a few things."

Logan nodded, but it seemed like the old elf sagged a bit at the request. "He's pretty gung-ho to get started. He'll appreciate the visit."

"Get started?" I asked.

"Jonathan's found himself a new job," Logan said, keeping his voice even. "After what happened with Paula, he feels he needs a fresh start. Once he's wrapped up his school year, he's going to work with MyTH."

CHAPTER 14

I'M SORRY, LOGAN, I DIDN'T know. Jonathan never said anything to me about leaving," I said.

"Well, he's hitching his wagon to a good team," Logan said, getting to his feet. "Come on over, Taylor. I'm across the field. You two need anything tonight?"

"We're good," I said to Logan.

Logan nodded. "Rider and Vincent are on site. They'll be stopping by tomorrow to let us know what they've found. AIR knows there was an altercation and the clean-up team is ready to step in once Rider has done what he can. But we can deal with the paperwork tomorrow."

I nodded. "Thanks for your help tonight, Taylor. If you see Neil, let him know I'll get in touch."

"Ice those muscles before you sleep. Let me know when you're in town." Taylor waved and followed Logan out the back door.

Once they left, the kitchen was so quiet it was almost deafening.

"Can I get you anything?" I asked Ethan, trying to fill the void.

"No. Thank you, though."

After a few more silent moments ticked by I got myself a glass of water to give myself something to do. "You're okay, though, right?" I asked.

"More bumps and bruises than I'd like. How about you? When Logan brought you out, I thought...well, it looked bad."

"Bruises and sore muscles. Sorry I worried you," I said.

"You all act like it's another day at the office, but for me, the last few days have been more than worrying. It doesn't help that

I feel like I've been left hanging out in the dark with nothing but my drawers on."

I blinked and my lip curled up. "Can you say that last part again?"

Ethan grinned and shook his head. "It's something my grandpa used to say. I'm serious, though. I've been taking a lot of things on good faith, but I opened fire on someone tonight. In my world, that's a rare occurrence."

"We don't go around shooting people. I don't even carry a real gun most of the time. We carry tranq guns mostly," I tried to reassure Ethan.

"Speaking of tranquilizers, why did your partner knock you out?" Ethan appeared to be trying to keep his voice level, but I could tell he was trying to add two and two together and getting five every time.

"It's really complicated."

"Trust me when I say I believe that, but I think it's time you fill me in. It might also help to know why, when I shot a man, nothing happened. And why you appeared to be replying to it when it hadn't spoken. At least for starters."

Crap. I looked at my glass of water and tried to figure out where to start.

"I see," Ethan said. He sounded dejected, and he stood up. "I should go."

"No, wait. I'm only trying to figure out where to start." Ethan didn't make a move to sit back down. "Please stay."

"You're going to explain it all?" Ethan asked.

"You have to understand, there are some things that I can't talk about."

Ethan tensed and gripped the back of his chair.

"I can tell you anything you want to know about me." I glanced out the back door and back to Ethan. "I'm pretty sure there isn't an issue with me telling you about the case, but some things aren't my stories to tell."

"Anything about you?" His lips curved up with a hint of a smile.

"I'll tell you. I'm not sure what you'll think of me once it's all out in the open."

"You're really worried about that, aren't you?"

"I'm sure it doesn't come as a surprise to you that I like you. The last person I let in was my former fiancé, Zander. You see how well that turned out." Ethan's brow furrowed and he started to say something, but I quickly continued. "I don't think you'd be like him. You already know things aren't quite normal, but things were much less complicated back then."

"I like you as well. Us working together isn't quite like I thought it might be, and you're right, I'm nothing like the guy I met tonight. I'm not saying everything is going to come up roses, but I've seen enough to know you're not crazy."

"Where do you want me to start?" I was resigned to jump in and get this over with.

"I heard Dr. Taylor mention ice?"

"What? Oh, yeah, for my arms," I said dismissively.

"Let's start there, and you can tell me why your partner knocked you out and refused to take you to a hospital. Dish towels?"

"I'll get them."

"Sit back down. I've got this." He smiled and winked at me. "I don't want you to get distracted."

I pointed out the drawer. "It does look bad, doesn't it? I promise you it's for a good reason."

Ethan grabbed the towel. "Freezer bags? And those reasons are?"

I pointed to the cabinet. "It'll be best if I start back further and work my way up to tonight."

Ethan put ice in a bag, along with a little water, wrapped it in a dishtowel, and then came over and sat down next to me.

"What are we icing?" he asked.

"My arms."

"Both?"

"Yeah."

"Hold on to this one, I'll make another. You can start wherever you're most comfortable starting."

I wanted to soak this moment in before spoiling everything. It was even tempting to reach for the Path to see how he really felt, and see what changed as I told him as much as I could, but that would be intrusive.

How would a man react if the woman he's seeing has a broken soul? Worse yet, having a bunch of other pieces of souls stuck inside her.

I guess I was going to find out.

Starting with being a Reader was the easy part. He already knew a little bit about it.

Ethan pressed the new ice pack to one arm while I held the other and talked.

"That explains a lot about what I saw at the construction site," he said when I paused.

I blinked at him. "That's it?"

"Well, I assume you're not done. You haven't said anything that would give Logan a reason to knock you out. Unless you tried to take things too far. I'm assuming that's what happened early in the day. And why you went home?"

"There's definitely more. It's just that..." I shook my head and couldn't help but let a small smile escape alongside the hope that was welling up. "Well, what I told you was all that Zander knew. The rest is new territory for me."

Ethan surprised me by putting his hand on my cheek. It was cold, but I leaned my head into it and closed my eyes.

"That guy is an idiot," Ethan said.

I nodded in agreement and opened my eyes, looking into Ethan's concerned face. Then I kissed him, basking in the warmth of his lips. He returned the kiss, but I stretched back after a moment. I tried to shove the hope back down, but it stayed put.

Next came the shredding of my soul.

"Workplace accident?" Ethan's concern was mingled with shock. "What kind of place do you work at?"

"That's a whole other story." I yawned and caught the look in his eye. "One that I'll tell you," I assured him. "Not everything. Not specific cases or people, but enough that you'll know what I do."

"Did it hurt?" he asked.

"No, but I should tell you that it's the reason the officer almost shot me the other day."

"I'm not following."

"Do you remember the first time we met?"

"At the station, yeah."

"Do you remember how much you liked me at first?"

Ethan frowned. "I remember it had been a rough day." Then he started to grin. "As you left I remember thinking you were cute, and I was kicking myself, thinking I should have asked you out, but then figured I'd never see you again."

I laughed. "You almost dodged the bullet there, but I came back. Do you remember how the rookie officer acted that day?"

"Yeah." Ethan was turned inward now. "And the DEA when you came back. Our first few dates were pretty odd, too. You were almost shot over this? That must be hell."

"It makes it pretty hard to make a good first impression. Luckily, most people get over it pretty quickly."

"So, the officer the other day, him almost shooting you, that wasn't his fault?"

I raised an eyebrow at him. "Have you seen anyone else try to kill me? I wouldn't say it's entirely his fault, but something's not right there if he was using his weapon so freely."

"Yeah, I guess you're right." He didn't sound entirely convinced, but I let it drop.

"That leads us to this spring. Around the time we met. This is where things get...strange."

After yawning widely, which Ethan picked up and mimicked, I gave him the briefest of overviews about not exactly being alone inside my own body.

Ethan's face paled. My heart constricted.

"I'm not sure I understand. You somehow ended up with other people's souls inside you?"

Feeling like a giant freak, I went for broke. "People, yes. Human, not exactly."

"I'm still not following."

I cleared my throat. "You asked who I worked for. The agency is AIR, the Agency for Interdimensional Regulation. We work with the Lost, Mythological creatures that come from other dimensions."

"I'm— what?" Now Ethan looked like he was adding two and two and coming up with frog.

"Elves, werewolves, fairies, gn—"

"Hold on."

Knowing I had pushed too far, I shut my mouth and waited.

"What you're talking about...those are kid stories," Ethan said.

"Well, yes and no. People made up stories over the years about what..."

Ethan held up a hand and I stopped again. He appeared to be struggling hard.

We sat in silence for a few moments before I took the ice pack from Ethan's unresisting hand and went to the sink to hide my face.

"You're telling me that these things are real, and you think they're inside you?"

"People, not things." I didn't raise my voice, and I couldn't bring myself to address the second part of his question.

"What?" Ethan sounded more confused than angry, but his frustration was definitely there.

"The Lost, they're people. Not things or-"

"Things or people, whatever. I'm not sure what I'm supposed to say here, Cassie."

"I know it's not what you expected." I wanted to add that I had warned him, but I didn't think telling him, I told you so, would help anything right now.

"Why are you telling me this?"

"What?" Not really understanding the question, I turned to look at him.

"This story, whatever it is. Why aren't you telling me the truth?"

He thought I was lying to him. "This is the truth. You asked, and I'm telling you."

He didn't say anything for a while. I took my time emptying and drying the bags. When I looked back at him, Ethan appeared to be lost in his own world of thoughts.

"How are you feeling?" I asked, joining him at the table.

"Confused," Ethan said.

"I meant your injuries."

"Oh, yeah," Ethan said. He looked like he was coming back to our world. "I'm alright. Nothing that won't heal."

"You should know that I am telling you the truth." I put as much sincerity as I could into the statement. He had to understand that I wasn't lying or crazy.

"And your other team members, they all know this?" Ethan asked.

A corner of my mouth threatened to turn up. "They do. It's our job to know." I could have told him about my partners, but those were secrets that weren't mine to tell.

"So, if I go home tonight and I don't know, I get mauled by a werewolf or something, your team would show up?" The forced smile he put on was so strained that it looked like he was in pain.

"You're not going to be mauled. But yes, if something happens that involves one of the Lost, you might see us around." My stomach was a tight little ball of uncertainty.

"The Lost?"

I rushed to explain. "It's misleading. Some are Lost, they came here by accident, but some are here on purpose, but they're still lost from their world."

"The thing that attacked tonight? Was it one of them?"

Thing and them. Even if he did come to believe, he was already sorting people into categories of them and us. It wasn't a good sign.

"We don't know who he was. I'm sorry you were pulled into this mess."

"And you? You're, um… you…" Ethan let the words trail away.

"If it matters," I said, filling in the blanks, "I'm human."

Ethan nodded and his eyes focused in on me for the first time since rejoining him at the table. "I don't know what to think about all of this."

Swallowing hard, I nodded.

"I should go," Ethan said. "I think…I think I need some time with this."

"Okay," I said, surprised that I was able to keep the tremor out of my voice.

He slowly rose to his feet and I walked him to the door and let him out. He stopped on his way out and turned to me. That tiny bit of hope clamored in my chest.

"I didn't expect…I mean…I'm sorry."

I plastered on a smile and lied. "I understand."

Ethan nodded and looked at the ground.

"Will I see you tomorrow?" I felt sick to the stomach and my heart felt squeezed, but I had to ask.

"Uh…well, it sounds like you're research bound tomorrow."

"Right," I said, the defeat clear in my voice.

"I'll just need some time with this."

"Of course," I said, trying to keep my voice level.

I thought he would say something else. Instead, he turned and walked away.

I shut the door before he got to his car and leaned against it, listening intently. It felt like a giant lump was in my throat. It seemed like an eternity.

This was Ethan. Surely he'd come back. He wouldn't leave like this.

My heart hammered in my chest.

A few minutes later, the eternity ended. Ethan started his car and drove away.

Any hope I held evaporated. The lump in my throat didn't die away, and it felt as if my heart was as torn as my soul. There had been a chance there. I was certain of it. Ethan was a fantastic guy. He was smart, caring, and understanding. At least to a point.

And now he needed time to think. Sure, I had told him a lot. Actually, no. We didn't get very far at all before he shut down, but I could give him time. If a relationship couldn't work with a guy like Ethan, there's a chance I'd be spending a lot of time alone.

The home phone rang, which was a welcome distraction. "Hello?"

There was a crackle in the line and then the caller was disconnected. I looked at the caller ID, but there was no name or number. Since there was no diversion there, I cleaned out the coffee pot and got it ready for the morning.

The home phone rang again and again there was nothing but crackling. As soon as I hung it up, my cell phone rang.

"Hello."

"Hello," Rider said. "I wanted to call to find out how you were doing."

"It sounds like we have a good connection now," I said.

"We do have a good connection," Rider said.

"I'm glad you and Vincent were able to check the area on campus."

"He dropped me off at home a few minutes ago. We retrieved the bullet fragments and shells left by Ethan. They will be back at the office for testing. Vincent said that Ethan would want to know," Rider said.

My chest felt tight. "I'm sure he will want to know." There was no way I was going to ask my partners to call him, but I know Ethan didn't want to hear from me. "I'll text him and let him know."

"Ethan is not there?"

"No, he went home." Rider was my best friend; could I talk to him about what happened with Ethan? "He, um…" The lump started to reform in my throat. "He was pretty sore, so he went home."

Even if I could talk to Rider about Ethan, the day had been too long already. There was no way I wanted to talk tonight.

"What are you doing tonight?" Rider asked.

"It's late, so I'm going to take whatever it is that Taylor left for me, and I'm going to sleep."

"I see. I will call Vincent. Goodnight, Cassie."

"Goodnight…"

Rider hung up before I got the rest out. Shrugging, I stowed my phone in my pocket in order to put it on the charger upstairs later.

Knowing that if I put it off now, I would put it off tomorrow as well, I took a few minutes to straighten up Gran's bed from its use as an impromptu exam room.

While I busied myself, I got lost in my head. Why did I have to tell him everything? Why all at once? I knew it was too much for anyone to take in one sitting.

Tomorrow would be better though. Even if Ethan didn't call, I'd have a case to focus on.

For tonight, it was medicine and off to bed.

When I reached my room, the doorbell rang. My mood went from depressed to aggravated in a heartbeat. Who would stop by this late at night?

Even more important, would they go away if I ignored them. Then I had a thin thread of hope that it was Ethan, so I hurried back downstairs.

"Who is it?" I called on my way through the living room.

"It's me, Cass."

Shaking my head, I opened the door. "What are you doing here so late?" Then I put the pieces together. "And why did Rider send you?" Despite the words, I ushered him in.

"He called, he didn't send me," Vincent said. He saw my bandages. He didn't say anything, but he looked like he wanted to.

I rolled my eyes. "I'm fine. It's been a rough night."

He nodded. "Worse than I thought."

I shrugged. "Can I get you some coffee?"

"Do you want to talk about it?"

"Not really." There was no part of this night that I wanted to talk about. Although, the muscle relaxers were kicking in, so I was starting to feel better.

"Want me to talk to him?"

"To who?" I asked, not quite following.

"Ethan. I'm guessing this night interrupted your date."

"You could say that." I shook my head, but my lips twitched up at the thought of Vincent and Ethan talking about tonight.

"That doesn't sound like the best idea." I cleared my throat. "You didn't have to come by, but thank you."

"Can I get you anything?"

I wanted to ask for a new life, but that was far too dramatic for me, so I shook my head.

"Let me know if you change your mind. I'll be down here."

"You're staying?"

CHAPTER 15

I 'LL BE ON THE COUCH," Vincent said.

"Don't you want to go home?" I didn't put any emphasis on the words. The truth is, the house felt far too empty.

"I'll be on the couch," Vincent repeated adamantly.

Knowing that I wasn't completely alone in the house tonight would make me feel better. "Why—"

"Cass, I'm staying."

I rolled my eyes. "What I was going to say was why don't you stay in your room upstairs."

"My room?"

I shrugged my shoulders, then winced. "That's what I was going to say. You did live here after all."

Curling up and going to sleep was tempting, but the need to get the dirt and grime of the day rinsed off was greater. Yawning, I started up the stairs. Before I made it to the top, I remembered the compression wraps on my arms.

When I turned back around, Vincent hadn't moved. He looked caught up in his own thoughts.

"You are going to stay in your room, right?" I asked. "Not down here."

He looked at me for a few moments, but I couldn't read his expression. Whatever muscle relaxers Taylor gave me were doing their job.

"Sure," Vincent said. "I'll be up later."

Trying not to look relieved was difficult, but if he noticed, I could blame it on the drugs. Whatever the reason, it was nice to know that Vincent would be down the hall.

"Night," I said.

"Goodnight, Cass."

After retreating to my room, I stripped off my socks and shoes. Sleep sounded divine, but I still went straight for the shower. After stripping the dirt from my skin, I stood in front of my mirror and looked at all the bruises. This was definitely not the way I had expected the night to end. I balled up the wraps for my arms and tossed them in a corner. This day needed to be over, and my bed looked inviting.

The next morning voices filtered up from downstairs. I couldn't make out anything they were saying, or even whose voices they were. After yesterday morning, it probably wasn't the wisest decision to assume the voices belonged to my partners, but, since the plan had been to meet here, I expected it to be them.

I didn't bother getting out of bed. Instead, I decided it was past time I called Gran. Luckily, my phone was nearby, although reaching for it caused such deep aches in my arms, I wasn't sure if I would even be able to pick it up.

"Mornin', sugar," she answered on the first ring.

"Morning, Gran. How is everything at Mom's?"

"As good as can be expected. Your mother has decorated with some sort of fake plants. It's almost as if they want to suck the life out of you to become real plants. Dee Dee is springing me for a few hours later today."

"That's good."

"I forgot to ask if you dropped off that package the other day."

"Yeah, I was able to get it over there."

"I appreciate that," Gran said. She sounded relieved.

"It's no problem."

"How was your date last night?" Gran asked.

"It...it didn't go so well. In fact, it ended badly. I think I caught Ethan off guard by telling him the truth. Now he wants time to think."

"I didn't know," Gran said. She sounded surprised she hadn't known about it ahead of time.

"You can't see everything all the time," I said, trying to sound more upbeat than I felt.

"Why don't you tell me all about it," Gran said.

She received a brief overview of the evening. Not the stuff about the case, but everything with Ethan.

"And Vincent came over?" Gran asked.

"Yeah. I think he stayed in his room. I told him he should take it instead of the couch."

"Don't you worry. You may have only overwhelmed Ethan last night. It can be a lot to take all at once."

"Maybe."

"You're a strong, capable woman. If that man doesn't see what he's missing, you can always show him. If you want to, that is."

"Thanks, Gran."

"I swear your mother's house is sappin' the life out of me."

We chatted about Mom's enthusiastic decorating skills before we said goodbye and I got my day started. The first thing I did was send Ethan a quick text saying our office had removed the bullets and casing from the site.

The second order of business was to take a pain pill and a muscle relaxer. Who knew muscles could hurt so much? I got dressed, found the wraps for my arms, and hunted down the source of the voices. In the kitchen, research was already underway. Logan, Vincent, and Rider all had laptops open.

"Morning," I said, going straight for the coffee pot.

"Howdy, partner. You need help with those bandages?" Logan asked.

"Yeah, it's not so easy with one arm. Thanks."

I took the seat next to Logan and he started helping me wrap an arm.

From my other side, Rider lifted my other arm lightly and inspected it. I'm not sure what he was looking for, but he sat it back down after a few moments.

I wasn't sure if Vincent had mentioned anything about the previous night, but I wasn't going to bring up Ethan. After what Gran had said, I felt somewhat cheered up. If I wanted Ethan back, it was worth a try. I couldn't imagine myself walking up and kissing him out of the blue, but there had to be something.

"So, where are we?" It was best to press my personal life aside. "Was there anything else about last night?"

"Nothing," Vincent said without looking up from his computer.

"That is not entirely correct," Rider interjected, frowning at his partner.

"What did you find?" I asked.

"Your scent changed," Rider said.

"My scent?" I asked, trying to follow. I could tell I was going to need more coffee.

Logan finished up one arm and I shifted so he could help me with the next.

"You were not you," Rider said.

"I guess that makes sense. Sort of. That happened before when a fragment got out, right?" I didn't wait for an answer. Being reminded how far from normality my life had traveled didn't make for good morning conversation. "Nothing about Einar?"

Rider shook his head and went back to his deficient typing skills, hunting and pecking as slowly as ever.

"Vincent and I are researching through the office. Rider is online, and we thought you'd go through MyTH," Logan said as he finished my other arm.

"Thank you, Logan, and yeah, I can go through MyTH." I went to get the laptop Neil gave me.

I had been using it to email Quin, another Reader that I had contacted. We had been swapping information for half a year now. It was nice to have another Reader to talk to, even if I didn't have any idea who she actually was. I knew I could track her down, but I wasn't comfortable with that. She'd let me know who she was when she was ready. It wasn't like I had to let her know my real name either.

When I came back to the kitchen, Logan was on the phone.

"Yeah, we'll mosey on down," Logan said before hanging up.

"Where are we heading?" I asked.

"Local police found a body. Hank called and he wants us to check it out to see if it's related," Logan said.

"Any details?" I asked.

Logan shook his head. "Too soon to tell. I thought you'd be sticking around the house today."

I rolled my eyes. "It's my arms. I'll be fine."

"Maybe we should drive separately, in case someone needs to leave early," Logan said.

"And by someone you mean me?" I crossed my arms.

Logan shrugged. "It can be a bit uncomfortable in the truck with four."

It was a blatant lie. The truck had two rows of seating up front.

Rider looked like he was going to say something and Vincent kicked him under the table. Rider's eyes widened, giving Vincent a hurt look.

"Subtle," I told Vincent.

His expression was wooden.

I could feel my cheeks flushing and looked away. "I'm not supposed to drive on the pain pills until I know how I'll react. I took one this morning."

"I'll drive," Vincent said.

"Sure," I said, feeling defeated. Being hurt and not being able to do my job effectively sucked.

I stowed the laptop and grabbed my stuff before leaving the house. Vincent needed to stop at his apartment before catching up with the others. We rode in silence. I couldn't help but wonder what Vincent's apartment might be like. He'd moved in a few weeks ago, and housewarming parties definitely weren't his style.

His complex was one of the newer models that were popping up all over town. There were eight buildings and some sort of clubhouse at the entrance. More buildings were still under construction.

There was a passing thought that I should wait until he invited me in instead of assuming that I could walk in with him. Then I decided that I could grow old and die before ever getting that type of invite from Vincent, so I followed him in. Since he didn't object, I figured it was as close to an invite as I would be likely to receive.

Vincent lived on the ground floor, for which I was grateful today. My legs might not have been mummy wrapped, but the muscles still ached and the bruises had firmly settled in. He unlocked the door, and I sensed a moment of hesitation before we entered.

I'm not sure what I had been expecting, but I'm certain this wasn't it. The walls were a soft white, the carpet had that just-installed look, and every piece of furniture was new. More surprising, it all matched.

"You missed breakfast. There should be some fruit in the kitchen if you'd like. It's...well, help yourself to anything." Vincent crossed the living room and disappeared down a hall.

The blinds were mostly open, and bright, morning sunlight filtered in. It was an open floor plan, but it was hard to find anything that could be considered personal. I went to the kitchen to get something to eat. I wasn't hungry, but it was an excuse to be nosy and get a bit more insight into Vincent's life. The fridge was mostly empty save for a few pieces of fruit, some vegetables that looked like they all belonged together in a salad, condiments, and bottled water. The six pack of beer off to the side looked out of place.

I closed the door. The kitchen was in perfect condition. No dishes in the sink, no crumbs on the counter, no mail stacked up anywhere, and a bowl of fruit looking almost decorative. Wandering into the living room, I saw artwork on the walls. On closer examination, I discovered two of the pieces matched the furniture a little too well. I'd be willing to bet money that it was part of the set.

The third piece drew me in. It was different. At first glance, it looked like the sun setting in a forest. When you looked closer, though, the shadows in the woods had shape. Some of the trees had sharp thorns. There was a dirt path twisting through that darkness. The shadows seemed to line the trail, trying to crowd it out. If you stared at a shadow for too long, another one, one that you hadn't seen before, captured your attention, when you looked back, though, the first shadow seemed to meld into the scenery and only the new one you noticed remained.

It was beautiful and terrifying at the same time. There was no person on the trail, but I sensed it had been painted from the perspective of someone walking the path.

"An old friend of mine painted it," Vincent said. His voice was quiet.

"It's amazing," I said, still trying to pinpoint a shadow for any period of time, trying to discover what it might be. Then I caught sight of a shadow much larger than the others. It seemed to loom over the entire picture. It was unnerving the way it suddenly appear. I took a step back before I caught myself, realizing I had let a picture startle me.

I glanced at Vincent, who had moved up beside me, then back at the painting. The looming figure was difficult to pick out again.

"Your friend is an amazing artist," I said.

"Was," Vincent corrected. "He was going to marry my sister."

I felt the sorrow in his voice. "I didn't know you had a sister." Mentally, I was kicking myself. How did I not know he had a sister?

Vincent said nothing, but it looked as though he regretted saying anything. . I wanted to know more, but this was definitely not the time.

"I'm sorry about your friend." I put my hand on his arm as a comfort. A feeling of warmth and charged energy started to radiate up from where I touched him.

Vincent didn't say anything, but he didn't move away and he looked more at ease than he had a moment ago. I wanted the force that rose between us to permeate through me, but I knew it couldn't, so I stepped away. It wouldn't have been fair to him or me. Vincent had made it clear that he didn't want to get too close. Besides, who knew if it was real?

"Um, thank you for coming over last night." I moved to the next piece of art and took a cursory glance.

"It was no problem." He kept his voice even and looked at his painting.

"I guess we should go to the site?"

"Did you get something to eat?"

"No, I'm good."

"Do you mind getting us some water?" Vincent asked.

"Sure."

I gathered the water, Vincent took his bag, and we left.

Vincent put the bag in my trunk and we drove to the site.

"I thought your gear was in the truck," I said.

"It's an overnight bag. I didn't have one last night."

"Are you staying over again tonight? Not that I mind," I added quickly, "you can stay whenever you'd like."

"It's possible at least one person is targeting you. Possibly another if Einar isn't the one that magicked your house."

"If that's the reason you're staying, you might as well move back in." I was trying really hard to avoid being aggravated by the thought. "If you had planned on staying last night, why didn't you bring a bag?"

Vincent gripped his steering wheel hard. Was that a pink flush on his face?

"What?" I asked.

He cleared his throat. "I didn't...I mean..." He stopped talking and gripped the wheel harder.

"What?"

"We thought someone else would be around last night."

I could feel the blush come over my own face now. "We?"

"Cass, how many times have you been almost killed in the past few days?"

"Never mind that. You said, 'we thought.' Which 'we' were discussing who might be staying over at my house?"

CHAPTER 16

I T WASN'T LIKE THAT," VINCENT said. "Rider thought we should stop by on the way home to check on you last night. I thought that it might be better if we waited. Rider didn't really understand why I said we shouldn't. He wasn't going to take no for an answer."

Picturing Rider not understanding why Vincent didn't want to stop by was an easy task. It would have been an interesting conversation, especially with Vincent doing the explaining. I turned to face the window and bit my lip to hide my amusement.

"It's not like we were standing around discussing it. He was adamant that we stop by."

Swallowing hard, trying to keep the laughter out of my voice, I asked. "And when you told him?"

Vincent frowned. "He was still adamant. It was a long conversation. And since he called you after I left, not an effective one."

Trying to hold the laughter back only caused me to snort. Then all the laughter came pouring out.

The corners of Vincent's mouth turned up, and his eyes appeared to lighten.

"Poor Rider," I said when the laughter started to die away.

"He was going to call Margaret to double check."

"I guess werewolves do things differently. I wonder what types of social interactions the government goes over during the integration process."

"We might want to find out. With some of the questions he's asked lately, I think he might want to ask someone out."

"That's a good point. I wonder how werewolves differentiate between dating and friends. I know things didn't go well with Jonathan and Paula." Elves usually have one mate for life. When Jonathan and Paula got engaged, I don't think he really realized how often couples split up. I'm not sure if Paula was his one true love or not. I was almost afraid to ask.

"I never thought of that," Vincent said, stopping behind the AIR SWAT-style truck. "Let me know how that conversation goes."

"Wait, what?"

There was a hint of mirth under his blank face. "I'm his partner, we haven't hit friend status yet."

"Oh. That's fair, I guess." Werewolves were hard to make friends with, but once you were friends, you were friends for life.

We got out of the car and looked up the street where the police had set up obstructions to keep people away from an alley.

"I don't know if our world meshes well with the normal world." I tried to keep my voice light, but it was true.

Vincent came up beside me and followed my gaze to where Ethan stood. He was inside the barrier, talking to an officer on the other side of the ugly yellow and orange sawhorses that blocked the sidewalk.

"Hey," Vincent said, putting a hand on my arm. I looked up at him while soaking in the current running through us. "Sometimes the worlds can mix. Try to give it some time."

When I looked back up, Ethan was watching us.

I nodded. Vincent's lips had moved up infinitesimally into a half grin, but there was a sad look in his eyes. Then he dropped his hand, and we went to the police tape.

Several reporters had set up across the street.

"Are those types of microphones legal?" I asked as we approached the crime scene. "They look like they could pick up voices from the International Space Station."

"I'm not sure," Vincent admitted, "but I doubt they'll get too much over the street noise."

My stomach was starting to churn before we reached Ethan. It was bad enough having to face him hours after he walked out, but the idea of reporters listening to what we might be saying left me uneasy.

"Let them through," Ethan said, nodding towards us. The officer waved us through, and he followed my gaze to across the street.

"They've been here for an hour already," the officer said.

"Yeah," Ethan agreed, "they set up there to get a better view of the crime scene."

I watched the reporters point in our direction. Microphones were raised and aimed our way. The last thing I wanted was AIR business caught on microphone. The thought of them picking up any conversation with Ethan and I wasn't sitting well either. I turned to face the alley, glanced at Vincent, and scratched my head. His look of unease turned into a smirk, although I could have been the only one to see it.

Closing my eyes, I reached for the Path. There was a bit of a struggle, but not as bad as it had been the past few days. Half turning to the reporters, I read their Path. My nose curled at what I saw. Any remorse that they may have felt was being overwhelmed by eager jumbles of emotions as they worked.

"If you all want to step this way," Ethan said.

I ignored him, but Vincent replied. "We need a moment."

It was petty, but my concerns were real. I sifted through the Paths for the duller and almost unnoticeable traces of equipment. I'd never done anything like this before with electronics, but energy is energy, and their battery packs were live. At least they were for about a minute. Twisting the Path around each little energy source allowed their power to drain away into the atmosphere.

"Well, I feel a bit better anyway," I said to Vincent. I glanced across the street and saw people replacing batteries, only to find the replacements dead.

"It's a shame it won't stop them for long."

I watched someone dash to a van down the street. Cocking my head, I twisted the Path again and felt satisfied that by the time he reached the others, their new power source would be dead as well.

I shrugged, "I just wanted a little privacy."

Ethan was watching an argument break out across the street. He glanced at me and back to the reporters. I couldn't read his expression and the little pieces of Path of his that I couldn't avoid didn't look promising. I was willing to bet I had made things worse.

My heart sank, but work called. I made my way into the alley watching patterns in the Path. Logan was crouched and looking under a white cloth on the ground. Rider was pacing around, looking up the sides of buildings and into windows. I could see the issue immediately. It was the same black trail as the job site, but sliding up the building.

"Those news crews aren't anything compared to what's going to come down on this town if we don't find who's doing this," Ethan said.

Logan stood and came over to talk to Ethan. "Think this is going to go national?"

"We've had four bodies in three days, and the day isn't over yet. Yeah, I think it could get bad. What can we do to help you?" Ethan asked.

I wandered down the alley towards Rider. "What are you finding?" I asked.

"It is what I am not finding that is bothering me," Rider said.

"You know where the victim entered, right?" I asked.

"From the street. His head left at the other end of the alley."

My hand clutched my stomach as I stared into the smoky black Path. "Head?" I asked.

"That is the only part of the body that is not here."

Shimming threads of bright color rolled through the blackness, curving out, and then folding back under the dense Path. "Whoever did this was here and then moved out this way."

"But no one came here and took the head." His frustration rolled out from him in waves of amber.

"Do you smell what you did at the job site?"

"I smelled only objects there, except where the bones left."

"Do you smell the same object here?"

"There are some similar smells. But they are smells that are all over the city."

"What about from last night?"

Rider shifted and looked up the side of the building again. "There was a strong smell of clay, dirt, trees, and plants last night. Less so here. There was very little clay at the job site, but many more smells of dirt and trees."

"But that links all three," I said.

Rider shook his head. "There is clay everywhere. In the brick, on the street, even at our homes."

"I'm going to see where this leads," I said, following the black cloud through the alley and out the other end.

Rider kept pace with me. "I smell only the exit of the head."

"I see the person leaving. It's the same Path that was at the construction site."

We were on a less populated street once we left the alley. A few times I reached out as though to touch the Path, but my skin prickled and I dropped back. The black cloud didn't feel evil or vile. I had seen that type of darkness before and the emotion radiates. This was different. Almost dull and condensed, but with some emotion or power trying to break away.

We were a block away and well outside the police barrier when my phone rang. Caught up in the Path, I answered it without looking at the caller ID.

"This is Cassie."

"Cassie, this is Felicity. You have to come." Felicity's voice radiated fear.

I reversed directions and moved quickly back the way I came. To keep my concentration all on the call, I dropped the Path.

"What's wrong?"

"There's someone here…" Felicity started crying, "…here in the house. I'm with the girls hiding upstairs, but there's someone downstairs tearing things up."

I started running. I dodged under the police tape and sprinted down the ally. "Tell me what's happening."

Logan and Vincent saw me running.

"It is Felicity," Rider called out to Logan and Vincent.

I put my finger over the phone so Felicity couldn't hear what the others were saying.

"We need help," Felicity said.

"We're only a few blocks away, and we're already moving your way. We'll be there in a few minutes."

There was relief in the sob that Felicity let out.

"Vincent and Rider, wrap up here, quick. I'll call this in," Logan said.

Ethan looked worried, but I didn't say anything as I rushed by.

"Tell me everything you saw," I repeated to Felicity.

"It was—"

The phone went dead.

"Felicity?"

My heart beat fast and my feet pounded down the sidewalk.

Logan was faster. The truck was starting when I flung myself inside, and we rushed away.

"Get the coms," Logan said, concentrating hard as he weaved in and out of traffic.

I snatched a box from behind the seat and took out our comms units. I twisted one of the small earpieces, handed it over to Logan, and put two others in my pocket. After readying the fourth, it sprang to life when I put it into my ear.

Hank was already talking, asking what we had.

I repeated the information from my call with Felicity.

"This could be a random burglary," Hank said. "Be careful. Keep your eyes open and your ears tucked in. Get our girl out as quick as you can."

I took a holster from my gear bag and snapped it to my belt, took my gun from the lock box, checked the magazine, and then chambered a round before holstering it.

By the time Logan stopped in the circle drive to the sorority house, I was ready to go. There were a few girls out on the lawn, several on cell phones. Sirens blared in the distance.

"Hank, I think we have locals on their way here."

"We're talking to them now. They know to stand down."

We ran up to the front door, which had been left open. Logan had his gun in hand, I drew mine, and we strategically entered the house. The large entrance was eerily still. There was noise, music playing somewhere, whispers, and someone crying while trying really hard not to be heard, but there was a stillness that I didn't think was possible in a sorority house.

A crash came from upstairs. Looking back, I saw a girl ran down the stairs, fear evident. When she turned and saw us, she let out a squeak and covered her mouth quickly.

"He's, he's..." She pointed upstairs.

We nodded and she ran outside. We were familiar enough with the layout of the house to know that there was more than one way upstairs. Logan motioned for me to go towards the kitchen, where the other staircase hid. He started climbing the stairs, keeping his attention split between the upstairs and down.

I filled Hank in on my way through the kitchen. When I opened the door that hid the stairs, two girls screamed.

"Shh," I said, trying to keep the harshness out of my voice. "Backdoor. Go. Now."

They fled.

"The locals are all out front," Hank said. "I'll send some around to the back. They're working on getting the civilians out of the way."

"I'm at the landing," Logan said.

I hurried up to the door to the second floor. "I'm entering the hallway," I said.

My hand was shaking, so I took a meditative breath before opening the door. There was nothing in sight.

"Hallway's clear," Logan said.

It was a temporary relief. I still opened the door with great care, checking both directions before stepping out. Another crash sounded from one of the rooms.

CHAPTER 17

L OGAN TRIED TO USE A few hand signals, but they were nothing like any of the signals in the manuals, so I was lost.

"Check the rooms. Send anyone you find down the nearest staircase," Logan whispered.

Before I opened the first door, I reached for the Path, but got nowhere.

Once I opened the door and I waited for a breath before poking my head in. For each room I steadily worked through, I used this tactic. At the third door, the pause saved me from being pummeled with the objects hurled into the hallway.

Unfortunately, there was nothing I could do about the yells, which echoed down the hall.

"Shh," I hissed into the room when the throwing ceased. "Kitchen stairs. Run out now. Straight out the back door."

They were out the door the moment the words came out of my mouth.

"Hank, do they have a role call yet of who's outside?"

"Not yet. The locals are working with someone from the sorority. Vincent and Rider are on their way. We have another team en route as well," Hank responded.

I put my hand out in a gesture to stop one of the girls. Thankfully, she was one of the few that weren't freaking out.

"Do you know how many others are up here?"

She shook her head.

"Felicity, have you seen her?"

"She was in her room."

"Thank you. Backdoor, straight outside. There's someone there to help."

She ran off.

Closing my eyes, I concentrated as hard as I could, stretching my mind, but there was nothing, only darkness.

Frustrated, I looked around and saw that Logan was already standing outside of Felicity's room.

"Hank, we need the backyard cleared of civilians. We gotta get our guys back there," Logan said. "We also need a fast and thorough check of the first floor. Get in and get out, unless they're ours."

I joined Logan by the door.

"Four locals will be clearing the first floor. Rider's in the back, and Vincent's on his way inside," Hank said.

"Entering," Logan said.

My heart threatened to hammer out of my chest as Logan held up fingers to count down. He was focused on the door.

Holding up a balled up fist for zero, he kicked the door in. After a quick glance in the room, I entered, concentrating on one side and trusting Logan to cover the other.

Felicity was sitting on a bed in the small room. She looked like she had been crying at one point, but now she looked more ticked off than distressed. The room was a disaster, and it was steadily growing worse. Logan had his gun trained on a closet. Clothes, shoes, and everything else was being tossed onto the floor.

"Hands up and come out," Logan said.

The closet exploration didn't stop.

You know as well as I that we would not hurt an Other if it can be avoided.

"Logan, get back!"

We know their pain. We caused them much pain.

Logan took a step away. "What is it?"

"It's him." I moved across the room to Felicity and held out my hand to her. She jumped up, took my hand, and positioned herself behind me.

Logan's features began to contort. Both ears were at their points and his face stretched to become more jagged.

"Felicity," I kept hold of her hand and made sure that I was always between her and Einar, "stay behind me. When you reach the hall, go straight for the central staircase. It's closest. We have someone downstairs that can help."

"Vincent will meet her at the stairs," Hank said through my earpiece.

"His name is Vincent. He'll make sure you get outside. Talk to no police officers. Other AIR agents will help. Are you good with that?" I asked.

"Yeah, I'm good," Felicity said.

We made it out the door and I watched as Felicity dashed towards the staircase. Once she was out of sight, I entered the room again. My arms were screaming in protest from the weight of my gun, but I wasn't about to let it go.

"Hands up and back out of the closet," Logan said again.

The flurry of activity in the closet stopped and Einar came out. He paid Logan little attention.

"Put your hands up!" Logan hissed. His voice was almost as alien as his appearance.

I struggled not to look at him. When an elf let his true appearance show it brought out a chilling fear that tried to override everything else.

I will assist you shortly.

Gooseflesh broke out on my arms. "What's that supposed to mean?"

An end to your suffering.

My step back was involuntary.

"Is he talking?" Logan asked.

My creators thought allowing me to speak would be a mistake. Now they do not know why they must die.

"Why who must die?"

The creators. Those responsible for the travesty that is our existence.

Einar was looking around the room. When he turned his back to Logan, the elf took his chance and tried to grapple Einar's arms from behind.

There was a deep sigh from Einar before he turned, picked up Logan, and then tossed him effortlessly into a wall.

Logan hit with enough power that the drywall buckled.

There is nothing here to explain.

"Explain what? Why are you hurting people?"

Not the people. Those in charge. Einar appeared downcast. Then he turned his face to me. *They allowed you to speak.* His resentment was tinged with disgust, and he took a step towards me.

"No one allows me to do anything. I speak because I want to speak."

This seemed to stop Einar. *Explain.*

"Explain what?"

He took another step towards me.

"Come any closer and I will shoot," I said.

Logan hurled himself at Einar. When the pale man reached out, Logan dodged under his arm, brought one arm against Einar's throat, and using his other arm as leverage, started to squeeze.

I do not wish to hurt him, but he leaves me little choice.

Einar twisted around with incredible speed, breaking Logan's hold. As if Logan were a rag doll, he slung Logan out the door where I heard the elf make full contact with the opposite wall.

Then Einar rushed at me. I fired three shots, which made Einar screech in my head, but it didn't slow him down.

You will tell him that I wish to harm no Others.

The words reached my mind as Einar seized my arms. I fired until my gun was empty.

"Let her go." Behind Einar, Logan gripped the doorframe. He looked ready to jump back into the fight.

I do not understand. The Others fight with you and not against. Einar's features didn't change, but the confusion was evident.

Trying to reach for the Path was a struggle that got me nowhere. I didn't know what Logan could do against Einar. I didn't know what any of us could do against him.

I am not done here.

The movement was so slight, yet so fast that my brain had trouble catching up with what was happening. My feet left the ground as Einar threw me straight into the window. When his hands left me, my back struck the glass. I might not have gone through, but Einar had launched himself after me. Our combined weight hit the window and it shattered.

When I slammed into the tar tiles of the roof outside the window, I skidded down them. Einar loomed over me, standing on the roof, but I was sliding away. As I reached the edge I made a panicked grasp at the gutter, which slowed my fall, but gravity quickly dragged me down and I took the gutter with me.

I hit the ground, back first, and all the air was knocked out of my lungs. There was noise above me on the roof and yells from ground level. More shots rang out.

My lungs burned as I struggled to breathe. Logan flew off the roof. I strived to move as the first ragged breaths of air returned to my body, but my arms collapsed when I tried to leverage myself up. In the air, Logan twisted like a cat and landed on his feet. He hit the ground not far away from me and turned to aim.

Clutching at my chest, I tried to roll over and get my gun. My injuries caught up with me and pain lanced through my body, almost taking my breath away again.

Logan glanced at me, but he didn't need the distraction. Einar was the priority, so I waved a hand at Logan indicating he should get moving. Logan ran off while giving orders through the comms.

Lying on the ground, I stared up at the sky for a few moments, trying to bury the agony that seemed to scream from everywhere at once. My biggest issue was the fact that the Path hadn't opened. It put my partner and me at risk each time I tried and failed.

A shadow fell over me as Vincent knelt on the ground next to me. His eyes were slate black and his face tense.

Gritting my teeth, I pushed myself up. "Logan went that way."

"Did you hit your head?" Vincent started probing.

"Ouch. What are you doing?" I shoved his hands away.

The flash of anger from Vincent nearly bowled me over. I was grateful that it didn't stick around.

"I'm fine. Bumps and bruises. Go!"

Vincent balled up his fists.

"Here." I dug around in my pocket and took out a comms unit. "I'll let you know if I need anything."

"Dammit," Vincent said under his breath. He turned on the comms unit, gave me one last look over, and then ran off.

Sitting up wasn't the most comfortable thing in the world, but there was no way I was going to lie back down on the ground. I looked in the direction the others had disappeared. Sound was coming in and out on my comms, so I was having a hard time figuring out what was going on.

Grimacing, I picked up my gun and then forced myself to my feet. I released the magazine and stowed it in my pocket before taking out another, sliding it home, and then chambering a round. Guns seemed useless against Einar, but it made me feel marginally better to have at least some weapon in hand.

The decision not to follow the others was an internal struggle. The need to help was battling with the understanding that I was a liability in my condition.

"Are you hurt?"

Jumping, I turned and almost stumbled over. It wasn't one of my finer moments, and it was made worse by the fact that I stood face-to-face with Ethan.

"Oh, uh, yeah." I could feel the heat rising to my face.

Ethan shook his head. "You're bleeding."

I rolled my eyes, tugged out my useless comms unit, and then dug around my pocket to find the last one. Twisting it, I could finally catch up to what the others were doing.

Logan was issuing orders, but it didn't take long to discover that they lost sight of Einar.

"Hank, my comms are sketchy. Does someone have Felicity?" I asked.

"She's on her way to the Farm," Hank said. "Satellite will be available in three minutes."

I muted my comms and turned back to Ethan. "Has the house been cleared?"

"It's empty and everyone has been accounted for," Ethan said. "Interviews are being conducted, but no one really saw much of anything. No injuries reported beyond you and Logan."

"Did Logan look hurt?" I stared in the direction he had disappeared as though I could see through the buildings and find him.

"He looked like he'd been tossed around." Ethan looked uncomfortable. "Logan, um... His face? And ears..."

"Crap." I thumbed my comms on again. "Hank, remind Logan he elfed out."

"Got it," Hank said.

Ethan looked around before dropping his voice. "Elfed out?"

"Yep." I holstered my gun and didn't offer any further explanation.

"And Vincent's eyes, they were... I mean they looked..."

"Black. Yes."

"And Rider? The tracking or whatever he does?" Ethan asked.

"He's good at it." I crossed my arms and tried to hold back my hostility. My anger shouldn't have been directly aimed at Ethan, but my partners were gone and I was feeling useless. His timing wasn't great.

"He growled at me."

"Don't aggravate a werewolf." I tried to shrug as though the answer should have been obvious, but the gesture sent a jolt of pain up one arm.

Ethan opened his mouth and shut it again. It was vindictive, but I enjoyed watching him struggle with that one.

"And you..."

"I told you about me. You wanted time." I glared at him as my anger rose.

"You took me by surprise," Ethan said.

He looked repentant, but I wasn't giving him an easy out. "And today, here you are jumping in with both feet."

Ethan ran a hand through his hair. "Look, you're still bleeding. Let's at least find a medic."

My arms did appear to be oozing. "I scratched myself on the roof tiles."

"How's your back?" Ethan asked.

"It was already bruised."

I held a finger up to stall Ethan's next question and listened to Logan through the earpiece. "They still haven't found him," I said.

"What can we do to help?" Ethan asked.

He sounded as relieved at the change of conversation as I was and for the first time that day, I liked the way he thought.

Closing my eyes, I reached out to the Path. I wavered on the precipice before my mind finally decided to make the jump.

I un-muted the comms for a moment. "Hank, let Logan know I'm reading and moving his way."

"Passing it on now," Hank replied.

CHAPTER 18

T HE INKY PATH ON THE roof was out of place in the brightness of the midday sun.

"Hold up," Ethan said.

I didn't look at him, but kept my eyes on the dark cloud of the Path. If there was any doubt that it was Einar that left the Paths at the other murders, this put the issue to rest.

"What is it?" I asked, continuing to follow the trail from the ground.

"Put this on," Ethan said.

He slid a jacket it onto my shoulders.

"It's really warm out. I'm not cold," I said.

"No, but you are covered in blood. I'm pretty sure standing out isn't what you had in mind."

"Oh, thanks," I said, turning to him.

It was the first time I had done more than take a glimpse of his Path since we started to see each other. His core was swirling with color and it rippled away from him in waves. Warm oranges were wrapped in blue and they reached out to me, wanting me to know that he cared. Uncertain greens and browns chased each other around as though he wasn't sure if he should follow his own instincts. There were dark smudges and signs of other emotions that flared up. It was fascinating to see that the dominant oranges and blues threw off golden sparks as they worked to overpower the rest.

"Something wrong?" he asked.

"Oh, no." I wrenched my eyes away. "Sorry."

I looked around and picked up Einar's trail from where he jumped off the roof.

"Can they hear us?" Ethan asked. "On your microphone I mean?"

"Only when it's not muted." I followed close to the black cloud, once again feeling the urge to reach into its depths even though the thought made my skin crawl. "We're muted now. The others have split up to search the area."

We left the sorority house property and started to move away from campus.

"That's good to know," Ethan said.

"You don't have to follow me," I said.

"That's funny. I think the others might disagree."

That made me crack a smile. "They might at that."

"Pretend they're here now. What would your partners want me to know while following you around?"

"Make sure I don't get lost?" I suggested. "And make sure I don't wander into the street and get hit by a car or something."

"I can manage that," Ethan said.

We walked without talking for a while. Ethan was especially wary when we approached a busy intersection, worried that I might actually walk out in front of a car.

Ethan took a phone call. My inclination was to snoop and listen in, but this time I didn't pay much attention, staying intent on the Path. The call was followed by giving instructions through his radio.

When we entered a park, the hustle and bustle of the busy campus and surrounding streets faded away. The Path itself was lighter, and I felt some tension fall away.

"If I talk, will it distract you?" Ethan asked.

I shrugged. "That probably depends on what you say."

He seemed to mull that over. "Fair enough."

When he was quiet again, my curiosity became piqued. "What did you want to talk about?"

Being deep in the Path, I could not only sense his anxiety, but also see and feel it fill the area.

"I wanted to apologize for last night."

I slowed and my grip on the Path wavered. "Oh." It was lame, but I couldn't think of anything to say.

"But then I figured it wasn't the best time," Ethan said. "Maybe we can talk later?"

"Um, yeah, maybe later." I picked up speed again while trying to drive thoughts of my personal life out of my mind.

"Cassie." Hank's voice seemed farther away, but I'm sure the comms was still in my ear. "Logan's pulling back. Are you at the sorority house?"

I started to talk, but then remembered the comms was muted. "No, I'll be a little while."

"I'll relay the message." Hank didn't sound happy about it.

"The others are meeting back at the house," I said.

"Should we do the same?" Ethan asked.

I shook my head. A part of me knew I could help if I followed a bit farther. Another part was telling me that was stupid and I had already done too much.

Looking ahead, I tried to see how far the Path ran, but there appeared to be no end. Knowing I had to walk away made me feel worse than the pains that were radiating through my body. Still, I knew it had to be done.

From experience, I knew that with the dense black cloud of Path beside me, I wouldn't be able to stop reading. I tried anyway, but I didn't expend too much effort.

"We need to move away from this Path." I peered closely at it one last time, watching the brilliant, waving strands of color, then turned my back to it and walked away.

Ethan stuck beside me. He was quiet, but I could tell he was watching me carefully. I didn't know what he was looking for. Maybe he thought I was going to grow another head or something.

When we reached a bench, I sat down to hide the fact that I was becoming unsteady on my feet. Hopefully I was far enough away.

"The Path goes that way," I told Ethan, "but I don't see an end to it. I can't tell where he stopped or went."

"Got it," Ethan said. "That's more than what we knew before."

Nodding, I closed my eyes and thrust the Path away. The moment it was gone, my pain rammed home, back in full force, and I could feel myself sway. Gripping the bench stopped the swaying part.

"How far away from the house are we?" I asked.

"I'd say about a mile. Maybe a bit more."

"Lovely," I muttered.

"Should we go back?"

"We should," the next part was like pulling teeth for me to admit, "but I need a few minutes."

Ethan got another call. He answered, but then walked away to talk.

Leaning my head back, I stared at the sky for a while. Puffy white clouds shifted across the blue backdrop. It was calming to watch. Ethan was still talking, so I closed my eyes and concentrated on feeling the warmth of the sun across my skin.

It was a beautiful day, but I was covered in bruises and sore as hell. You can only drive that kind of thing aside for so long.

I couldn't open the Path when I needed it, and couldn't follow it as long as I needed to. The stronger the flow, the faster my energy drained away. Coffee helped, usually. Maybe I should start carrying around caffeine pills or energy drinks.

Then again, what would happen if I kept taking them and then kept going? Not being able to do my job was one thing. Killing myself while trying to do my job didn't sound like the smartest way to move forward.

"Logan wants to know if you're still reading," Ethan said.

Being lost in thought, I hadn't heard Ethan come back. I also hadn't heard the comms.

"I'm not. Do you mind letting him know where we stopped and which direction Einar left the park?" I plucked the small piece of plastic from my ear and examined it before turning it off and stowing it away.

"No problem."

I yawned and started to stretch, which turned into a wince and a groan. Carefully, I laid my head on the back of the bench and closed my eyes again. I was feeling steadier, but I wasn't ready to start moving around yet.

Ethan settled down on the bench beside me. "You didn't tell me you could die from what you do."

I didn't open my eyes and tried to let the remarks flow over me without getting frustrated. "I'm an agent, you're a lieutenant. We could both die from what we do. For that matter, so could anyone on the street."

"Fair point," Ethan said after a while. "They should be wrapping things up at the house soon. You all have a forensics unit on the scene already. Another house is taking in the residents overnight."

"And from the scene this morning?"

"Logan and Vincent are going to the morgue."

My brow furrowed and I lifted my head. "Did he say where Rider was?"

"Bringing us your car."

"Thanks for that. And sorry, I should have called him. I'm pretty sure you're supposed to be working with your guys, not following me around."

"I went where I was needed. Logan seemed to approve anyway."

"They all would," I muttered.

"Besides, my side of things is a little...less complicated."

"You can catch up with Logan if you need to," I said, stifling another yawn. "I'll meet up with Rider and work with him."

"I'm on strict orders to take you home."

I raised an eyebrow, but I was too tired to feel any real frustration. "Did Logan give you an order? You don't have to listen to him, especially not if it gets in the way of the case."

"Technically, Logan made a suggestion. It was one that I happen to agree with, though."

"So you ordered yourself?"

Ethan nodded. "Orders that I intend on following."

I couldn't help but chuckle. "I'm fine. Just tired. We can go back and help out."

A horn honked. Rider was at the edge of the park, waiting for us. Being incredibly stiff made standing an ordeal, and after a few steps, I was grateful that we didn't have to walk back to the house.

Ethan opened the door for me and I slid in without comment. Rider's nose curled as Ethan slid into the back seat.

"You are bleeding."

"Still?" I asked, feeling aggravated by my body's limitations.

Rider leaned over and helped me tug off the jacket Ethan had given me. My scrapes burned in the places the where the fabric had to be peeled off the skin.

"I think I ruined your jacket," I said as Rider lifted and turned my arms until he found the spot he was looking for.

"Don't worry about the jacket," Ethan said, leaning forward in the seat.

"It has slowed," Rider said. "Are you injured elsewhere?"

"Bruises and scrapes," I said.

"Your bruises have their own bruises now. Have your muscles healed?" Rider asked.

"Those take longer. I'll re-wrap them when I get home," I said.

Rider swerved in and out of traffic and I felt Ethan grip the back of my seat.

"We need a plan to fight Einar," Rider said.

"Yeah, we really do," I said.

"Vincent has volunteered—"

"No." I put all my resolve into the response. There were two options for Vincent, take Einar's soul, or take him between the worlds, and I didn't want Vincent to do either of those things.

"I agree," Rider said. "He has not gone back to his old work since he came to this office. That should continue. We will meet and come up with another plan."

"That sounds good," I said.

Rider parked in front of the sorority house, but didn't get out of the car. "I am working here with the clean-up crew. Ethan is driving you home?"

"I could drive—"

"Yes," Ethan said over me.

Rider looked in the rear view mirror at Ethan and then back to me. "I have not spent much time with Ethan. Do you trust him to help with your injuries?"

"I know first aid," Ethan said. "It comes with the job."

Rider pretended not to hear, but continued to look at me until I answered.

I patted Rider's hand. "I trust him."

Rider didn't look completely satisfied, but he nodded and got out of the car. Ethan followed suit and came around to the driver's side. There was a brief exchange of words between the two before Rider moved back and Ethan got behind the wheel.

Ethan looked a little pale and he watched Rider in the rearview mirror as we drove away.

We were a block away before Ethan said anything. "So, werewolf, huh."

"Yep." I looked out the window to hide my grin.

"I don't think he trusts me."

"He doesn't know you."

"You two seem to care for each other. A lot."

"Of course. He's my best friend."

"He takes his friendship seriously."

"You could say that. We both do."

"How did you become such good friends?"

I had to think about that for a minute. About where the friendship actually started to form.

"I shot him," I said finally. "That's where it had all started anyway."

"You what? Why did you shoot him? How did that make you all friends?"

I wondered if Ethan was going to get pushed too far again. He had walked away last night when I had answered his questions.

In the end, I decided I wasn't going to tip-toe around in my own life. "He was going to kill me. Actually, I think he wanted to eat me, but I'm not sure if he was serious."

Ethan started to say something and then stopped. The rest of the drive to my house was made in silence. At some point, I must have dozed off because I missed a great deal of the ride.

Yawning, I hauled myself out of the car and into the house, straight to the coffee pot. Unfortunately, we had left the house in a hurry, so I had to clean out the current pot before I could start another. Once the coffee was brewing, I turned to find Ethan leaning against the kitchen entry, watching me.

"You don't have to stick around," I said. "You can take my car and ask one of the others to bring it back."

"Actually, I was hoping we could talk."

CHAPTER 19

I F ETHAN HAD STARTED SPEAKING in tongues, I'm not sure my look would have been any different.

"Not right this minute," he assured me.

Waiting for the coffee wasn't an option, so I grabbed the pot while it was still brewing and poured a quick cup.

"Help yourself to anything," I said, knowing full well that Gran would be shocked by my poor manners. Still, I felt grungy. "I'm going to get cleaned up."

I wasn't at my best today. Hell, the last few days were varying levels of depressing. Taking time to contemplate what I wanted, I didn't rush through my shower and I inspected my bruises and scrapes. There was a lot to contemplate. My job, my social life, my on-again, off-again powers as a Reader, and not the least of which, the fact that someone seemed intent on killing me.

Again.

Looking in the mirror and seeing bruises marring my skin everywhere didn't help my mood. After running a brush through my hair, I threw on some loose-fitting clothes and then went downstairs. Ethan was waiting for me in the kitchen.

"I hope you don't mind," he said, gesturing to the table, "but I rummaged around your bathroom for supplies."

Strewn across the table were different sizes of adhesive bandages, alcohol, peroxide, and a giant bag of cotton balls. He had enough stuff to disinfect a small platoon of goblins.

"Thank you for helping out," I said as I poured myself a cup of coffee.

"Consider it self-preservation at this point." He grinned at me and winked. "Oh, you received a package while you were upstairs."

I looked around and didn't see anything.

"I left it at the front door. Let's start with your arm."

He had a careful hand, but I hated him seeing all the bruises and scrapes. It made me feel distinctly not pretty. It wouldn't be so bad if I had been capable of taking down the bad guy, but alas, that was not the case.

"You've had a busy few days," Ethan said, moving to the other arm. "Or are things always like this?"

"Only when someone's trying to kill me."

Ethan looked up at me, startled.

"In other words, it's not often like this," I said.

Ethan nodded, but when he spoke again his voice was softer and slower. "When you were on your last big case in the city, things got bad there, too."

Memories flickered through my mind. The basement. Being tied up. Pain.

My breath was shaky and my veins started to fill with ice. "What do you mean?"

Ethan rubbed my arm with one hand before moving to the next scrape. "Rider mentioned..." He didn't look me in the eye.

"What?"

"When you got back into town, he said things got bad. That you were hurt. He wanted me to keep an eye on you."

I shook my head trying to dislodge thoughts that rose up and threatened to overtake me. One disaster at a time. That was all in the past.

"Rider gets worked up over little things," I said.

Ethan didn't say anything.

"Trust me; it's not every day that this stuff happens. Most of the time I'm doing house calls and checking in with people. I told you before; I usually don't even carry a gun."

Ethan nodded, but still didn't look directly at me.

"Would it be an issue if it was like this often?" I kept my voice level because I was curious about how he felt about my job. Then I realized that this was the exact opposite of giving him time. "Not that you have to answer that. I'm not trying to…" I tried to get my brain to catch up with my mouth and it wasn't working.

Ethan ignored my babbling. "It would take some adjustments."

That sounded promising at least. Now, I needed to figure out exactly what I wanted here.

I winced when Ethan put alcohol on a particularly nasty gash. He leaned forward and blew on it to take the sting away.

"Did you learn that in training?" I asked, letting a smile escape.

"Sure. The guys really appreciate it when I do that." Ethan chuckled. "No, that I learned from my mother."

"Get into a lot of scraps when you were a kid?" I asked.

"A fair few. How about you? I picture you as hell on wheels. Hanging with the guys and giving your mother fits."

I laughed. "Maybe a few small incidents, but I didn't give Mom fits until I quit my job as an accountant and started to work for AIR."

"She doesn't approve?"

"Not exactly. She'd rather I forget about what I can do, and get a job where she works. After Zander, I started in that direction, but it wasn't for me. I didn't even last a full year at my firm before AIR recruited me."

"Zander's the guy from last night."

"Has it really only been one night?" The thought made me tired.

"It was a long night," Ethan said. He sounded dejected, which started to fill me with tension.

"Yeah," I agreed. "A long night. Followed by a long day."

"Turn around and lift up your shirt."

"Uh…what?"

He started to turn red. "Your back. You slid down the roof on your back, I wanted to check…"

"Oh, right." I turned and lifted up the back of my shirt.

Ethan's fingers felt cool as he traced a few lines onto my back. "Rider wasn't wrong. Your bruises have bruises."

I twitched away and let my shirt drop. "It's fine. They'll fade away soon enough."

"Yeah. I guess they will."

This wasn't improving the atmosphere.

"Let's get your arms wrapped," Ethan said.

"I'll get it." I was getting self-conscious of Ethan seeing my injuries.

Ethan raised an eyebrow. "Self-preservation." He snatched up a long wrap and started to wind it tightly around my aching muscles. He worked for a while, looking very intent on the process.

Then he waded into the deeper waters, ones I was hoping to avoid. "I need to apologize for last night."

"I understand," I lied.

"I shouldn't have left the way I did."

"I'm sure it was a lot to take in all at once."

Ethan cleared his throat. "As soon as I drove away, I knew it was a mistake."

Since I agreed, I didn't say anything. He picked up the second wrap and moved to the other arm.

"I seem to be tripping myself up where you're concerned," Ethan said.

"I'm not always the easiest person to get along with."

A ghost of a smile flickered across Ethan's face. "You're plenty easy to get along with. I'm just a little on the slow side and having a hard time catching up."

"You kept up pretty well today."

Ethan let out a grim laugh. "When I saw you fly out the window, I thought I was going to have a heart attack. And I barely recognized Logan. And with Vincent...well, I'm not even sure what happened there."

I nodded sadly at his description and became uneasy.

"I'm betting I've seen more unreal things in the past few days than most people do in a lifetime."

"You're not wrong," I said, trying to keep the looming stress out of my voice.

Ethan finished the arm and tentatively took my hand. "I really want to say that I won't fall over myself when...I don't know...when a fairy jumps out at me or something. But I'd be lying if I said that."

It felt like my throat was starting to constrict.

"Still," he continued, "I'd like to at least try to understand your world. That is, if you're willing to give me the chance."

Some of my concern over where the conversation was going changed directions. "Are you sure you still want to see me after all that's happened in the past few days?"

Ethan's hand gripped mine a little harder. "Yes, if you're okay with that. I'd like to stay."

My brow furrowed as I reflected back on the past few days. "Why?"

"You want the list? You're smart, driven, and tough."

I couldn't help but laugh. "I've spent the past two days having my butt handed to me."

"You also have a great laugh." The cutest little half grin rose on Ethan's face. "And you're beautiful. Plus, you've managed to put up with me for a few months now."

I shook my head, but I was still smiling.

"What do you say?"

I kissed him. It turns out I didn't have to say anything.

He grinned through our kiss. "Is that a yes?" he asked when I pulled away.

"I don't know," I said coyly. "Maybe we should see how you deal with the fairy first."

"Point me in that direction and I'm there."

I bit my lip to keep from looking too pleased and I pointed out the back door.

It was Ethan's turn to look confused. "Here, in the backyard?"

"Really, Gran has a stray fairy in the garden."

The confusion slowly deteriorated into an amused look, and he stood up. "You'll introduce us?"

"Let me find something for you to give her."

Ethan looked out the window in the back door.

"It'll be better if you meet her without me," I said as I started to dig around in the fridge.

"You two don't get along?" Ethan asked.

"Not exactly." I hesitated, but decided it was best to forge ahead. "Fairies have really short memories. Since she doesn't remember me... well, you've seen how people react when they meet me." Not seeing any fresh fruit, I turned to go to the pantry and found Ethan behind me.

He wrapped his arms lightly around my waist and kissed me. "It's a shame she doesn't get the chance to get to know you."

"Hmmm." The contented sigh was all that I could manage before he kissed me again. This time it was shorter.

"What can I do to help?" Ethan asked.

"We usually have some chocolate chips in the pantry. She'll like those."

Ethan let me step away. "What do I do? Do I hand it to her?"

"You can call out to her. Her name is CiCi. Once you see her, talk to her like you would anyone else you're meeting for the first time. Introduce yourself and then put the chocolate chip down on top of something."

"I shouldn't give it straight to her?"

"She'll want to make sure it's not poisonous first. She might not even take it while you're out there." I found the bag and selected a small piece of chocolate. "Are you allergic to any plants? Poison ivy or anything?"

"Sumac," Ethan said.

"I'm not sure if she'll have any of that, but if she starts flying over you and dusting you with something or throwing things at you, come back inside."

"Fairies try to poison people?"

"Not only people," I said. "When you're not much bigger than a butterfly, you fight any way you can. They like to try stuff out to see if they can add new plants to their dust. Think of it as a greeting more than anything else."

"She's that small?" Ethan was starting to look nervous.

I handed him the chip and pointed at the door. "Go face the fairy," I said.

When Ethan stepped outside and closed the door behind him, I watched for a minute. Remembering the package out front, I went to retrieve it, and got back to the window in time to see Ethan set down the chocolate. He talked to CiCi for a short period while she approached the lone sweet with clear suspicion.

It didn't take her long to decide she'd rather be on the safe side and chase Ethan away before trying the food. She disappeared and quickly reappeared buzzing around his head. Ethan made a quick retreat into the house.

He took a deep breath and looked back out the window looking exhilarated. "I don't think she liked me much. But wow!"

"Don't take it personally." I took out a knife to open the package. "Even Logan gets dusted from time to time, and I'm pretty sure he speaks her language."

"Pretty sure?"

"Pretty sure," I repeated without elaborating. Logan could be cagey when he answered some questions.

"So," Ethan smiled wide, "did I pass the test?"

I laughed and sat down the knife. "You faced the fairy. That means you passed." Tilting my head up, I kissed him.

It was a long, slow kiss, that made my toes curl.

When Ethan's phone rang, he groaned and put his forehead to mine. "Hold that thought," he said.

Ethan took the call and I snatched up the knife thinking wistfully about how tingly the kiss had made me. I cut the tape off the box and put the knife in the dishwasher. Ethan smiled at me from the just outside the kitchen as he talked on the phone. It sounded like work, but thankfully, it didn't seem urgent.

Watching Ethan, I opened the box. My hand felt something soft and I looked down. Mounds of soft white fur topped with long pink ears. A rabbit? I leaned closer and saw that blood was coming out of its little pink nose.

CHAPTER 20

I SCREAMED AND CLAPPED A HAND over my mouth, backing away. Ethan frowned and came into the room. Seeing where my panic was aimed, he looked into the box.

"I've gotta go," Ethan said into the phone. "Yeah, tomorrow morning."

It took me backing into the table to realize that I was still moving away from the box. Tears fell freely. My stomach started to heave, but thankfully, I hadn't eaten anything. My lips were locked tight and covered by my hands anyway.

Ethan was a bit pale, but all business. He took out a pencil and moved it around inside the box. I didn't get close enough to see what he was doing, but I was hoping it would somehow end up with a stuffed bunny and a bad joke.

From the look on Ethan's face, I knew it wasn't a joke. Once that realization settled over me, I couldn't take my eyes off the box. There was nothing special about it. Brown, with brown packing tape.

"Cassie, do you have gloves?" Ethan asked, trying to look at the underside of the cardboard flap without touching it. I had a feeling he had said something else as well, but the words lost their meaning before they got to me.

My cell phone rang, but the noise sounded like it was coming from far away.

"Cassie?"

My eyes were still glued to the box. Ethan must have stepped out of cop mode, because he moved in front of me, breaking my eye contact with the box. My house phone rang as Ethan gathered me into a silent hug. My tears ran unchecked and my mind was full of this high-pitched screech.

"Let's go into the other room," Ethan said.

I nodded, but started to tense when we neared the box. Ethan shifted and put himself between the counter and me.

In the living room, I sat on the couch and stared at the wall to the kitchen. It was there, not thirty feet away.

"Want me to call Logan?" Ethan asked.

I sniffed and tried to pull myself together. "That's...that's them trying to call." My cell phone rang again in the kitchen.

Ethan stood and went for my cell when his own rang. I wasn't sure who it was beyond AIR calling. He moved into the kitchen, talking quietly. My mind was full of nothing but white fur and that loud buzz. Scrubbing the tears from my face wasn't doing any good. New tears arrived to take their place.

I took my hands from my face and looked at them. Panic welled up. My hands, one of them at least, had grazed the soft white fur.

Throw me out a window, drug me, or take away my powers, and I have something to get angry about, or pain to propel me forward. Dead bunny? Sent to my house? To me? The only pathway my brain seemed to want to take was to freak out, and it's always better to lose it alone.

Trembling, I went upstairs, closed the door to my bedroom, and then locked myself in my bathroom and scrubbed my hands until they were bright red. After that, I sat on the floor next to my tub and let all the fear and trepidation fall on my shoulders. For the next ten minutes, I was a sobbing wreck of a human being.

There was a soft knock on the door.

I cleared my throat and said, "I'll be down soon."

"It is me," Rider said through the door.

Maybe they voted him most likely to succeed or something. "I need a few minutes."

"Certainly."

There was movement behind the closed door and I thought for a moment that he would go back downstairs. Instead, he had chosen to sit down. Then I heard him lean against the door.

There needed to be a manual on how to be friends with a werewolf. Would asking him to go away be a horrible thing to do? In the end, I wasn't willing to take the risk. I slid across the floor and leaned my back against the door as well. It was comforting to be back-to-back with Rider, but still alone in the bathroom.

My tears started to dry up and that high-pitched noise, surely a defense mechanism to give my brain something else to concentrate on, quieted down.

Minutes ticked away and Rider let me take them in silence.

"How did things go at the house after we left?" I couldn't muster the energy to speak loudly, but I knew Rider would hear.

"The cleaning team picked up all the smears of blood and any evidence from you, Logan, Felicity, and Einar. All blood and fibers are gone."

"That's good to hear." I sniffed and laid my head back and stared at the ceiling.

"Why were there so many females in one house?"

"It's a sorority house. They have them for guys too, that's a fraternity. It's a place to live...well, I guess it's a place to live with people that think in a similar way to you. It's like a club, but sometimes it comes with room and board."

"There were no males in the house, although I could smell that they had been there."

"A werewolf would either make the best house mother or the worst," I said, "depending on whose point of view you were looking at. I think there are areas of the house that are out of bounds for men. Probably the bedrooms and anywhere else upstairs."

"That doesn't seem to work well."

"Heh, yeah, I suspect it doesn't."

"Why would Einar search through a house made for women?"

"I think he was looking for Felicity. Well, maybe not specifically her, but she is one of the closest Lost around."

"Do you believe that he is targeting the Lost?"

I thought that through. "He seems to think that the Lost have some information he wants."

"Did he say that?"

"No, he said that he didn't understand. He's trying to find meaning in something. He said he wouldn't hurt the Lost, although he called them Others."

"Yet, he seems to have no issues in harming humans."

"He said he had caused enough harm to the Lost, er, Others. Actually, he said that he and I had both caused them damage."

"I do not understand what that means."

"Me neither," I said, which was sort of a lie. I didn't directly hurt anyone, but each time I didn't work hard enough or fast enough on a rough case, more Lost were put at risk. "I think he was the one that trashed the Palmer's house as well."

"What makes you think that?"

I shifted uncomfortably. "The few times I've been around Einar, I haven't been able to reach the Path. Anytime I've been around the Path he leaves I've also been unable to reach the Path. It's blocking me somehow."

"I am sorry. It is not a necessity, but I know that you want to read to work."

It felt pretty necessary to me, so I didn't bother to reply.

"Should we warn other Lost?"

"That's a good idea," I said. "There aren't too many more living in town, but the smaller towns and surrounding areas have quite a few. Maybe we should set them up with alarm systems or something."

"Maybe, although some of the Lost will have better methods than the electronic alarms and surveillance systems that buildings use. For instance, humans think that the Farm is secure. But I believe it would be a mistake to assume so."

I mulled that over.

"Oh, sorry, Logan has asked me to never repeat that message."

I grimaced, knowing that Logan was listening in. "The secret is safe with me. Um...did he...with downstairs..." I stammered unsure of what to say that didn't start or end with fluffy dead bunny.

"He and Vincent are processing the box. Dr. Taylor is in the area and he will assist this evening."

"Ethan?"

"Watching and helping where Logan has allowed."

"He brought in Dr. Taylor. I guess that means Logan doesn't think it should go through AIR?"

"They are trying to decide if it is part of a case. If it is, AIR should be involved. If it is personal, AIR and Ethan may or may not need to be involved."

"Do they think that Einar did this?"

"I do not think so. I am starting to associate some trace element scents that might be related to Einar. His smell is not in your house."

"He said he was made. He wants to get revenge on the people who built him. He thinks they created me too. That's why he wants to kill me. He thinks he's going to be doing me a favor by killing me."

"Einar is targeting you?"

"The way he talks, I'm on his to-be-killed list. He said he would end my suffering, but he couldn't leave this world until he's finished with whatever it is he's doing."

Moments later, I winced as a burst of rage exploded from downstairs. If Vincent couldn't keep himself in check, my whole house would turn into one great blight of anger that the Path would have trouble moving away.

"Logan seems to think you should have mentioned this before now."

I rolled my eyes, even though I knew no one would see. "You mean while we were chasing Einar earlier today? Logan knew last night that he had tried to kill me. Last night we would have needed Gran to know that he actually intended to make my death a priority."

Rider sighed.

"What is it?" I asked.

"They are arguing over the best course of action. My partner is extremely agitated."

"Your partner is confusing."

"I am glad I am not the only one that thinks so." Rider shifted. In the silence, he moved again as though uncomfortable.

"You think we should go downstairs." It wasn't a question, but more of a glum statement.

"Not yet."

Knowing I didn't need to face anyone for a little longer was a relief. "Downstairs, did you...around the rab-uh...box. Did you notice anything familiar?"

Rider was silent for a few moments. "I did not have much of a chance before I came up here. I did not smell Einar and I did not find anything familiar, but I cannot be certain yet."

My face was fully dry now. With Rider to distract me with the case, it was becoming easier to adjust to and accept what had happened.

"Who would do something like this?" Rider asked. "They said this was not for food. I am afraid I do not understand."

"Don't try to understand it." My heart broke for Rider while he tried to grapple meaning from an insane act. "Whoever did this is sick. Their mind doesn't work right."

"So there was no reason?"

"Nothing that will make much sense. The person could be trying to scare me, which I guess worked." I wasn't even sure if I was scared, freaked out, or just lost as to how someone could do this sort of thing.

"It has managed to upset a lot of people."

For that, I had no reply. Rider and I sat in silence for a few minutes.

I listened to the muffled sounds of voices downstairs. Signs of my tears and distress would surely be gone by now. Maybe it was time to leave my bathroom.

"Did Ethan help you with the cuts?" Rider asked.

"Yeah, but he might have overdone it with the bandages. What did you say to him?"

"Downstairs?"

"You know where I mean. When we dropped you off at the sorority house."

"Oh, I asked him to look after you."

"That's it?"

"That is all."

Before the rabbit, I had it in mind to ask Rider what he told Ethan about our last case, but it didn't seem necessary anymore.

"Things sound a little quieter down there," I said, letting the subject drop.

"They are discussing the case now."

I peeled myself off the floor and stared into the mirror. Thanks to Rider's intervention, I looked almost normal again.

"May I come in?" Rider asked.

CHAPTER 21

S URE." I UNLOCKED THE DOOR and opened it, then went back to the basin to wash my face. "I shouldn't have stayed up here so long."

"There is no need to be down there." Rider leaned against the frame of the door and watched me.

Rider was starting to look more confident than he had when we met. He was growing and settling into the dimension and the job.

"How are you doing?" I asked.

"The animal is unsettling. Einar is as well. What kind of person smells like an object? And kills?"

"I'm not sure. The only thing I can think of is an android, which doesn't actually exist. Not one like Einar anyway. Maybe we'll find something when we finally get the chance to do some research." I brushed my hair to stall for time. "What about outside of work? How are things going elsewhere?"

Rider shrugged. Something so human that he picked up quickly. "There does not seem enough for a life at work and one outside of work. I do not know how you and Ethan manage it."

"We're not doing too well at it. Our last date ended up with Einar trying to kill us and Ethan...well, we didn't exactly argue. He wants to try keep dating, though. To see if we work well together."

"Is that how it works with humans?"

"Sometimes it's less complicated. Sometimes two people meet, fall in love, and then promise to spend the rest of their lives together. Most of the time that's for TV and romance novels. The real world is messy. Humans tend to make things more difficult than they need to be. I know I do."

"You and Ethan are not friends?" Rider asked.

"Not like you and I are friends. Most humans, lots of different types of people really, have temporary friends. Even families don't always stick together."

Rider looked troubled. "It sounds very lonely. How do you decide you want to be with anyone?"

"Sometimes, you have to take a leap of faith. People throw around the words friend and love pretty freely. When you're ready to take the plunge, make sure their definition of friendship is the same as yours."

"But we are friends?"

"We are your type of friend, the kind that doesn't go away. At least as far as what I understand our friendship to be." I hated saying the last part, but I wanted to make sure Rider knew that I didn't have all the answers.

"That is the core of any friendship with my people. We assume that the other person will always do whatever they can to help. Even if it is help that the other does not want to have."

"That sounds ominous."

"Not everyone knows what is best for them."

"That's true. Just be careful out there. Dating here doesn't mean you have to be friends with the other person, just friendly towards one another. Once you date, you see if you're compatible and decide if you want to move on from there."

"Are you and Ethan friendly?"

"We are firmly under the friendly-towards-each-other category. Every now and again, I don't know if we've made it even that far."

Rider appeared lost in his own thoughts.

"If you ever have any questions, or need anything, I'll help where I can."

"Yes, we are friends."

"Yeah," I said, unable to stop a small grin. "Thank you for coming up here and keeping me company."

Rider nodded.

"Are they still talking about the case?" I asked.

"Mostly," Rider said.

"Did I miss anything?"

"Frustration, aggravation, and many questions."

"Well, at least we know that going in. We should probably join them. Maybe we can give a few answers."

On the way downstairs, the doorbell rang. I froze on the steps. Thoughts of a deliveryman with multiple packages popped into my head and chilled me to the bone.

Logan came out of the kitchen and saw us. "We ordered up some grub."

"Oh, good. Thanks." I could breathe again.

When I walked into the kitchen, my eyes went immediately to the counter, but the box had been removed. I should have asked where they moved it to, but I decided I really didn't want to know.

No one looked very happy, except Logan when he returned with the pizza. Ethan appeared worried, so I forced a smile on my face when I sat down next to him.

Ethan looked like he wanted to say something, but worried about the subject, I steered the conversation to safe waters. "What do we know about Einar?"

"He's stronger than anything I know of," Logan said.

"He's fast," Rider said.

"He wants you dead," Vincent said, his voice flat. I noticed a bit too much black in his eyes.

"Also, he thinks he's made," I said, "and Rider only smells an object, not a person."

"But he's obviously a person of some sort," Ethan said. "He moves, thinks, and acts like a person. A monster, maybe, but still someone that's alive."

"Can something be made that is alive?" I asked.

Logan shifted uncomfortably. "It sounds like we're nearing Walker territory again."

"A Walker can remove a soul and put it into something else," Vincent said, "and we saw this a few months ago. But the objects made don't come alive."

"Could they have, though?" I asked.

"No." The finality in Vincent's voice was clear.

I changed gears, leading the conversation away from Walkers. "Is there anyone else we know that could create something and make it alive?"

Vincent's phone rang and after checking the screen, he left the room to take the call.

"Not that I can think of, not alive," Logan said.

"Is it possible that Einar is not alive?" Rider asked. "Could he be a representation?"

"Like a puppet?" Ethan asked.

Rider shrugged and we mulled it over.

"It's possible," I said. "But he appears to be acting, thinking, and talking on his own. There's no pause in processing."

"It doesn't rule it out," Logan said, "but it does tend to lean towards something living."

"I guess it's research time," I said.

"We have to go," Rider said. He looked like his spirits had been lifted considerably.

Vincent walked into the room. "We have gremlin duty." He looked at Rider and shook his head, but I saw the small grin that crept onto Vincent's face after looking at his partner. Rider loved the gremlins.

"We've got plenty of zip ties and metal in the truck if you need it," Logan said.

"We'll be back when we can. Stay safe," Vincent said.

"Einar came from the job site," I said after Vincent and Rider left. "I mean, from the Path I read, he was in the ground and climbed out."

"Like a zombie? Do you have zombies?" Ethan looked alarmed.

"Never confirmed," Logan said. "They're only a rumor."

"I'm pretty sure a zombie would have a distinct smell," I said.

"Even after all those years?" Ethan asked.

"Do we know how long the graveyard was there?" I asked.

Logan slid a tablet over to me. "It wasn't your typical bone yard, more like a battlefield."

The file was open, so I started flipping slowly through the pages, worried about what pictures I might see. This part of the job sucked.

"They're bones." The relief in my voice was obvious, but I didn't care.

"The few items excavated from the site give us a tentative timeline around the Civil War," Logan said.

"I guess we can rule out cyborg," I mumbled and flipped past the photos of skeletons.

"Could something disguise its scent from Rider?" Ethan asked.

"Huh." I had never thought about that possibility.

Logan nodded. "Disguise, yes, but very few could actually get rid of their scent altogether. People are more apt to overwhelm the senses of a werewolf than mask the scent."

"Overwhelm it how?" Ethan asked.

Logan hesitated. He hated letting anyone know more about the Lost, even at the office.

"Would that be on file?" I asked Logan.

"Yeah, I guess it would be. To overwhelm the senses, someone would have to cover themselves or an area with as much potent scent as possible. Make it strong enough and it would override Rider's sense of smell, so he'd smell that and nothing else," Logan said.

"Rider smells objects, clay and stuff, so that doesn't seem like it's happening here." I thought for a while. "The other day we talked about a warlock. Could they do something like this?"

"Warlock?" Ethan asked.

"I suppose it's possible," Logan said, ignoring Ethan's question. "Both Einar and the warlock have an interest in you."

"Could they disguise the scent?" I asked.

"It's within their skill range, I'm sure, but I don't think they'd bother with digging something like Einar up."

"Einar thinks and reacts on his own. What else do we have?" I had an answer as soon as I asked. "There's the body parts. Einar has picked up bones, a head, uh..."

"Hands," Ethan offered, "the other body had hands missing."

My shiver was involuntary. "And we interrupted him last night on campus. So he didn't have a chance to take anything there."

"The victims all work for the government," Logan said.

"The type of jobs and branches of government aren't related," Ethan said. "We're also pretty close to the capital, and we have a federal building here in town, not to mention all the local government. It could be a coincidence that they are all government employees. Not likely, but it's possible."

Logan crossed his arms and leaned back in the chair. "If this thing came from the Civil War era, I'm not sure it'd make much difference to him."

"Are we suggesting that Einar was alive that long ago?" I asked.

"It's a possibility we have to consider," Logan said. "You saw his Path climb out of the ground."

Ethan shook his head. "I'm not sure my brain can make that big of a jump. This goes back to zombie territory. What could live that long?"

Once again, I turned to Logan.

"The Civil War wasn't as long ago as humans seem to think. The war ended around 1865. Not even two hundred years ago."

"Are there things that can live that long?" Ethan asked.

I did some quick mental math and realized that Logan was a kid at the time of the Civil War. Not in this dimension, but he was still alive.

The air turned thicker and I took a quick glance at my partner. "People, not things. Lots of people could have lived that long."

Ethan let out a disgruntled sigh. "This is so far over my head I can't see the top. I don't think I'll be much help here."

"Want to check the job site?" Logan asked. "Once we're sure all the bones are out of the ground, they'll be excavating the hole Einar came out of."

"It's past time I check in at the office anyway." There was some tension in Ethan's voice.

If Logan noticed the strain, or the fact that Ethan seemed to want to make it clear he wasn't taking direct orders, my partner didn't comment.

I automatically got up to walk Ethan out, but didn't say anything till we got to the door. Logan would be able to hear us even if he went home.

This day had had more ups and downs than a roller coaster. We stood awkwardly for a moment. The reluctance to talk came from not knowing what to say.

"Thank you for calling Logan earlier," I said.

Ethan took my hand. "He beat me to the call. I wish there was something more I could do. Are you going to be alright?"

"Yeah, it's...yeah." I didn't want to say, 'yeah, it's just my life.'

"And, us? Are we..."

It sounded as though he was as lost as I was, so I strained to smile. "You faced the fairy, remember?"

He grinned and kissed me. It wasn't a toe-curling kiss, but then, it hadn't been the best day for us.

"Will I see you tomorrow?" I asked.

"You will."

I squeezed his hand before dropping it, and I watched from the door until his car was out of site.

Back inside, Logan was on the phone with Hank. My partner's voice was low until I came into the room. I got the distinct impression that the subject was changed. Before I walked in, there was whispering, and now Logan spoke in normal tones about work.

The cagey elf was good at keeping secrets and had over one hundred and fifty years of practice. I poured a cup of coffee and thought that over. To be this bad at hiding something, he must be doing it on purpose. Maybe he was actually leading up to confiding in me.

About him and Hank? It would be about time. Elves chose their mate for life, but Logan's wife had passed away more than fifty years ago, not long after Gerald was born. He may never have another true mate, but that didn't mean he couldn't have a relationship.

If that's what this was, I wished him more luck in his relationship than I ever found with mine.

With Logan on the phone, I gave Gran a call. She didn't answer, so I left a message. Her cat must have sensed the attempted contact with Gran. He came tearing into the room and jumped onto my lap.

Logan looked surprised, and then gave the cat a long, calculated look before signing off with Hank. "What got into him? No offense, but I thought that cat hated you."

"I think it's because I've been feeding him." I stroked the cat's fur until he started to purr. Even I was surprised by that, since he never purred for me.

"Maybe." Logan looked into the other room.

I followed his gaze. "What is it?"

Logan's ears unfurled slowly. When the thin tips had reached their points, the skin on the back of my neck began to rise.

Ding-Dong.

I jumped at the sound of the doorbell. This didn't make for a happy cat. He sunk his claws into my legs and stretched before jumping down. Even with his claws sinking into my skin, it was a vast improvement over my previous relationship with the cat. He hadn't tried to hamstring me in days.

Logan sat watching the other room intently.

"I'm going to answer that." I'm sure Logan would have given me some sort of warning if I shouldn't have been going into the other room. Still, I felt uneasy walking across the living room to the door. It was only late afternoon, so the house was brightly lit, but I felt like there should be shadows lurking throughout.

I opened the door and plastered on another fake smile. "Hi, Taylor, thanks for coming."

Taylor looked me up and down. "I see you've been following my instructions to the letter."

I winced, remembering that it was doctor's orders to have a research day and take it easy. "If it helps, I'm researching now." I moved aside and waved him in.

"Was the rest of the day spent fighting?" He didn't sound angry or insulting, only resigned. He knew my job, and even more, he knew me.

I shut the door. "Thrown through a window."

"And this window was where?"

"A sorority house," I said, leading him into the kitchen.

He was looking at me expectantly, waiting for more details.

I sighed heavily. "The second story window of a sorority house."

"That looks more accurate. I should examine you."

"Hey, Doc," Logan said. His ears were back down, but he didn't seem his happy, smiling self.

"I presume you both had an interesting day?" Taylor asked.

"Yeah, couldn't be helped. Well, maybe in hindsight," Logan said.

Taylor looked at Logan for a few seconds before continuing. "Should I take a look?" He had never been Logan's doctor, but with Jonathan joining MyTH, he was probably becoming familiar with elven physiology. There may even be a few elves in the city.

"Just bruises, Doc. I don't break easy," Logan said.

Taylor continued to watch the elf with the same expectant look that he had given me.

"If it'll put your mind at ease," Logan said. "I wanted to ask you a few questions about Jonathan anyway."

Taylor nodded.

"You can use my bedroom upstairs."

While they went upstairs, I checked the cat's water and left a treat in his bowl. He was content lounging in the kitchen. I chanced petting him twice on the head. From the look he gave me, I assumed that a third stroke would be one too many. Since I walked away unscathed, I called it a victory.

When Logan came back downstairs, I took his place with Taylor in my room.

"Tell me everything," Taylor said.

I gave him the run down, but directed him first to the gash on my arm that had taken so long to stop bleeding.

Taylor inspected the bandaging. "It seems as if someone has already looked after you. Logan?"

"Uh, no. My, uh, well, it was Ethan from last night." I think we were landing in boyfriend girlfriend territory, but I wasn't positive.

"Was he there today as well?"

"Yeah, he showed up."

Taylor nodded and started to re-bandage everything. "Was he injured?"

"No, only Logan and I were in the center of the action."

"Tell me about this afternoon and the package."

The smile whipped away from my face and a cool chill passed over me. "There's not much to say really."

Taylor took out a penlight and shined it into my eyes. "Go on."

"What is it with doctors and trying to blind their patients," I mumbled.

"You're stalling."

"It was...unpleasant. That's all." Just thinking about it left me shaky.

"Start from the beginning," Taylor said.

I took him through the arrival of the package and my discovery of its contents. I left off the part where I went upstairs and lost it.

Taylor finished his examination as we spoke.

"Was anything found when the box was processed?" Taylor asked.

"Not that anyone mentioned, but I wasn't in a rush to ask," I said.

Taylor nodded. "Is there anything else I need to know?"

"I can't think of anything," I said. "Maybe Logan has something more."

It was an excuse to stop talking about my 'present' and turn things back over to Logan. It was hard to stop thinking about the box if people insisted on bringing it up.

Logan met us at the foot of the stairs.

"Where did you put the package?" Taylor asked.

"It's in the laundry room," Logan said.

"Down the hallway and to the right," I said, making no move to join Taylor.

"Do you have all the evidence you need before I get started?" Taylor asked.

"It's all yours," Logan said.

Taylor nodded and left the room while Logan and I returned to the kitchen where I settled back into my chair and woke up my laptop. It was past time to get into research mode.

The computer was still mostly unresponsive when Taylor returned looking troubled.

"Need anything?" I asked.

"You said it was in the laundry room. In the box in the laundry room?" Taylor asked.

"Yes," Logan said.

Taylor frowned. "It's not there."

CHAPTER 22

T HE BOX ISN'T THERE?" I asked, not really wanting an answer.

"The box was there, on the floor, but it was empty," Taylor said.

My stomach churned. "Gran's cat must have-"

"We closed the door." Logan stood up slowly, but his ears shot to their points in an instant.

"It was still closed when I went in," Taylor said. "When I left the room, I left the door open. It must have been stunned or drugged."

Relief turned my legs to jelly. "That's so good to hear. Maybe something in shipping? What kind of idiot..."

Logan was shaking his head. "Sorry, I know it is dead. It wasn't breathing and had no heartbeat."

"There's someone in my house?" Dammit, once again my gun wasn't close at hand. That might be a good thing. My scales were starting to tip from freaked out to pissed off. It had been a long day. I started out of the room.

"Where are you going?" Logan asked.

I didn't bother stopping. "I'm going to get my gun and shoot whoever broke into my house."

I dashed upstairs, and snagged my holster and gun. When I went back downstairs, the kitchen looked empty. I could hear Logan and Taylor down the hallway.

"Did you all find, um, anything?" I called.

"There's no one else here," Logan said.

It sounded like he was in the laundry room. Maybe Taylor had overlooked the rabbit. I wasn't about to join them.

It felt better with my gun handy at my side, though.

My coffee was still warm when I sat back down next to my computer. They could handle...well... they could handle everything else. Research was what I needed. Dull, mind-numbing research that would scour the past few days out of my thoughts.

Using the links Neil had set up for me, I did a quick search in the MyTH data banks on created life forms and clicked into the first research report.

It was dull, which I could handle, but it didn't take me long to figure out it was about bacteria splicing and had nothing to do with what we were looking for. I backed out and tried door number two.

Gran's cat brushed up against my leg while I started reading the article. It was more like he ran into it, but I'll take what I can get. While reading, I reached down and scratched his head.

The fur was too soft. The ears too long. The skin, far too cold.

My breath caught and I yanked my hand away. I didn't want to look down, but there really wasn't a choice. I saw the white fur of the rabbit and the dried red blood on his coat.

Shoving away from the table I nearly tripped over my feet while putting distance between the bunny and me. My heart hammered inside my chest like a troll's fist. Somewhere between leaving my chair and reaching the wall, my gun ended up in my hand.

The gun was already pointed at the rabbit, which was watching me. At least it appeared to be looking. The thing's eyes looked cloudy. It half-jumped half-lurched forward. One back leg didn't appear to be working well.

Fear hobbled my thinking, but reaching for the Path was instinct. The turbulent shimmer of the Path cascaded over my world.

After the extremes of the day, I couldn't handle my own strength. My vision started to gray around the edges, but I focused hard on the creature before me.

What Logan had said was true. The thing trying to lurch towards me wasn't alive. It had the Path of a creature, but no spark and there were signs of decay in the Path.

Reading drained me to a standstill, but there was no way I was dropping the Path. Adrenaline surged when the dead rabbit bounced again, aimed at me. It gave me the strength to move towards the living room, but within seconds, it left me even more exhausted, and only the wall kept me upright.

My vision became narrower, and there was only the rabbit from hell and me. If I started to read its Path, really read it and follow it, I might get some answers. There was no way I would make it back to share what I found. I wanted to pull the trigger to force the little fluffer away, but the gun may as well have been a hood ornament at this point. I didn't know where the cat was, much less my partner and Taylor. Who knows what I would hit if I shot.

At the next lurch of white terror, instinct made me jump back. Since I was already against the wall, the only thing I managed was to smack my head.

Taylor gripped my shoulders and hauled me away. Bright lights popped into the Path and it was only Taylor's arms keeping me on my feet. My gun was taken away and Taylor let me fall unceremoniously onto the couch.

It was still in there. The Path grew brighter while I watched Logan and Taylor at the entrance to the kitchen. Soon, they turned gray and disappeared, leaving bursting lights behind.

Then the world began to fade.

Shadowy forms lurched around in the darkness, always out of sight. My body felt like it was being drawn downward. A heavy weight was crushing me under the ground, deep into the earth. I could smell dirt and decay. The air felt cold, only to be followed immediately by intense heat.

At some point, my brain kicked into gear and told me that nothing was real. Then the shadows started to close in, and any hints of rational thought flew out the window. Darkness swirled together to form some semblance of an old man. He cackled before fading away. A gray rabbit sprinted across the edges of my vision, but was gone before I turned my head. Einar stepped out of nowhere. He took my hand. When I tried to wrench myself away, I could see that his hand had melded into my own. Einar moved towards me, then into me. He sank into me everywhere that his pale cold skin touched mine.

Screaming, I struggled to get away.

My eyes opened.

The shadows in the darkness were gone. The room was dim, but the normal kind, caused by the lack of light. I was still on the couch in the living room even though I felt as though I had been running. My heart was beating rapidly, but the Path was gone, and I was alive.

Even more importantly, when I peeked at the floor, there were no animals scurrying around.

"How are you feeling?" The concern and admonishment curled together in a way that only Vincent could manage.

Across from me in the chair, Vincent looked no more stressed or angry than he normally did, which put me more at ease.

"I've had better days." I stretched and tried to seem casual when I looked back down at the ground.

"They put it in the other room."

"It's still in the house?" I sat up, but curled my legs under me, too afraid to put my feet down.

"We're not sure what we're dealing with yet."

The dim room momentarily flashed with bright light from the windows.

"The living dead?" I suggested. "Is everyone else fine?" I asked.

Vincent shrugged as distant thunder grumbled like an old man. "From what I understand, nothing happened."

I frowned and crossed my arms.

He held up a hand to stop the flow of comments that were forming in my head. "I mean besides the rabbit. They're still puzzled as to how it reached the kitchen and why no one saw it get there, but it didn't attack anyone. And it's...you know... a rabbit."

"It is a *dead* rabbit." I stated each word slowly and clearly. Emphasizing the dead part shouldn't have been necessary.

"Which is disconcerting."

"Huh," I scoffed, "I guess disconcerting is one way to put it. What's it doing in the other room?"

"Logan and Taylor built it a cage of sorts. They put it back in its box, but it ate through the cardboard."

"How can you be so calm about this?"

Lightning flashed illuminating the room once again.

"With Einar out there, the rabbit doesn't rate very high," Vincent said.

"It is a dead rabbit." I repeated it slower this time in case he was missing some part of the concept. "A dead rabbit that moves."

Vincent shrugged again. "It's little."

"What if it bites someone and spreads some sort of zombie disease? What if it tries to kill me in my sleep?"

"You've been watching too many movies. Dr. Taylor doesn't seem to think it will be an issue. It's locked up. That should keep it from biting, or smothering you in your sleep."

It was frustrating how calm he was about this. "Whoever sent this isn't exactly thinking warm and fuzzy thoughts about me."

When Vincent tensed, I knew I hit a sore spot. The rain began to fall outside, hard and fast. I listened for a few moments.

"It couldn't be linked to Einar, could it?" I asked.

"Logan doesn't seem to think so. I think he may be right. This seems more like someone...like someone messing with you. Like Logan said the other day, a twisted way to introduce themselves."

"It's perverse. An early morning surprise and a lovely new pet."

Vincent froze and I watched the darkness swirl out, filling his eyes.

"What?" The cold feeling of his anger made me twist in my seat.

His voice was flat. "Those are things you might do for someone you are dating."

Lighting flashed. The thunder wasn't far behind.

My stomach churned. "That's sick. Someone you're in a relationship with doesn't do these things."

"That could depend on the person. Ethan gave you the package?"

"Ethan signed for the package. Normal. Human. Ethan."

Vincent seemed to think that over and I watched some of the whites of his eyes return. "There are some sick minds in this world, both from here and that have arrived here. It may be someone you don't yet know."

I wanted to stand and yell, but I wasn't quite ready to put my feet on the floor. "You were going to try to blame Ethan!"

Vincent had the decency to look slightly abashed, although that may have been wishful thinking on my part. "We don't know who, or what, can use magic."

I glared at Vincent. The rain sounded harder. Heavier. Vincent went to the window next to the front door and looked out. I twisted around to watch him over the back of the couch.

"It's hailing," Vincent said.

I liked seeing the little balls of ice bouncing off the ground. After taking the time to look around on the floor, making sure the coast was clear, I put my feet down. I padded over to the window on the other side of the door and watched the hail leaping off the sidewalk in the light of the porch.

We watched the little pea-sized chunks of ice falling and rebounding off the concrete. Every now and again, I'd check the ground around my feet to be sure the floor was clear of bouncing white balls of fur.

"Where is everyone?" I asked as the hail started to subside.

Vincent didn't say anything right away. He looked lost in thought while watching the storm.

"It doesn't storm like this much on the west coast. Even then, I don't remember feeling the urge to watch."

"Things have changed a bit in the past year," I said. I thought about the piece of my soul curled around his own and wondered how much that had changed him.

Vincent shook his head and walked away from the window. "Do you want some coffee?" His voice was more stiff than necessary.

"Sure, um, where is everyone?" I asked, following him into the kitchen where my eyes were immediately drawn to the cage by the back door.

Vincent avoided looking at me. "Taylor took some samples back to his lab. Logan and Rider left not long before you woke up. Hank sent them somewhere."

"This seems unhygienic." I stared at the cage next to the back door. The ball of white fur floundered around the enclosure.

A cabinet door slammed shut and I jumped. Vincent still wasn't looking at me.

"Everything okay?" I asked.

"It's fine. I'll move the cage back into the laundry room later." His voice was steady and level, but even without the Path, I could feel tension building around him.

It was best not to dwell on how much either of us had changed in the past nine months, but I couldn't help but wonder if that's what Vincent was doing.

And I wasn't helping matters. "Uh, don't worry," I said, watching Vincent carefully, "I'll move it."

Vincent only nodded as he watched the coffee pot.

The rabbit was in some sort of metal animal cage. I had no idea where it had come from. There was an extra layer of chicken coop wire on the inside, and then it was wrapped around the outside twice as well. The rabbit occasionally moved around in a small circle inside.

I looked closely at the handle and the layers of metal between where my hand would be and how close the rabbit could get to it. I thought about asking where my gun was, but I looked back at Vincent and he was focusing intently on the percolating coffee. After glancing around the room and not seeing the gun, I cringed and lifted the cage.

Holding it as far away from me as I could, I rushed to the laundry room and sat the cage in the middle of the floor. Vincent looked like he needed a minute alone, so I sat down next to the rabbit. It didn't do anything beyond attempting to bound around. It looked almost confused, or sad.

Who would do such a thing to a bunny?

I went back to the kitchen. Vincent was still studying the coffee, so I didn't say anything. It took a while of digging around the refrigerator to find some lettuce. It was rather wilted, but then, wasn't the rabbit? I tore off a few leaves and took it back to the laundry room.

Sitting back on the floor, I stared at the rabbit. It was dead. Except for the part where it was still moving, it even looked dead. Shaking my head, I folded the lettuce and shoved it through a hole, careful to keep my fingers well away. The lettuce leaf fell next to the rabbit. It made a shrill squeak and picked up the leaf with its teeth. It settled down and appeared to be oddly contented.

I shoved the other leaves in. When I got up, Vincent was watching me at the door.

"You fed a dead rabbit," he said, shaking his head. He looked calmer at least.

"It's not his fault he's dead," I said defensively.

The smallest hint of a grin ghosted across his face. "Coffee's ready."

A part of me wanted to ask what was wrong, but I think I already knew. Vincent had changed a lot over the past year. I had changed as well, but I was good at actively ignoring difficult issues until I had no choice but to confront them. The method didn't work for everybody. It's possible that Vincent missed the person he was before.

After making sure the door was firmly shut, I followed Vincent towards the scent of coffee. Lightning flashed and the lights of the kitchen momentarily dimmed. Thunder growled through the room.

"Rider and Logan were sent to an old church," Vincent said.

I settled down with my coffee. "A church?"

"Hank dug up records of landmarks that had been around during the Civil War. The church was the first one he found. Rider and I had returned to drop off the gremlins. Hank called and asked us to check out the church."

"We have a church in town that was around during the Civil War?"

"Part of it was. I stayed and Logan went with Rider." After a few moments of silence Vincent quickly added, "I thought we should meditate tonight. You've been having trouble reaching the Path."

The rain picked up again and lashed at the windows.

"It's the other Path that causes it," I said.

"Other Path?"

"Einar's. The black Path that he creates somehow prevents me from reaching the Path, or dropping the Path once I have it."

"This happened at the Palmer's house too, though."

"Einar went to Felicity's place. I think he's the one that trashed the Palmer's house as well."

Vincent thought that over for a while. "I believe we can work with that. We can't practice the application without going somewhere Einar has been, but we can explore a few theories."

I hated to admit it, but not that long ago I was falling over from exhaustion in the kitchen. "It might not be the best idea for me to read the Path tonight." It seriously sucked having to say that out loud.

"You won't need to. In fact, it might be better if you didn't."

"I guess I'll give it a try."

We went back into the living room where we could hear the rain starting to fade away. We had only meditated in here once, but we each gravitated back to the spots we had taken up last fall. We kept the living room lights off, but left the kitchen ones on.

Closing my eyes, I took a few deep breaths before I began to wonder if Vincent was watching me, and my eyes popped open. His eyes were closed and his attention was turned inward. His face and body began to relax while I watched. My mind wandered back to last fall. Meditating together and feeling our energies reach out to each other wanting to combine. I remembered our kiss upstairs and the feel of his hand in mine.

CHAPTER 23

PUSHING THOSE THOUGHTS OUT OF my head wasn't easy, but push I did. Closing my eyes, I mimicked Vincent and turned my thoughts inward. Life was hard enough without dwelling on what once was, or what could have been.

It had been a while since I really sat down to meditate. My mind felt cluttered and unkempt. Thoughts kept jumping out or even slipping away. Then my brain pointed out shoulder pain and back pain. My bandages were too tight and I had an itch.

Struggling to beat back my own thoughts reminded me that I needed to make this a part of my everyday routine. When my mind was more serene and under my thumb, Vincent started to talk.

His voice was calm and quiet. "Think back to last fall." It also held a soft warmth that Vincent didn't usually let escape.

Thoughts of last fall filled my head again and I let out a sigh of regret.

"Back to our first meditation session." His voice was a bit quicker and lost some of the mellowness this time. "We concentrated on what happens right before you reach for the Path."

My brain shifted gears.

"Go there now," Vincent said, "and tell me what you see."

I knew what he was looking for here, but I took my time. The very edge of the knowledge that I had of our world. It's the only way I could explain it. Inwardly, I stared out over the vast space and looked for the telltale signs of my soul.

My mind's eye saw emptiness, but I had expected this. Moments of time ticked by with me mentally staring over an empty abyss.

A glimmer appeared. Then a patterned network of gleaming shards twinkled into life.

"I see it," I said, keeping my voice low. A sense of awe stole over me when I saw the patchwork soul stretch out before me. Then I noticed the pieces that didn't fit. "It looks different, though."

This close to the Path I could feel Vincent's anxiety slowly leak away from him.

"What do you see?" Vincent asked.

"It's like..." I struggled to find the right words. "Like sparks trying to find a place to settle down. Where my soul rolls and flares, the sparks try to find holes they can fit into."

"What do they feel like?" Vincent asked.

Tentatively, I sensed the nearest glowing wisp. A buzz started to fill my head. My body didn't want to sit still. It wanted to move. Running suddenly seemed like a good idea. My breathing increased. A small hole began to form under the flare and it started to propel its way through. Yanking myself back made me open my eyes to the world again.

Vincent was watching intently. The rush of energy began to flow away. Once I was sure I was still me, my breathing slowed to the point I could talk.

"Fragments of other souls." My heart felt heavy at the thought of all those small rays of life not being able to find their way home.

It took Vincent a while to respond. Signs of reining back his own burdensome thoughts flickered across his face.

"Did you sense anything else there?" Vincent asked.

I cleared my throat to keep my voice from cracking. "Nothing else."

Vincent nodded. "Are you... Do you want to continue?"

"We need to. I need to find a way to reach the Path when Einar is around. It's the only thing I have that might be an advantage."

"Okay," Vincent said, "this time, take a good, long look."

Already closing my eyes, I asked, "At my soul?"

"At everything. You don't need to go close, only watch, and study what you see."

It took me no time to pick out the patterns of light that tried to hide between the Path and me. "Each piece of my soul fits in smoothly with the next, but the lines move slightly. Like an ever-changing puzzle. The other balls of light glide across the surface and stop here and there to try to pry their way through."

"Without getting too close, how many of the fragments would you say there are? That aren't yours, I mean." His voice wavered.

That was something I didn't want to tell him. Having more than one made me feel like a big enough freak.

"They're kind of fast," I hedged, "it's hard to say."

"Take a guess." Vincent's tone was more direct.

I frowned. Watching them zoom around, everything looked the same. There were no colors to distinguish one from another, so they tended to blur together as they mingled.

"Trying to estimate is hard." Which was true. I had nightmares of hundreds of shards swarming over me. I tried to stretch my mind up higher to see the full effect, but I was having difficulty. My mind was so used to the trip I could feel the urge to jump the gap and reach the Path.

"Take your time," Vincent said.

"Huh." Easy for him to say. "There seem to be...I don't know, around fifty, maybe a little more." *Maybe a lot more.* I kept that thought to myself. "Taking them all in like this, though, I see that some aren't moving fast. They shift at different paces. There are even a few pieces that appear to be..."

"Yes?" Vincent said after I trailed away.

"There are a few pieces that aren't moving. It sounds crazy, but, it's almost as if they are waiting, or watching the other pieces moving around." I shivered at the thought. "They seem, I don't know, bigger somehow. The others don't get too close, but the odd ones appear to be at the fringes. It would make things so much easier if I could see my own Path." That thought made me cringe. They were a part of me now, even if they didn't fit.

"Let's step back some. This spot is where you make the jump to the Path, correct?" Vincent asked.

"Yeah, my mind jumps over, though. I don't look at it as I pass."

"That might become easier with practice," Vincent said, "and I think you should practice. Become more familiar with what you're seeing."

The thought didn't make me comfortable. It was a beautiful sight, but it was so hard to watch those small pieces scramble around. I knew there was no consciousness to them. No thoughts. It was only a small part of their essence left behind.

"It may be difficult at first," Vincent continued, "but in the long run, I think it's going to help."

"How so?"

"I think this is the area that Einar's Path blocks. At least from your description."

My eyes snapped open. "You think Einar's Path gets that close to my soul?"

"Not necessarily," Vincent rushed to explain. "Something about him cuts you off. Not his Path directly, but like an echo it leaves behind. Or a vibration."

Vincent's explanation didn't help my feelings of trepidation.

"It sounds like some sort of pollution," I said.

"It's only an obstacle. Something you need to jump over or move through. Once you are more familiar with what you normally pass by, I think you'll find it easier to go through barriers."

This thought rolled around my head. "I guess that makes sense."

"Want to try again?" Vincent asked.

"Uh, yeah." If Vincent was right, maybe it would help the next time I faced Einar. If we could figure out which Lost he'd be checking in on next, it might help us find him. Wild animals could be netted and brought down. Seeing Einar's victims made me think more and more that a wild animal is precisely what Einar was. And he had to be brought down.

Two more times I went to the edge of my mind and stared out at nothing. Each trip made me tired, both physically and mentally. After the second time, I came back with a dodgy feeling, as if I was being watched.

"I'm done for the day," I said, yawning and stretching out.

Vincent looked at me for a few moments as though contemplating what to say.

"What?" I asked.

"Nothing. I mean, I'm going to get my bag from your car."

After Vincent left, I checked the time and decided to chance calling Gran.

"Hi Gran, how are things going at Mom's?"

"Darlin', I'm going to be happy to get back home and out of this house."

Einar wanted to kill me and someone was sending me dead bunnies that spring back to life, the idea of Gran coming back home was terrifying. "What time tomorrow does Mom get back?"

"Late in the evenin'. With any luck, I'll be home tomorrow night."

"We have a guest staying with us. He may still be around tomorrow night."

"Is it that man of yours? I should already know these things. I threw out four of your mother's fake trees, but it hasn't done a lick of good. I keep runnin' into more." Gran tried to sound light-hearted, but her frustration came through loud and clear. "Maybe Anala keeps them around to block her own ability, because it sure as heck blocks mine."

"It's Vincent."

"Oh, I knew he'd be back at some point. It'll be good to see him back in his room."

"Hmm." I didn't want to comment on Vincent being back. Mostly because I didn't know how I felt about him living down the hall.

"I've been in the dark for days. We'll catch up tomorrow night."

"Sure thing, Gran. See you tomorrow."

"Is Margaret coming over tomorrow?" Vincent asked.

I jumped and turned, nearly tripping. "Don't sneak up on people like that." A trace of a smile slid over Vincent's face. "Gran's done with house sitting tomorrow. She's coming home."

His smile was gone. "You look worried about that."

"Aren't you? We have balls of violent energy floating around and a dead rabbit in the laundry room."

"Can you suggest that she extend her visit for a few more days? It wouldn't be a bad idea for you to stay out of the house for a while, too."

"No one is chasing me away from my home. Gran's going to be even more adamant about that. Besides, she hates it at my mother's house."

"Tomorrow we can see about getting some extra security for the house."

"What type of security?"

"We'll have to figure that out. Maybe do some research. Rider said this is magic, maybe there's some way to repel the effects."

"Do you really believe there's magic?" The question had come to my mind several times in the past day.

"You read marks no one can see. I walk between dimensions. Who says that isn't magic?"

"Those are abilities, not magic."

"I've seen a lot of things so far in my life. The idea of magic is simplistic next to some of the things I've witnessed."

My interest was piqued. "Like what?"

The shadows of a frown formed and Vincent took his time answering. "Like trees made out of energy, ripped through from an ethereal world."

I rolled my eyes. It was obvious he wasn't going to tell me anything I didn't already know. "Well, we're not going to solve this tonight. Do you need anything?"

Vincent shook his head, still looking agitated by my question.

"Well, help yourself to anything. I'm going to go check on the rabbit."

"There's nothing you can do for it."

I put my hands on my hips. "It's not his fault this happened." To myself I added, *besides, I want to make sure he's still in the cage.*

Vincent looked like he was going to say something. Instead, he shook his head and went upstairs.

"Goodnight to you, too," I muttered.

The rabbit was still safe in his cage. It was pretty obvious he was still dead, even though his little nose was scrunching up as he stared at me.

I firmly shut the door. Then I leaned on it, rattled the doorknob, and then opened the door and started the whole thing from scratch again. The idea of going to sleep when Night of the Living Dead: Bunny Edition was taking place in the house wasn't easy to digest.

Upstairs, I paused in the hallway before going into my room. It was strange to have Vincent back. Somehow, it felt right, though. Even when he was cranky. I wasn't even sure what I had done to aggravate him. It was only a question.

Sleep didn't come easy. The storm had died down, but the rain continued.

And Vincent was down the hall.

Last fall, on his final night here before he disappeared, we were kissing in the hallway and I had been hoping for more. Now, I've had those feelings shoved down for so long, it was hard to know what I wanted.

I rolled over and twisted my pillow into a more comfortable position. Thoughts of Vincent had to stay shut away, he made that clear. It was a stupid decision, but it had been made all the same.

Luckily, I had Ethan. At least I think I had him. It seemed to change by the hour. Still, we had parted on a good note tonight. That was promising. It wouldn't be easy with Ethan, but could it be easy with anyone? Not someone normal. It would never be easy with a human, unless they had a special ability or were familiar with the Lost.

Still, Ethan was cute, smart, and he was trying his hardest to get a grasp on the craziness that is my life.

My eyes shot open, seeing nothing but darkness. My heart was pumping fast and I laid there, still and silent. Rain blew hard against my windows. Had I fallen asleep? Had the storm woken me up?

Listening for sounds in your house, in the middle of the night, is a recipe for unease. Especially in a storm and with a dead animal that doesn't realize it shouldn't be moving anymore.

My heartbeat started to slow. Lightning illuminated someone sitting in my chair and my breath caught. I wasn't alone in the room.

"Dammit, Vincent! What are you doing?" My anger shot straight through the roof, and I threw off my blankets. He didn't move. Thunder reverberated around the room and it was lit once again.

I thought my heart would stop. "You're not Vincent."

CHAPTER 24

I DO NOT UNDERSTAND THIS WORLD. The words were clear in my mind, and Einar sounded somber.

"What do you mean?" I scrambled back onto my bed to put more distance between us.

Vincent walked into the room wearing nothing but PJ pants and his gun, which was pointed straight at Einar.

Einar didn't even look up at Vincent. *The citizens are despondent towards their government, yet they do nothing but watch it grow larger.*

"Is that why you have been killing government employees?" Vincent asked.

Einar stood with a speed that couldn't be followed. One moment he was sitting, the next standing and watching Vincent.

I closed my eyes and shook my head, trying to dislodge what had to be a nightmare playing out.

What is this before me? Am I no longer doomed to have only this broken female to speak with?

My fury began to rise in earnest. "Excuse me?"

"Cass, move behind me." Vincent's eyes never left Einar.

A part of me wanted to argue. Guns were useless against Einar. Still, putting some distance between this monster and myself seemed like a good move. Especially now that I wanted to smack the crap out of him.

When I slowly began to move back away from my bed and toward Vincent, Einar leaned forward. He was keeping his distance, but inspecting Vincent.

I reached Vincent's side, ready to stand beside him and face whatever was going to happen here. Vincent took my hand and began to yank me around behind him. I was willing to take a step back, especially with Einar so intent on Vincent, but there was no way I would hide behind him.

"Idiot," I breathed. I gripped Vincent's hand and didn't move any farther. It would have been more convincing if my hand wasn't trembling.

The momentary flash of a grin told me that Vincent had heard. He returned the pressure of my grip then eased his hand away.

Are you Einar?

"I was under the impression that you were Einar," Vincent said.

I am Einar. She is Einar. You are...something else."

"I'm the one that is taking you on a trip between the worlds," Vincent said.

Air sucked into my lungs.

Between the worlds?

"Like hell you are." I reached for the Path and struggled against the darkness blocking my way.

Vincent ignored me, focusing on Einar instead. "The monsters there will make short work of you."

Einar shook his head. *I name you Walker. None was thought to have survived. Yet, you are here. Broken, but standing before me.*

Knowing how poorly I react when someone calls me broken, meant that I was ready for the sudden burst of anger that exploded out of Vincent. Something in the shadowy darkness between my mind and the Path stirred.

"You will know the meaning of broken before the day is through." Vincent stepped forward.

Instinctively, I reached out and put my hand on his waist. For the first time since entering the room, he was distracted from Einar. Some of the anger swirling around the room melted away.

If I am taken between the worlds, I shall only return. Those old roads are familiar to me.

"Only Walkers and those they bring with them can travel between the worlds."

This is true. Alas, Walkers, as with the Einar, cannot be allowed to continue. I do not cherish the task that is set before me, but know that I will make it painless for you both.

"Wait!" It came out more of a screech than I anticipated. "You are Einar."

Once my tasks are complete, I will join you in the next life. Einar stepped forward.

"Wait!" Einar's expressionless face looked at me and fear took hold. "Why can't the Walkers live?"

They are tools that will be wielded against men and Others. Einar turned his attention back to Vincent. *In another time, we would have looked upon each other as friends. I will not make you suffer by watching me take the woman. She shall follow behind you without pain.*

No, no, no. My mind ran against the darkness as Einar walked forward. Vincent fired the gun eight times. Einar continued towards him.

May you find peace.

I scrambled for Vincent's hand and felt the warmth of our connection. My energy and his reached out towards each other. It sped through the blackness between my mind and the Path and swirled around my soul. It was a tiny fragment of a break, but I charged through it.

Naked, raging Path poured over me. As Einar reached towards Vincent, I snatched Vincent's Path and yanked him backward, bodily. It was sloppy and burned through more energy than I anticipated, but Vincent was out of the way.

Einar's darkened Path surrounded him. The radiant threads wove in and out quickly. Around his core, they were brighter and thicker.

Einar looked at me as though he were trying to solve a puzzle.

Vincent said something behind me, but I couldn't hear him over the roar of the Path around me. The storm raged through the Path as though seeking vengeance. Vincent grabbed me from behind. I shoved him back. With a glance, I burned through more energy to put a bubble of pure energy around him. He would be safe while I stood against Einar.

Anger and frustration began to fill the room. I soaked it up, adding it to my own power. Deep inside me, something shifted and butted up against my soul.

I do not understand what it is that you do.

Cocking my head, I grinned and stepped up to Einar. An arrogance that wasn't my own was trying to move forward. What I wanted to do was reckless, so I drew on that foreign ego, but strove to maintain control.

Up close, the bright tendrils of Path around Einar reached towards me. "There's a lot we don't understand about each other. I'm going to fix that and find out what you're all about."

Vincent cursed behind me.

My hand stood a breath away from Einar's Path. Colors drew themselves out of his darkness and stretched.

"Vincent, if this doesn't work, I'm sorry." There was so much more I left unsaid.

But, this would work, right?

My hand plunged into the eager twirl of colors in Einar's Path. They wriggled, gripped my hand, and then sunk into me. I'm not sure if the scream was Einar's or mine. Maybe it was both.

A white void spread over me and my world was gone.

When I opened my eyes, the sun hung high in the sky. Breathing deeply, I expected to smell the grass on the breeze. For some reason, smells of a storm reached my nose. Had there been rain? Blue skies wrapped themselves from horizon to horizon.

It must be that old witch next door. It raised my hackles to live so close to that woman. It was unnatural how she twisted the world. Like so many others, she wanted to find a way home, but now she was bending things too far. My nose, indeed the nose of any werewolf I know, had never been tricked.

The trees in the distance hid her house from view. Maybe Ellen would talk to the old crow. It was a well-known fact that the witch hated men. She would probably make everything smell like decay if I approached with a complaint. My wife, on the other hand, had a silver tongue and could quell the old woman.

Clouds started to form in my mind and a calm settled over the grassy hill. It took moments to realize that the animals no longer stirred. Birds ceased their chirping and burrowing creatures stopped shifting below ground. A growl formed in my throat as unease drifted over the landscape.

Ellen. Something was going wrong in my territory, and every particle of my being screamed at me to get home to my wife. Everyone knew trouble was looming. Perhaps it arrived earlier than anyone else had expected.

Turning, I almost walked directly into Henry and took a step back.

"Henry, where do you come from?"

"You must have had your mind on other things and missed my approach."

"Yes, other things." It's no wonder the day went strange. Everything turns out that way when you have a Walker around.

Henry was looking off into the distance towards the witch's house.

"Do you sense the oddities as well?" I asked to Henry's surprise. "The old woman is up to something."

"Maybe she found her way home." Henry's voice was devoid of emotion. "I pray that she does before I get there."

I felt myself take another step back and stopped. "Of course," I said uneasily. "I'm sure many feel the same when approaching her home."

"Why do you live so close?" Henry asked.

"Someone has to." When Henry said nothing I continued. "Ellen enjoys her company."

"Upon reflection, it was an unwise decision for the Others to live so close together."

I let out a bark of nervous laughter. "And we should reside among the humans?"

"Perhaps things would have turned out differently if you had." Henry met my gaze.

I was looking at someone who was staring into the face of hell. "What is it, Henry?" The hair on the back of my neck began to rise.

"I am sorry, old friend."

Henry grasped my wrist, and I watched his eyes turn black. I started to struggle, but weakness was already coming forth.

"What is the meaning of this?" I asked, trying to wrench my hand away.

"We must sacrifice a few for the benefit of many."

Punching as hard as I could muster would not break his hold. He didn't try to fight back. I felt myself draining away. My thoughts flew to Ellen, and Henry seemed to read my mind.

"Do not fear for Ellen," Henry said, "you are joining her."

"Ellen!" In my mind I was screaming, but to my ears, it was a mere whisper. "You will pay for this." My world began to grow dim around the edges.

As the last feelings of myself flowed away, I heard Henry say, "When my task is complete, I promise you, everyone will pay for this."

My bones ached more fiercely than they had all summer. The sun was shining, but there was a storm on its way. I took a pinch of ash and threw it on the ground. It was the largest curse I dare lay on the land while my feet still walked on its surface.

There was a knock on the door and I sighed. It would be that fool from next door. Anytime I made an attempt to return home, he would come over and raise a fuss. Maybe Ellen will have a word with him.

I took my time heaving my tired bones out of the chair. The knock came again before I reached the door.

"Who's there?" My voice was scratchy. When had I become old? Even if I made it home, Oris would want to see the young woman who had gone into the woods. Not the old crone that was still trying to return.

"It is Henry."

Henry. Not the type that I would normally want to visit on his own. Still, maybe the man would be of some use. He walked between the worlds. Maybe there was some way he could help me bore my way between them.

My hand hesitated on the door handle. There was something in the air that had not been there last night.

"Has that wolf sent you?" I asked.

"He has not. I have come to see you."

My skin prickled, but I opened the door. As I aged, my fear had grown. It seems that you can't get one without the other.

"Good day, Henry. Would you care to come inside?" Years ago, I never would have dreamed of letting a man into my house. I was a married woman, though no one in this wretched world had met my Oris. Still, if I wanted information from the man, I would have to get him inside and comfortable.

"I am sorry to say that I am unable to stay. I've come to deliver a message."

Some trick of the light made my tired old eyes see what could not be there. "Just a moment." I tried to keep my voice calm, but a tremor came out. Henry was not alone. There were at least four, no five more, twisting around inside him. "Wait right here." Steadily, I closed the door, but Henry put out a boot and prevented me from latching it in place.

"Please forgive me, Mrs. Brown," Henry said. Then he threw the door open.

I fell back and hit the table. Pain shot through my back where it made contact with the rough-hewn wood. Scrambling around the edge of the table, I endeavored to put something between the Walker and me.

Henry reached out.

I swiped madly through the air. A symbol blazed only for my eyes before rushing at Henry and throwing him back.

"Come at me again young man, and you will coat my walls." It was a bluff. Between trying to open a doorway home last night and the spell I just threw at him, the charge in the air was depleted. In my younger days, the latter would have done much more than knock the man off his feet.

I could feel myself sag. When had I grown old?

Henry rose to his feet.

"You're not alone in there anymore, boy." My mind raced to find the spell that would cause the most damage.

"What do you mean?" I couldn't see if he was nervous, but I could hear it in his voice.

"Are you the one in charge in there?" I forced out a cackle, trying my hardest to unnerve the lad.

"I am always in control," Henry said. He had tried to drain the emotion back out of his voice, but I heard the tinge of fear around the edges.

"Better than most could say." I laughed at him again. "Especially at your age. Still, I see a bit of elf in you. Old Bill would be my guess." I swallowed hard and tried not to think too hard about that. "Is his daughter in there with you?"

"Shut up, old woman." There was fire in Henry's voice.

That was good. Fire from the man could fuel my next spell. At least if there was enough of it.

Henry started forward.

"The others are lively as well. What is it that you have against our community?"

He stood opposite of the table from me. "I work to protect the Others."

"By killing us all?" I grinned at him, trying to put him off balance.

"The lives of a few shall save the rest."

"Oh, good for the others, I suppose." As Henry moved around the table, I did as well.

"It is good," Henry spat. "They will be left alone. Given freedom. The Others will be safe."

"And you will live in safety with them?" I chuckled and could feel him grow angrier. "It's good to have an idea to cling to while you murder those around you."

"Shut up!" Henry roared. He dove over the table.

I jumped back. Maybe I had pushed things too far. One spell came to mind.

Oris, I am sorry I could not live to set eyes on you again.

Backed up against a wall, there was nowhere else for me to move. Henry clamped his hand around my wrist.

I didn't bother to struggle. Being too old to run meant that I was too old to put up a good fight. But, at least I could do some damage on my way out.

"Have you heard of the Triani Curse?" I asked.

Henry appeared unnerved that I stood and stared him. "I've not."

His eyes watched my hand trace the symbol into the air. It started to gather all the fury that had filled the room. It also soaked up the anguish that was pouring from my broken heart. Oh, Oris, I am sorry.

"Triani is a death curse." I could see a look of panic in his eyes, but he didn't let go. "The moment I die, the spell ensures that your darkest nightmares are played out."

Henry stopped staring at the empty air and looked straight into my eyes. There was pain there. "My darkest nightmares?"

My knees started to wobble. "Evil finds evil."

Henry caught me and gently lowered me to the floor. "Madam, my darkest nightmares are happening now."

I felt myself sag farther into the ground. I tried to say something else, but only a gurgle came out.

"I will take your curse, Mrs. Brown. Please know that I will make all those responsible pay."

My eyesight began to dim.

"That includes myself," Henry said.

My stomach churned as I stared at the body of clay before me. The barn door was open wide, and the light of the full moon clearly illuminated the entrance. It mocked me as it danced across the sky. The air itself felt heavy, as though a storm was on its way. Raging wind and the thunder of gods was out there somewhere.

It should be here, storming over me and over the men who stood watch from the shadows.

"We have one chance at this, Walker."

It was William talking. William was forever speaking for the others. If another man attempted to speak, he sternly took over and yelled until the man was properly cowed. He had spat the word Walker out as if it were a curse.

It was certainly a curse to me.

"This thing," I gestured to the statue before me, "it will move like flesh?"

William gathered all the superiority that he felt his station in life had warranted him. Because he was issued out by Stonewall Jackson, he felt he was significantly superior. "We do not have time to go over the particulars."

Anger flashed, and I froze to the spot. Slowly, I turned to face the man, allowing my eyes to go pure black.

William's dominance flailed under my gaze. Inside, I could feel the souls of the Others stir. Staring down a man like this didn't alter the iron grip that I used to hold onto those inside. I wanted to tell those inside me once again that I would make this man pay, but I knew they were beyond hearing.

A throat cleared. "It will move." A thin man stepped out of the darkness.

"And you are?" I asked, not taking my eyes off William.

"Friedlein, sir. Samuel Friedlein."

"What makes you certain, Mr. Friedlein?" I asked.

"I created him."

"I see. It sounds as though you are the man I must speak with. The rest of you may go." I was pushing it, I knew. I held no authority here, only threats. Still, all but William and Mr. Friedlein left the barn without a word.

"Go to the house," William called at their retreating backs, "I will meet you there."

"You wish to stay?" I asked.

"This is done under my authority," William said. "I stay."

I nodded curtly and released William from my gaze before my own fear was put on display. Focusing in on the statue, I started to walk around it, examining every inch.

"How was this made?" I asked, not looking at the others.

"Mysticism," Mr. Friedlein said. "It was—"

"These are things that are not necessary," William said stiffly.

This time, I let my anger get the better of me.

CHAPTER 25

G ENERAL," I SAID, CATCHING HIM once again in my gaze, "I do not think you understand the situation as it stands now." Once again, my eyes filled with blackness.

William went rigid when I moved towards him. He stood taller than I did, but only by a hair. By the time I was close, I had drawn myself up enough that it felt as though I loomed over him.

To his credit, William didn't move back.

"Let me explain things to you. You have asked me to enter into this creation of yours. As you know, to make this thing," I gestured at the lifeless form, "move, it will take us all and we must remain together." I said.

"In return—"

"In exchange for the freedom of the Others. The Vice President has confirmed that all shall be released. I still believe that this hell is worth the price."

"If you—"

"What you have failed to grasp, General, is that it would take no effort to bring you into the fold. Would you like to have a closer look at my process?" While I watched my words sink into him, I let a smile slowly spread. "In order to understand the need for my questions?"

William's jaw clenched tight. "Ask your questions."

"Once I have your assurances that we will not be interrupted again." Again, I felt as though I were pushing things too far.

A scornful smile spread across William's face. "I'll stay quiet and watch you as you pave your way to hell."

I'll see you there. Out loud I said, "Mr. Friedlein, please continue." I gazed at William for a few more moments, trying to drive the threat home, and then I turned towards my new prison.

"Jewish mysticism," he continued, as though he hadn't seen the whole exchange.

"It came from humans?" I asked, genuinely surprised by the fact.

"As far as we know, that is correct. The knowledge falls from one to another throughout time."

"You've seen others built then?"

Mr. Friedlein hesitated. "No. What we do here is forbidden."

"Then why is the knowledge kept?"

"It is a choice. As you are sacrificing yourself, I too will be losing any hope of an afterlife."

"You are forsaking your soul for him?" I asked, gesturing to William.

Mr. Friedlein looked horrified. "For the cause. We have the chance to put an end to this war. On the battlefields, brothers are fighting brothers. Men are falling to these creatures."

"People." I put steel into the words to make sure the man remembered. "These people were slaves and have been forced into this."

Mr. Friedlein didn't look me in the eye. "Battles are now slaughtering grounds. What chance do men have against ogres and trolls? These are things...people of legend. This country cannot continue in this way."

"So you give yourself for this country?" I asked.

"What is one soul if thousands of others are saved?"

It was the same idea I had been clinging to for days. "I've taken many souls in the past week. I hope that yours finds the peace that I shall bring to the Others when this task is complete." I studied every inch of the statue, ignoring William's growing impatience. "This will hold up in battle?"

"If you are against a Howitzer or Parrott rifle, you will not survive. A Minie Ball or other shot might penetrate the core, but it can be repaired."

"And swords?"

"Will have very little effect."

"The strength of those that I will be fighting against is great."

"If I had doubts that it wouldn't hold, I would not have forsaken my soul or yours."

I nodded and inspected the face that would become my own. "How will I go about repairing myself?"

"Most any material can be used. Take whatever you may have at hand. In the end, I would suggest that you get clay. However, it is said that you may use..." Mr. Friedlein grimaced. "Uh, body parts. But that is unnecessary."

My stomach clenched. "Clay is easy enough to obtain."

"If you come to me, I shall repair you."

"And if the war continues for years to come?" The thought wasn't appealing, but I would endure. When the conflict was over, the Others will be free and left in peace and I will make all these bastards pay for their folly.

"My heirs shall have the knowledge."

I didn't look at Mr. Friedlein, but focused on the statue. "You would task your children to forsake their own souls?" The energy of others inside me rattled their own frustrations at the thought.

"No!" The word broke off as though the man were choking. After a few ragged breaths, he continued. "They will have the knowledge. They will be able to mold the clay or give advice. As will their children, and so on. They will not participate any further in this business." In the end, his tone was resolute.

I took a moment to shove back any emotion that I, or those inside me, felt. "As you say." A breeze blew through the barn. Realizing that soon, I would no longer feel the breeze on my skin, I took a few moments to bask in the sensation. As it had for days, it felt as though a storm approached.

Perhaps I was the oncoming storm.

"How many, uh..." Mr. Friedlein started.

Even in the dim light, I could tell that he could see my expression. He nervously began twisting his hat in his hands. "Is the exact number of importance?"

"No, ah...no. But you must understand the more there are, the better chance..." His voice faltered under my gaze.

"Let's stick with the necessities." My voice was curt. So many Others had been massacred by my hand. Young and old. Powerful and weak. I would not degrade them by reducing them to numbers. I had shamed myself enough.

"I only meant to confirm that you can, uh, fill it. I can mold the clay. Make it bend and flex as though it were human. It will even move in a rudimentary way. I am unable to give it life, however."

"It will have life," I said stiffly.

"The rest is up to you then. You will be in control."

Drawing my hand over the clay, it felt smooth and cold. "You sound sure for a man who has never witnessed this."

"Truth is truth. Even if it is not seen with your own eyes," Mr. Friedlein said. He moved in closer to me and spoke in a low voice. "You are doing your country a great honor. Is there anything that you want to be done? You know...with your body."

I took one last look at my prison. This would be my new body. Our new body. I stepped away from the clay and took one last look at the starry night outside, one last moment to feel the air on my skin.

Then I turned to Mr. Friedlein. "Burn it."

He nodded. "Let's get started."

They would all pay for the actions forced upon the Others, as would I.

Lightning lit the room. Had the storm finally arrived?

My mind was muddled with so many thoughts that had been pressed into me. They were countless. The clay statue stood still before me. The prison cell for those countless voices in my head.

The Path was still there, but my hold was slipping. Other Paths twisted to reach me. They wanted to be heard.

There were too many. It was too much. They whispered their stories all at once. I felt them. I knew them.

They were a part of me.

Stumbling back, I fell to the ground. I looked up at Einar and he took a step back.

"Cass! You have to let me go." I could hear Vincent's voice above the rest.

My voice caught when I tried to speak. I cleared my throat and tried again.

I understand now.

"Cass?" Vincent yelled.

I could feel his fury, but I couldn't let him go. He didn't know. Einar didn't move when I rose to my feet. I stepped back to Vincent. I couldn't let him go, but I could join him.

Vincent turned to me only when he found he was still unable to move forward. He seemed to struggle with what to say.

I knew exactly how he felt.

While watching Einar, I took Vincent's arm. When he wrapped it around me, I leaned on his shoulder while I watched Einar. The clay man stood, staring into nothing.

"Einar." When I spoke, Vincent gripped me tighter. Einar didn't look up. "Henry?"

There was a screech that reverberated through my mind. Vincent gasped and held me protectively until the cry died away.

We are Einar.

My energy was fading fast and I was having a hard time picking apart all the voices in my head.

"What is it that you want? What do you understand now?" I asked.

My tenuous hold on our protection was starting to break down. If Vincent tried to attack Einar or Einar us, I'm not sure I could hold them apart for long.

This world has changed.

"It has."

Would he attack now? Would we be safe if I stopped reading? Would it be safe to continue reading?

The lines of color were flooding over the surface of Einar's dark Path. He seemed to be having trouble containing everyone.

There is much more to learn before I continue.

"Let it go, Cass," Vincent said.

I hadn't realized I was leaning so heavily on him.

"Let it go." Vincent's eyes were on Einar.

Judging by the hard line of Vincent's jaw, I knew he had a plan, and I was pretty sure it wasn't one I was going to like.

Einar looked us both over before moving. *I will take my leave for the evening.*

Vincent's surprise mirrored my own. Einar came trying to kill us and he was leaving as though an invited guest.

Einar was out the door before we could say or do anything.

With him gone, my choice was clear. Concentrating hard, I moved the Path away. As the shimmering ripples disappeared, I sagged against Vincent.

He didn't move for a while. Since higher brain functions were mostly on hold for me, I wasn't sure if he was trying to decide what to do, if he was angry, or if it was something else entirely. With my head against his chest, I could hear his steady heartbeat. Closing my eyes, I concentrated on that sound, trying to drown out the confusion in my head.

"We should call Logan and Rider," Vincent said.

"Umm hmmm," I murmured, not opening my eyes.

Vincent guided me over to my bed. "I'll check the house first. Are you good here while I'm gone?"

The word 'no' almost flew out of my mouth. My insides twisted painfully because I desperately wanted to ask Vincent to stay. Einar was gone, but the voices were still there. I didn't want to be left alone with them.

Vincent sat down next to me on the bed. When he hugged me to him, I felt him shaking. I wasn't the only one having a difficult time with this.

After soaking up a few moments of comfort, I tried to sit up. His muscles tensed around me.

In a voice no louder than a whisper, he said, "I can stay."

The voices were starting to fade, but that only made me more aware of how utterly exhausted I was. I was trapped in indecision. Did I want him to stay?

That's a stupid question. Of course I wanted him there. It was Vincent.

Did Vincent really want to stay? I think he did. At least that is what I wanted to believe.

Did it matter either way? Another stupid question. It mattered in so many ways.

My mind twisted. Thinking through something was one thing, understanding the answers I tried to give myself was another thing altogether.

Vincent relaxed. Maybe because I hadn't moved away?

I closed my eyes and noticed once again that he wasn't wearing a shirt. My skin was warm everywhere we touched. It pained me knowing that I would have to move away.

There was a clatter downstairs. Vincent gripped my arm, and our decision was made for us.

"Stay here," Vincent said. He stood and was across the room before I could protest. His gun was in his hand, but my fuzzy brain couldn't remember if it was still loaded.

Trying to stand up and follow was a mistake. My stomach swam almost as much as my head and I quickly sat back down.

Listening intently, I tried to decipher what was happening downstairs, but it was quiet.

After a few minutes, there were soft footfalls on the stairs. Relief flooded over me when Vincent appeared in my doorway.

"We need to call Logan," he said.

I took a mental note that he didn't enter the room. "Everything okay downstairs?"

"Einar's gone. Get some rest. I'll call."

Rest was something I could do. It was probably the only thing I could do. Trusting that Vincent had things covered, I slipped back into bed. I had barely tugged up my covers when I realized that Vincent hadn't said that everything was okay. Still, I trusted that he would let me know if he needed me.

Thunder rolled in the distance. The voices in my head were quieter, and focusing on the thunder helped me block out anything they might be saying.

After that long day, I should have slept like the dead. The real dead, not hopping-zombie-bunny dead. Instead, sleep came in fits of stilted dreams. I went from protecting my daughter in one dream to fighting Henry in another. When I woke up and saw the sun had come up, I decided to rise with it. The dream of running with the wind blowing through my fur left me feeling a little refreshed, but uneasy all the same.

The feeling of fur stuck with me so intensely that I checked the mirror twice to assure myself that there was only skin showing. After my shower, I had to resist the urge to shake myself dry.

My mind was too muddled from the night before. It was necessary to get up. I had to check on things, see what my partners were doing, and make sure everyone, especially Vincent, knew I was fine.

Then I could go back to bed.

Halfway down the stairs, the doorbell rang. "Come in!" I hollered, not wanting to be bothered with actually answering the door. Thankfully, Gran wasn't here to see me do that.

Rider came in. He looked almost as tired as I felt, but there was something else too. I narrowed my eyes and saw him do the same. Carefully, I moved towards him. Something was wrong, but I couldn't put my finger on it. He looked, I don't know, darker somehow, like a cloud was casting a shadow over his entire being.

Rider glared at me. His lip curled back and he let out a snarl that caused me to pause, but I returned a scowl and continued moving towards him.

It was the animal in him. That was the difference. I could sense the beast that hid below his skin. Taking a wide circle around him, I could sense the shifting wolf. Rider's skin stretched around his hands as they began to change shape. He didn't turn as I stalked around him, but when I stepped closer, he growled.

CHAPTER 26

T HE GROWL FROM RIDER REVERBERATED through my bones, making me want to step back, but I stood my ground.

"Move back." It was a command that Rider issued, not a request.

There was something inside me that wanted to move away, but another part, the stubborn, stupid part of my brain, made me take a step forward. The hairs on my arms and the back of my neck stood up. Rider, looking furious, took a step towards me. His hands were elongating, and sharp, thick nails protruded.

"Hey!"

Startled, my eye contact with Rider broke and I looked up at Vincent's glowering face. It felt like I had been doused with cold water.

"Cass, move back," Vincent said. There was a hint of uncertainty in his voice.

The stupid part of my brain was still in charge, though. I glanced up at Rider and met his gaze. My face grew hot as embarrassment took root.

What the hell was I doing? "Rider-" I started.

Rider's hand shot out with speed that I couldn't follow. He gripped my arm, and pain flared where his nails dug in.

My mind whipped forward almost as quickly and plunged into the Path. With as much strength as I could muster, I shoved a wedge between us. Rider didn't let go of my arm, but I could make certain that's the only part of me he'd reach.

But it wouldn't last. In moments, my grasp on the Path started to waver while Rider's became stronger.

"What's going on?" Vincent asked. I could see his eyes starting to darken.

"I don't know..." I started, but I wasn't sure how to finish the thought.

A loud, high-pitched whistle filled the room.

Wincing, I looked up and saw Logan making the noise.

The sound caught Rider and Vincent's attention as well. Rider's grip loosened and I let the Path fall away.

The wolf looked down at me as the world went dull. Aside from his nose flaring, as though I smelled bad, there wasn't anything different about him. He was Rider and nothing more.

The noise stopped.

Rider looked down at his hand in confusion before drawing it away. He didn't meet anyone's eye, and he didn't look happy.

"Someone needs to tell me what happened." Vincent looked like he was having a harder time letting go of his frustrations.

"I think I started something," I said, trying to draw Vincent's ire away from Rider, "I'm not sure what, though."

"Rider?" Vincent asked.

"Something is different." Rider still wouldn't look at anyone. I could sense his irritation, but his hands were back to normal.

The uncomfortable silence spread throughout the room.

"I'm getting some coffee," I said. Even the small reading of the Path had wiped me out. And besides, I really wanted out of that room. I felt as though I had broken some unwritten rule with Rider, which made my stomach squirm.

Logan followed me into the kitchen, but the others stayed behind.

"Vincent told me you had quite the night," Logan said.

"Yeah." I thought about Vincent's arms around me and felt my face grow warm. I put those thoughts out of my head and poured my coffee. Once I was situated at the table, Logan started again.

"Seems to me, there might be some blanks in the story." When I didn't say anything, he went on. "Vincent said there was a long span of time where he wasn't sure what was happening."

I glanced towards the living room. Nothing could be seen or heard from Vincent and Rider. "I'm not sure I know what happened myself. It was... I'm really not sure. I read Einar's Path and think I know what he is. He's a golem."

Logan frowned. "You mean the creature from Lord of the Rings?"

Could it be that I knew of something that Logan didn't? "Um, not exactly. It's something created. Out of clay."

"You mean he's not a Lost?" Logan asked.

All those voices that had called out from Einar. They had all been Lost. Henry had taken their essence and poured them into the clay man, along with himself. Henry had been a Walker. I looked towards the living room again. Would Vincent get upset if he knew? How would he feel if I told others?

"Uh, I don't think we can rule that out yet. Did you all find anything last night?"

"There was an old church, but nothing looked out of order. If you know what we're looking for, we should probably stop by again."

"I'm not exactly sure."

"I'll call Hank and see if he can-"

"No!" I hadn't meant to be so adamant, but it popped out of my mouth that way. "I mean, let's research a bit before bringing this to the office."

Was that approval on Logan's face? He doesn't like AIR knowing too much, so maybe he thinks I'm siding with him. Maybe I am. Sometimes I wondered why he works with the agency.

"It's not a big deal." I fidgeted with my cup of coffee. "I should go check on the rabbit."

"Your rabbit is gone."

"What?" Instinctively, I picked my feet up off the floor.

"According to Vincent, it seems like Einar took him last night."

"Why would he take the rabbit?"

"Maybe he was the one who sent it?" Logan suggested.

That thought wasn't appealing. If last night was any indication, Henry had the ability to put a soul into something.

"There's something you're not telling me." Logan didn't mean it as an accusation, only a statement. "Does it have anything to do with what happened between you and Rider?"

I shook my head. "I don't know what happened between Rider and me."

"Looked like the two of you were about to duke it out."

"I wasn't...I mean, I wouldn't..." I was stammering and had no real idea of what to say.

"Good." Logan's voice lost its musical tone. "Tell me what happened in there."

When I looked at Logan to repeat my answer, I saw that he wasn't looking at me.

Rider leaned against the kitchen entryway but didn't come any closer. "She is different."

"How so?" Logan asked.

"Her smell has changed," Rider said.

I rolled my eyes and went to get another cup of coffee. "I don't smell," I mumbled under my breath.

That got the first grin I had seen from Rider this morning, but he still seemed to be unwilling to look at me. "Everything has a scent."

"Great. Do I smell like Einar? I took a shower," I said. It seemed like a wise move to put a bit of space between Rider and myself, so I stayed behind the counter.

Rider shook his head. "I smell werewolf."

My mind flashed to the dream of the wind blowing through my fur as I ran. I felt rooted to the spot.

"Werewolf?" Logan asked.

"There are other smells. For me, the werewolf stood out. Especially when the wolf started to circle."

"You were going to attack her because her smell changed?" Vincent came in keeping his face blank. "I thought you two were friends?"

"I would have attacked the wolf." Rider glared at Vincent.

"Really? It certainly looked like Cassie you had hold of," Vincent said.

"It looked like Cassie, but the wolf was stronger."

"You only-"

Logan cut Vincent off. "Enough." They looked at the elf, but his gaze was on me. "Cassie?"

I felt like a teacher had called me out at school to 'share with the class' what I had been doing.

"My smell has changed before," I said, trying to stall. "Why is this different?"

"Her scent has changed before, but she was still there," Rider said, not looking at anyone.

"So what's different now?" Logan asked, his gaze fixed on me.

Glancing at Vincent, I mentally crossed my fingers, hoping he wouldn't get upset when I told the others about the Walker. About Henry.

There was no use hiding it, though. Filling them in took a while. I described how I stupidly delved into the Path and then what I had learned. Vincent's cold face became stiffer the longer I talked.

Glossing over the details of what the Lost suffered at the hands of Henry seemed like the best idea. Sadly, things don't always work out the way I want them to.

"You saw this through Henry?" Logan asked.

"No." I struggled with what to say. "Well, part of it I saw through Henry."

Vincent's anger was whipping around the room.

"The rest..." I took a deep breath. "The rest I saw through those that he took. Everyone."

"Walkers can't do what you described," Vincent said flatly.

"I'm sorry, Vincent." I meant it too. I was so sincerely sorry to have to tell him about Henry in front of everyone else. "But I think this one can."

"You've been tricked," Vincent said, his voice still level.

"Tricked?" I hadn't really thought about that. Was it even possible to trick a Path? "I don't think so. Einar didn't know what I was, or what I could do."

"If he thinks he did all those things, really believes it, his Path would show you what he thinks." Vincent sounded so sure of what he was saying. It was starting to throw me off balance.

"I went into those lives. The old witch who put up a fight, the werewolf that thought of his wife. There were others too. They were jumbled and confused, but they were there."

Vincent crossed his arms and shook his head. "It's easier for you to believe a Walker is a monster than it is to believe that you might be wrong."

Logan raised his eyebrows at Vincent. Even Rider, who still hadn't looked at me, was watching his partner with uneasiness.

"I don't think I'm wrong here," I said. "I'm not saying you would do this. I'm saying that Henry did this. He thought he was helping. At least in the long run."

"You don't take more than one soul at a time, and you can't animate a statue with what you have." Vincent's voice was starting to confirm his bitter anger.

Except we knew that Walkers could take more than one soul at a time, because we had seen it happen. Bringing up Vincent's friend now would only make things worse.

I tried a different tactic. "I don't think Henry tied their souls together with the clay. There was another man-"

"We heard what you said about the other guy," Vincent said.

My eyes began to sting. This was not the time to start tearing up. "This happened in the Civil War, right? Is it possible that Walkers could do different things back then?"

"Maybe what he is does not matter." Rider was watching his partner carefully. "Cassie could be wrong. I think we have to take that as a possibility. But, does it matter either way? He is a killer. We know that as a fact."

The doorbell rang. I hesitated, not knowing if I should walk by Rider, but then I decided it didn't matter. Anything was better than being in this room. Vincent and Rider both seemed to think I was wrong, my best friend wouldn't even look at me, and I had no idea what Logan thought about the whole situation.

When I yanked the door open, my spirits lifted. "Morning."

"I wish I could say it's a good one," Ethan said. "Is your team here?"

My heart sunk a little. "Everyone's in the kitchen." I closed the door behind Ethan, and when I turned around, he hadn't moved. "What's wrong?"

Ethan tugged me into him and gave me a kiss. I had momentarily guilty thoughts about last night, but I shook them off. Vincent and I hadn't done anything wrong, and we had gone through a life-or-death situation. It was enough to stir up anyone's emotions.

By the time the kiss ended, I was smiling.

"I thought we should fit that in before business got in the way," Ethan said, looking down at me in his arms.

"It's a shame that can't be the business of the day."

"I wish it could be. Once all this is over, we should go away for a few days. Unwind, just the two of us."

"That sounds like an excellent plan." Inside I was jumping up and down.

Ethan glanced towards the kitchen.

"Come on," I said, "I'll get you some coffee."

The guys had been talking at the table, but stopped when Ethan and I entered the room.

Logan tipped an imaginary hat at him. "Morning, officer."

"Sorry to stop by like this," Ethan said, "but we have another body."

Frowning, I transferred the coffee cup to a to-go tumbler, one for Ethan and one for myself. I thought about preparing more cups, but then figured the last thing my partners needed right now was coffee.

"Government agent?" Logan asked.

"A local judge. Found in his home last night," Ethan said. "The thing is I'm not sure that this is the same perpetrator."

"There are differences?" Logan asked.

"No missing body parts, but I have to cover all my bases," Ethan said.

Logan nodded. "We'll gear up."

"I'll finish getting ready. Give me two minutes." Vincent didn't waste any time leaving the room.

Rider followed Vincent, but hesitated. He turned his gaze on Ethan and studied him to the point that it became uncomfortable, and then Rider left the room.

Ethan didn't look happy. Then again, if I had just come from a homicide, I wouldn't be happy either.

It was going to be a long day. "I need to run upstairs and get my bag."

"Ethan, mind if I talk to my partner for a minute?" Logan asked.

"Yeah," Ethan said, "I'll be in the other room."

Frowning, I looked at Logan and waited for him to talk. I could tell from the tilt of his head that he was listening for the others.

"I think you should sit this one out," Logan said after a few moments.

My mouth dropped open. "What? Why?"

"You had a rough night last night and a rough morning," Logan said.

"Vincent had the same night and morning," I snapped.

"He hasn't been running himself ragged for the past few days."

"I haven't been-"

"You've been pushing yourself too hard. Take the day. Let Vincent and Rider cool off, or whatever it is they need to do."

I crossed my arms and glared at Logan. "You're sitting me out because of them?"

"Mostly for you to get some rest, but it won't hurt for you three to spend a day apart." Logan looked intently at me. It felt like he was reading my mind. "You know I'm right about this."

This morning I had told myself I would get some rest, but that was before a body showed up. Now I felt like I was being moved aside.

"It's probably not even connected," Logan said, "not if the signature is different. You could go out and check on Essy."

"You know that things could have changed after the confrontation with Einar last night," I said.

"It's possible. Last night he also said he had things to think about. We'll check it out. If he's our perp, we'll see about calling you in."

I shrugged. "Sure." What else could I say? He wasn't wrong, and we both knew it. "Tell Ethan I have his coffee ready."

Logan nodded and left the room.

Ethan came in with a look on his face that I couldn't place.

"What's wrong?" I asked, handing him the coffee.

"Did Vincent stay here last night?" Ethan kept his voice quiet.

I could feel my face flush. "He did."

"I see," Ethan said. "Something happened last night, didn't it?"

I still couldn't tell what he was thinking, but I took a guess. "He stayed in the spare bedroom."

Ethan gave me a wry smile. "I appreciate that, but that wasn't what I was thinking."

Nothing was making sense this morning. "Oh. Um, yeah. Something kind of happened last night. "

"We've got a case right now," Ethan said. "Can you fill me in on the way?"

"I'm sitting this one out," I said.

Ethan looked confused, but I could see some concern mixed in there, both of which were better than the unrecognizable look I had been getting. "You're alright, though?"

I could see his eyes darting around, trying to look for new bruises, so I forced a little smile and lied. "I'm fine."

CHAPTER 27

S TANDING IN THE KITCHEN, I twisted the coffee cup around in my hand while I listened to Ethan leave. A minute later, Vincent came downstairs, and everyone left. The vehicles drove away and the house was silent.

What the hell had happened?

I'm not sure what Ethan was thinking, but Rider wouldn't look at me, Vincent was livid, and I had been benched from my job. All before noon.

This was set to be a stellar day.

I dumped the coffee and worked my way through the kitchen doing mindless chores. Halfway through the dishes, the tears started to fall. After the dishes were done, I looked through the cabinets to see if we needed anything, then I set about making a grocery list. Gran would be back soon and I knew she'd want to have a stocked kitchen, even if she wasn't planning on cooking anything.

I thought about making cookies for Logan's family, but my tears were starting to slow. With the waterworks out of the way, I eased into thinking over the issues at hand.

First, I went to check the laundry room. The entire cage had been taken away. We could assume it had been Einar, but was it? The idea of checking the Path was discarded immediately. I didn't want to experience Einar's Path again. Especially not alone.

Besides, I told myself, I shouldn't be reading, I should be saving my strength.

Rider might be able to take a look, or sniff, or whatever. If he would do that for me. After his reaction this morning, I wasn't sure if he would.

How could my best friend not even look at me? Back in the living room, I replayed this morning's events in my head. I had come down the stairs, seen Rider...and then what?

I could sense the wolf inside him. The animal was there, wanting to get out. I've always known Rider was a werewolf, from the moment we met, but I had never seen him in wolf form. Sure, his hands changed from time to time, but I'd never seen the beast within.

Until today.

Looking at my arm, I had the bruises to prove it, but why this morning?

He said I smelled like a werewolf, but that wasn't possible. Seeing Einar's Path was one thing, but I hadn't taken in the souls.

My mind grew panicky at the thought. No. There was no way I could have absorbed those souls. They were whole and complete. They wouldn't have jumped into me, would they?

How would I know?

I'd know. Surely I would. I had known with the leprechaun. They'd be jumping around trying to be seen and heard. Besides, that wouldn't make me a werewolf. So why did Rider think I smelled like a werewolf? Why had I seen his wolf under his skin?

The Rider issue would have to wait for the others to be fixed. I would need help in figuring out what was wrong.

I would need Rider to talk to me.

I took out the laptop Neil had given to me and went to the kitchen. With a fresh cup of coffee in hand, I started to research golems. It was too bad I couldn't keep my mind on the task.

What had Ethan been thinking? He said he hadn't been worried about Vincent, but was that true? Even with that, my relationship with him seemed more solid than with anyone else this morning. That was saying a lot.

I began to rub little circles around my temples to relieve the building tension. How do I tell him what happened last night? Something like that might push him over his threshold or weirdness. Ethan needed and deserved someone more normal.

Or at least screwed up in a normal way. I'm no good at breaking up with someone, but I think it had to be done.

Then there was Vincent this morning. His anger seemed to escalate from almost nowhere. He had reason to be angry, but at me?

There was a rattle at the front door, and I froze. I heard the door open.

"I'm home!" Gran called. "I...oh."

"I'm so glad you're home!" I went to meet her in the living room. If anyone could help me sort out this mess, it would be Gran. "You're home..." Her voice had trailed at the end, but it hadn't sunk in.

My stomach almost rejected its contents. Gran was there, but standing next to her, holding her arm, was Einar.

"Get away from her!" There was a quaver in my voice that I wish hadn't worked its way in. I fought towards the Path, but this close to Einar, it wasn't an easy task.

"Well, look at you. Or you all." Gran seemed completely unconcerned that the man held her arm. She reached up and drew her hands over his face. "Isn't that somethin'?"

"Let her go," I said.

You are needed. I could hear the words, but Einar was looking at Gran.

Panic clamped down. "What do you need with my grandmother?"

No. Not her. You, Cassandra, are required.

"You're all clay," Gran said. "That's interestin'. Can I make you a cup of tea?"

My mouth almost dropped open. "Gran! You can't offer him tea. He's threatening you."

"These people aren't going to hurt me," Gran said.

Einar's features didn't change, or if they did, it was subtle, but he seemed upset. *I am Einar. One together. Not people.*

Gran looked at the clay man and smiled. "I'm sure we can whip up something for lunch if you're hungry."

235

"He says he's one, not many," I told Gran, "and he doesn't seem very happy at the moment. Look, Einar, leave her alone. If you need me, that's fine. I'll go with you."

Gran frowned. "We're okay while you all are here. I'm not sure what happens if you all leave."

"He's safe here in the house?"

"Safe may be a strong word, but he isn't going to hurt us here."

I do not wish to hurt the old woman, but I will if I must.

Gran had been off her game lately. How could I tell if she was right?

"I'll go with you. It's no problem. Once you let her go and she leaves the room."

Einar looked away from Gran. *You will get what you need.*

"What is it that I need?" I asked.

We will use the automobile outside.

"When did you learn what an automobile is?" My mind was running towards any exit advantage it could find.

They belong to this time. I have been inside them.

"I can't drive that vehicle," I lied.

I came to know you. Last night.

The thought made my skin turn cold. It was something that Vincent had said last fall. He had taken my soul into him and he knew me.

"Right. Let her go and I'll get my stuff," I said.

Einar shook his head.

I didn't want to leave Gran alone with Einar, not even for a second. But my gun was upstairs and my purse was in the kitchen. I guess up until this point, the gun had been ineffective towards Einar anyway. The only thing that I had was the Path, and that was useless at the moment.

I walked backward out of the living room. Once my purse was in sight, I ran, grabbed it, and returned as fast as I was able.

"Where are we going?" I asked.

You do not need to know.

"I do actually. I need to know what to bring." That was almost a lie. Apparently, it was close enough to the truth that Einar relented in the end.

Many miles away, there was once a town of Others. You will take me there.

"The town of Others..." I stopped and rephrased what I was going to say. Somehow, I didn't think Einar would be happy if I said 'the town of Others you killed.' "The town of Others from the Civil War?"

Yes.

"Is that town even still there?" I asked.

We shall see what remains.

"Right. Okay." My mind raced for something else, anything else that might get Einar to stay, but allow Gran to leave. The guys would come eventually.

But would that be any better? Logan had had little effect when fighting Einar, I doubt Rider would have much more. Vincent was the only one that could do anything, but that was far too dangerous to try. There was no point in stalling. I needed to get Einar out of here.

"I have everything I need. Let's go."

Einar cocked his head and looked at me. I could practically hear his brain working, trying to figure out if I had a trick or plan.

Outside.

I walked to the door, leaving plenty of room around Einar, and then I opened it and waited.

He looked over at Gran. *Tell the old woman that I apologize if I scared her. This was a necessity.*

"What?"

Tell her.

I glared at Einar. "Gran, he says that he is sorry if he scared you."

Gran frowned. "Takes more than that to scare me. But I don't want you going with him. I don't know what will happen." She turned to Einar. "Promise me that you'll bring my granddaughter back. In one piece, mind you."

Einar and I both looked at Gran. She waited calmly for a response. When she didn't get one right away, she opened her purse and started rummaging through it.

Tell her I do not wish to lie. I do not know what this day will bring.

That made my heart skip a beat. I had to swallow twice to keep my voice steady. "He said that he doesn't know what the day will bring and doesn't want to lie to you."

"Are you protectin' this hunk of clay?" Gran asked, elbow deep in her cavernous purse.

"No, he's a murder suspect."

"Not working out so great, is it? Sorry to hear he won't promise, though." Gran hauled out a revolver and shot Einar at point blank range.

I'm not sure if it was the recoil or her surprise of actually firing the gun, but she staggered. Einar steadied her and took the gun out of her hands.

"Gran! Where did you get a gun?"

"Huh? Sorry Darlin', got a whistle in my ears. I didn't see that one comin'."

Einar led Gran over to a couch and sat her down. Gran was tugging at her ear and moving her jaw around trying to restore her hearing.

The fact that Einar was being gentle gave me hope that he didn't intend to harm her, even though she had tried to kill him.

Einar stood and watched Gran for a moment. *We must go now.* Keeping the gun in his hand, he gripped my arm and hauled me out to my car.

"What's this about, Einar?"

You will get into the car and drive.

Rule number one. Never go to a secondary location with someone who you think might want to do you harm. Actually, it was probably more like rule number four. The trouble is, I was more worried about the damage that would be caused if we stayed in the current location.

"All right," I muttered, "but you're going to have to give me directions."

When I got into the car, a squeaking noise made me turn. My rabbit was in the backseat. He was chewing on lettuce that looked much fresher than the stuff I had given him yesterday. I furrowed my brow at Einar when he got in, but didn't say anything when I started the car.

You will drive left.

I did what he said, feeling resentment at being told what to do. When I reached the road to town, where I could turn left or right, I stopped and waited for the next direction.

Einar bounced the tip of the gun against the clay of his legs. With every impact the metal caused a clanging echo, which seemed to fill Einar. *You will keep going.*

"Do you want me to turn left again?"

Einar frowned. *We must go straight.*

"There's no road. We have to travel on roads, especially in this car."

Einar seemed to think this over. *We must go in that direction. Take me to a road that goes that direction.*

"Right," I mumbled, "this day keeps getting better and better." I drove to the Interstate and started heading south.

We sat in silence. Gran was safe. That allowed me to drop down a terror level. She also knew where we were going. Well, not knew, but she had enough details that she would be able to tell the guys.

Vincent would already know, but he found that kind of connection an annoyance. Today, he might choose to ignore it all together. There hadn't been a call on my cell phone yet. Usually, he called if he suspected something was wrong, or he'd make someone else call.

There was no way everyone was too mad at me to reach out. Right?

It would make it better if they didn't come. It was depressing, but the facts were, we still didn't know how to deal with Einar. At least this way, I was the only one of us readily available for him to kill.

You are deep in thought. You are reasoning out a means of escape.

I shook my head and kept my eyes on the road. "Why did you take my rabbit? Did you send him in the first place?"

An angry hiss issued from Einar. *I would not do something so foul.*

"You kill people and you call sending someone a dead rabbit foul?" Why did I say that? Never remind a killer that they're a killer.

Einar was quiet for a while. *It is the magic that brought the creature back to life that is unseemly.*

"What are you going to do with it? Kill it?"

It is not the animal's fault that this happened.

That was too close to what I had told Vincent last night. "What will you do with it then?"

I am not certain. Its creator is no longer available to undo the damage.

"You killed him? Was that the body my team went to see this morning?"

I do not know what body they saw. If it is new, it is not one I ended. The man did not die. He sensed the ending of our arrangement and has disappeared.

"Arrangement?"

Einar said nothing.

"So you didn't send me the rabbit. You got someone else to do it?"

Do you always speak so incessantly?

"Yes. At least when I'm... when I want answers." The word hostage almost slipped past my lips. At this point, I didn't think it would be a good idea for Einar to be reminded that I'm a hostage either. "Who did you get to send me the rabbit?"

What this creature is now, I would not wish on any animal.

"Why did your pal make it then?"

Einar slammed a fist down onto the dashboard of my car. I jumped as thick plastic and fake wood gave way to a huge dent and large cracks.

Enough! You will be silent. I will give you instructions. I've learned enough that I should be able to drive this thing without you if needed.

Panic tried to overrule my mind while I watched the thin cracks spread through the stiff plastic. This was trouble. Real, serious, this-guy-is-going-to-kill-me, kind of trouble.

At least Gran was safe. My eyes started to sting at the thought. Logan and the others would look after her. They would all take care of each other.

Crap, crap, crap, I thought as I sniffed. Going down that line of thought would get me nowhere. Vincent was probably already on his way and hopefully, dragging the others along.

And if he weren't, I would give him hell for it later, once I had gotten away from the mad man sitting next to me.

The rabbit squeaked and snuffled in the back seat. I adjusted the mirror to look back at it. Einar was already turned in his seat to watch the rabbit. It squeaked again.

When Einar reached back to the cage, I couldn't keep quiet. "Don't hurt it!"

This creature has done nothing to me. I will not harm it.

"And I have?"

You are an agent of the government and one of their botched creations. Killing you will be a release.

"Not the kind of release I want," I said. "Besides, what about Gran? You scared and threatened her."

It was a means to an end. A necessity.

"Whatever," I mumbled.

I do not know what you mean by those words.

I licked my lips and looked back again at the little ball of fur in the back seat.

Oh well, better to be pissed off and dead than weepy and dead. "It means I don't believe you. It means that I think you're telling yourself these things to justify them to yourself."

A cold clay hand reached out with blurred speed. It clasped around my neck.

Fear jolted through me as my air supply became restricted. I slammed on the brakes and took my hands off the steering wheel. My hands wrapped around Einar's straining to wrench his grip away. I might as well have been trying to push a tree over. There was no chance of having any effect.

CHAPTER 28

I T DOES NOT MATTER IF *you believe me. I need no further justification of myself.*
The hand loosened enough for a response and I hesitated. I didn't know Einar, but I knew Henry. At least a little bit.

Horns blared all around.

I rolled the dice and took a chance. "You're justifying it to yourself. You have to, or you would have to admit that you're letting those that created you control your-"

The pressure around my throat doubled. The edges of my vision began to dim. Then he removed his hand.

I coughed and leaned my head on the steering wheel, trying to suck in as much air as I could. I watched my own tears fall on the steering wheel and slide down. How much of Henry was left in there? How much of the others?

Another horn blared.

Drive. I had expected his words to sound harsh in my mind, but they weren't.

Still, I took my time. After sitting up, I wiped my face off with my hands, checked the backseat, and adjusted my mirrors.

Traffic was light, which is probably what saved our lives. Well, my life anyway. With shaky hands, I continued to drive where Einar had indicated.

It wasn't until we were moving again that I thought of running, but that wouldn't work. He knew Gran and my friends. Rubbing my throat, I thought through other options. Escape was out. If I crashed the car, I would be more likely to get hurt than he would. I wracked my brain trying to think of something I could do to get the upper hand.

We are traveling in the wrong direction.

"If you told me where we're going, I might be able to get us there."

Einar's thoughts seemed to turn inward, and he was quiet for some time. *You are driving us to the village.*

"The village?" Going with Einar to a place where he had already killed so many people was something I would like to avoid. "That was over a hundred years ago. I doubt it's still there."

Turn west.

Unfortunately, a road to take us west did not magically appear, and Einar's impatience grew.

"I'll take the next exit." I took out my phone and typed in the password while watching the road. "We can use the GPS to...Hey!"

Einar took the phone from my hand and casually tossed it out the window.

"We could have found a map on that." The frustration helped to shove away the fear. Better to be angry than scared.

People use that device to contact other people.

"It does a hell of a lot more than that." Scowling, I blindly took the next exit and started heading in a northerly direction. "See if there's a map in the glove box."

We are near. There is no need for a map.

There was a gas station at the exit and little else. We passed through a town so small that if you blinked, you would miss it. Fields with short green plants grew along one side of the road and dense forest covered the other. My agitation grew when I realized that work couldn't track me using the phone GPS now. I glanced over at Einar. Maybe he knew more than I realized.

Turn left.

"There's no road. I can't drive into trees."

Turn left. Einar's voice was insistent.

Up ahead, I saw a sign. I flipped on my blinker and we turned down a gravel road. A small sign read *Lost Hills Conservation Area.*

The road was rutted and looked barely used. About a half mile back it dead-ended and I turned off the car.

"Are you sure you want to see this?" I asked. Remembering the feeling of death from so many Lost, I knew I didn't want to go any farther.

Get out of the car. Einar got out and waited for me.

My stomach clenched and my mind scrambled to think of a way out of this. If I went into the woods with Einar, I wasn't sure I would ever come back out.

Einar leveled the gun at me. My heart skipped a beat. Go into the woods and maybe I don't survive. Stay here and I die.

"What is it that you want to do out here?" I got out of the car, but wanted to keep hold of my anger rather than slip into fear.

Take the cage.

After taking the rabbit, Einar motioned at me with the gun and I walked into the woods. The undergrowth was thick at the forest edge. I struggled through thorn bushes and tripped over hidden tree roots. Glancing behind, I saw that Einar moved through the terrain with ease. That gave a little heat to the fire. The least he could do was walk in front of me.

Although with him behind me, I wasn't walking directly in his Path. Maybe I had a chance here.

The Others were to be given the town.

"There's not a town out here." I slapped my arm where some biting insect had tried to take hold.

It was a part of our arrangement. What happened then happened for a reason.

I had to force myself to listen to what Einar was saying. There had to be something here that I could use to my advantage.

"The Others, I mean the Lost, they have a town with a bunch of land."

We began walking up a steep hill. It didn't take long before I was breathing hard and sweating more than any one person should.

They have a home?

"For the ones that want to stay there, sure. They have a home."

The government does not interfere?

That was stretching it, but I wasn't going to let Einar know that. I sat the cage down and leaned against a tree, trying to catch my breath. "I'm not sure. I haven't looked into it that much."

We are almost there. Continue.

"I need a minute." What I needed was to stall for time. As much as I could get. Still, it would be nice to catch my breath at the same time.

Einar watched me and I made a production of leaning over and breathing heavily. When he got tired of waiting, he shoved me to get me moving again.

Wishing that it was Einar's neck, I gripped the cage tightly and climbed the rest of the way up the hill. As we neared the top, the trees parted and a field stretched out in front of us before gently rolling down and back up again. Groups of trees were scattered around. With the sun shining, it was a beautiful sight.

Not where I wanted to die, though.

Looking up at the sky, I wondered if there were any satellites in the area. Would Hank have me up on a monitor? Would they have even brought Hank in on the search?

There was no way of knowing. If I were going to find a way out of this, it would have to be on my own. Einar was staring over the hills. Pretending to take in the landscape, I started edging away, holding the cage tight. For some reason, Einar was attached to the rabbit. I felt safer with it in my hands.

The Path was shrouded and I couldn't reach it, but I knew it was possible. It worked last night, and it would have to work here.

The witch lived down in that hollow. In that stand of trees. Over the next hill was the town proper. The elves lived there, along with most of the others.

"The wolves lived this way," I said, using it as an excuse to move farther away.

Did you see them all? Einar's voice sounded distant.

I shook my head. "They were jumbled together. I remember a few. Others were flashes that came and went. Were they your friends?" The moment the words were out I wished them back in. I tensed, waiting for Einar's reaction.

I have no friends in this life or the next.

That was Henry. "Why did you come here?"

This is where they all belong.

The darkness was starting to thin and I tried to be casual while increasing the distance between us. "I'm curious. Why didn't you bring them back years ago?"

I fell in battle.

"Then why didn't that release them?"

The opposing regiment had Others in their rank. I fell. I did not die.

"Why did you get back up?"

An old man found me and decided he could make use of me. He thought we would help each other.

"Who?" I turned to face Einar, unsure of what to make of this new information. When he didn't answer, I changed tactics. "What could you two do for each other?"

When I was created, I made a promise to the souls inside me. Those responsible would pay.

"Government workers?"

The world was different. The United States government was different. Those that need to pay are long gone. I found that out through you.

"What did you do for the man who woke you up?" I was almost there. My mind was stretching towards the Path.

Einar turned back the way we came. *Once they had perished, they had no use for the parts he requested.*

My stomach tried to revolt and I hugged the cage tighter to my chest. I started taking shallow breaths to avoid being sick. In its cage, the rabbit squeaked and wriggled its nose. The question 'why' was on my lips, but I couldn't make the words come out. The answer to 'why' was something I didn't want to hear.

Einar took a few steps in my direction. I copied his actions and moved away.

We were closing in on the only question that really mattered out here. "Why did you bring me here?"

Those you have inside you should be released. This area is as appropriate as any. Einar looked across the hills again before turning to watch the forest. *More appropriate than most.*

Gripping the cage, I took another step back. "If you know me, then you know those are not souls. They're fragments. Any whole soul I had, I returned." I tried hard to make my voice insistent, but the fear was creeping back in.

Einar's gaze was directed into the woods the way we had come. *I was concerned that I would not be able to take the Walker with us. The worry was unfounded. Come out.* The last two words rang louder in my head.

Frowning, I turned to the trees, but saw nothing. Quick movements out of the corner of my eye made me turn my attention back to Einar. He had moved closer, but was concentrating hard on the woods.

Tell him to come out.

Tell him? Einar wanted to take the Walker with us. Vincent had to be in the trees.

It wouldn't be me that drags him out. "No."

That seemed to surprise Einar. He aimed the gun at me.

You will tell him to come out.

"You're going to kill me one way or the other. Do you really want to kill him? Here of all places?"

Einar faced the woods and I heard him mentally call out. *Leave and you shall live. Stay, and you will die with her.*

Vincent stepped out of the woods and my heart sunk. Frantically, I grappled with my mind to charge through and reach the Path. Einar moved closer. His dark Path became thicker, effectively blocking my way.

Maybe Vincent had a plan. Please tell me he followed us out here with a plan.

You choose to die with her?

"I die without her." Vincent's voice was calm, but as he moved closer, I could feel anger boiling off him.

There was no way Einar was going to trade me for Vincent, and there was no way I would let him. Vincent had to know that.

Or maybe that wasn't what he meant?

The gun remained steadily aimed in my direction.

I gripped the cage. "What exactly is your plan here, Einar?"

As I said. The souls inside you will be released. It is a fitting resting place.

"What about the souls you stole?"

They will be laid to rest and I will die.

"If that was so easy for you, why didn't you let them go when you fell in battle over a hundred years ago?"

Einar stared at me. I didn't realize I had pushed him too far until the gun turned towards Vincent instead of myself.

Still, he watched me as though he were daring me to continue. A dozen different courses of action flew through my mind in seconds. My mouth went dry. They all ended in death.

At least for me.

I shook my head. "That's not a smart move." Einar pulled back the hammer of the gun and I rushed on. "You need him. You know as well as I do that it's the only way you can be sure that the souls are released."

My focus was solely on Einar. Even the flicker of activity in the trees didn't distract me.

Be sure?

"Cass, stop talking." Vincent moved in our direction.

Einar didn't look away from me, but the gun followed Vincent's movements.

I ignored Vincent. "How certain are you that when you die, they won't stay trapped inside that body. Vincent is the only way you can be certain."

Behind Einar, Rider ran out of the tree line and started up the hill. Logan followed close behind. To my ears, there was only silence. I didn't allow my gaze to leave Einar and I kept my face still.

"You know I'm right," I added.

You speak as though I would trust a Walker. Einar turned his head pointedly at Vincent. *Stop moving, or she dies.*

Vincent stopped.

If he had only taken a few more steps and I would have been able reach out to him. The contact of our shared souls would surely help me break through to the Path. In frustration, I mentally pounded on the black abyss swamping the edges of my mind.

The gun swiveled its aim. Without looking, Einar pulled the trigger. The bullet roared from the weapon. Rider fell to the ground before the sound had finished reverberating through the hills.

The cage fell from my hands and my mind went blank. Logan ran to Rider and fell down next to him. He pressed hard against the werewolf's chest, but even at this distance I could see his shirt already turning red.

I did not want to hurt an Other. You have forced my hand.

"No." There was a high-pitched scream. I wasn't sure if it was in my head or my ears.

Yes or no does not matter.

Logan was talking to Rider. I'd never seen the elf look so pale and unsure.

"No one made you do this, Henry." I wanted to yell the words, but they came out softer as I watched Logan helping Rider.

CHAPTER 29

M Y WORLD BECAME MINUSCULE AND focused. My best friend was on the ground, not moving. And I was standing in front of the thing that put him there.

Not Henry. We are Einar.

"You can tell yourself that," Vincent said, "but you know it is not true."

Einar let out a pained scream that beat against my mind.

"No one is forcing your hand now," Vincent said, "and no one forced you back then. You made the decisions. No one else."

I put the importance of the many above those of a few. The town of the Others exists now because of me.

"Did you even look for another way?" My voice sounded dull in my own ears. "And what about now? What have we done to deserve this? The people that you killed, what did they do?"

That was the necromancer.

Logan lifted one hand away from Rider and fumbled to get his phone. His palm was red and Rider still wasn't moving.

"Necromancer? Another excuse." Vincent's hands were squeezed into fists. "This was you."

Feeling numb, I stared at Rider's unmoving form. "It was always you, Henry. Each death, it was all down to you."

"Cass!" Vincent yelled.

Out of the corner of my eye, I saw Vincent surge forward.

Einar had gripped my arm before I looked away from Logan's frantic phone call. When I looked into the clay face, something broke inside me. He did this. He killed them all, and now Rider.

It had to stop now.

Anger welled up and ran through me. It wasn't only mine. The moment that Einar touched me, I could feel those inside him reach out. Their energy surged into my own and made it almost easy to tear through the black divide.

The Path was murky. It was stifling and tried to weigh me down. Those little flashes of colors, the lines of life from the Lost that Einar had taken inside him, pulsed around me. They strove to throw back the pitch trappings that Henry had created for them.

I tried to help. Moving the Path around me, I tried to eek out the individual strands of color, but they were tightly matted together.

Henry's grip became a vice. I felt a gentle tug in my core. It was eerily familiar. Henry was going to take my soul.

Panic started to well up. Trying to affect Henry's Path wasn't working. I couldn't separate him from the others, so I concentrated on the physical.

Getting him to let go was priority one. I drew on the power flowing around us, latching onto the flows outside the stormy Path created by Einar. By my hand, those natural currents were building into a raging tempest. Inside, I worked to keep hold of myself.

But maybe there was no defense against a Walker. Parts of my soul, and possibly fragments of others, rushed into Einar.

Vincent clutched Einar's arm before I could make a move. Looking into Vincent's flat black eyes, I could see his seething fear.

Chunks of my soul slid away and cold fragility started to take up residence. Keeping the Path bound together with enough power to hurt Einar was becoming a battle.

Einar tried to shrug Vincent away, but Vincent kept his hold. *You make things difficult where they should not be.*

When Einar let go of my arm, I staggered and nearly fell. By the time I caught my balance, Einar had Vincent.

Terror filled me and I lashed out. The Path snaked its way around Einar. My own energy dwindled to embers, but the outrage of the others inside Einar fueled my work.

There was a faint smirk on Vincent's face, which only made me work faster. Einar took Vincent's arm. I could hear a snap and Vincent's face grew pale, but he didn't let go.

Drawing in all the strength I could muster, I compressed the Path surrounding Einar. There was resistance, but I bore down.

What is it that you do?

Vincent said something, but it sounded like it was miles away. The noise was hollow.

Cracks began to form throughout Einar's body. Concentrating on the arms, desperately wanting him to let go of Vincent, I crushed down.

Lines splintered and small chunks of clay broke away.

"Let him go," I hissed, trying desperately to remain upright.

Einar let go.

I didn't.

He was still a threat, and one that we couldn't contain. I turned to Vincent in panic. There was no way to let Einar go free and no way that I could continue to hold him.

Vincent kept his injured arm close to him. I was certain he said something, but again, it was like he was too far away.

I can harm you no further. Defeat clung to Einar's words.

Einar looked down and I followed his gaze. Chunks of clay had broken off his legs as well. I was the only thing holding him up. I loosened the strangling Path I had around Einar, but when I tried to release the Path altogether, all those lines of color that twisted throughout Einar clung to me.

They still wanted to be heard.

Wavering, I took a step back. Drawing up an emotion of peace, I worked to calm those that fastened to me. An arm wrapped around me and gently tugged me further back. Looking up, Vincent was trying to keep me in sight while still watching Einar. The whites of his eyes were starting to make an appearance and lines of worry creased his face.

Once I convinced the others to let go, it became easier to move out of the Path. Vincent's arm was the only thing keeping me upright.

Nothing kept Einar up. His arms and legs were missing chunks of clay and he could no longer stand. Inside, he was hollow.

"Are you alright?" Vincent asked.

"Tired." My voice was flat.

Vincent stepped in front of me. His eyes locked onto mine and he looked as though he was searching for something.

Feeling as hollow as Einar, I had an idea of what Vincent was looking for. I'm not sure if I wanted to know what remained inside me. Vincent's intensity made me nervous, so I looked away.

In the distance, Logan was still putting pressure on Rider's chest. Now free from Einar, I lurched towards Rider. Vincent gathered me closer to him with his good arm, keeping me upright. Together, we made our way over to Rider.

When I reached him, I half knelt and half fell to the ground next to my friend. Vincent put an arm on my shoulder and I gripped his hand.

"A helicopter is on its way," Logan said, not looking up.

"Is he...Is there anything I can do?" I asked. The empty feeling remained inside me and tears didn't come.

Logan shook his head. "He's still breathing, but he's lost a lot of blood. Is our target down?"

"Down, but not out," Vincent said.

The three of us looked up when we heard the sound of helicopter blades slicing through the air.

"They're sending a team, too," Logan said, looking back down at Rider.

Vincent tensed behind me. "They'll pull him apart shard by shard."

"And study each one," Logan said, still concentrating on Rider.

"Why?" I asked. Then I realized it was a stupid question. "They'll try to make another one, won't they?"

"I've never seen a better soldier," Logan said, "and I doubt they have either."

The grip Vincent had on my shoulder increased. The helicopter came into view in the distance.

"He was crazy." As though I needed to remind them.

"They'll think they can do better," Logan said.

"What can we do?" I asked.

Logan shook his head. "It's a long shot, but if the magic were gone and Einar couldn't talk, would there be anything to find?"

"How do you kill magic?" I asked.

"What's holding it together?" Logan looked pointedly at Vincent.

"The souls, but he has..." Vincent started, and then died away.

He couldn't seem to bring himself to say that Einar had a part of me inside him.

I could feel Vincent's eyes on me, but I didn't look away from Rider.

"Didn't reach him in time?" Logan asked. The elf chanced a glance at me, but returned his gaze to Rider. "Will it be possible to retrieve anything if the agency has him?"

"No." The harshness of Vincent's voice startled me. "I'll take care of it."

Scrambling for Vincent's hand, I looked at him. My entire being felt indifferent, but I was very sure of one thing.

"You can't go between the worlds." My voice sounded as listless as I felt.

Vincent took my hand. "I won't be gone long this time." There was a bleakness to the promise.

"No. You have to release them here. All of them," I said.

"We don't-"

"This wasn't their fault," I insisted. I didn't know a lot about the area between the worlds, but it wasn't a place you'd want to hang out for eternity.

"Cass, it's not that simple."

"I'm in there, Vincent. Part of me at least." I didn't think it was possible for him to turn any paler. "Did you really think I didn't know?" The words sounded cruel, but I could feel empty areas inside myself. If he went between the worlds, there would be no chance of being whole again.

The helicopter started to hover nearby.

Logan broke the silence. "They need to know it's clear for them to land."

Vincent let go of me and took out his phone. He started talking on his way to Einar.

I looked to Logan for reassurance. "Was that wrong?"

Logan shook his head. "You said what you had to. You've got more to lose than he does. It might not be wise to leave him alone with all the AIR agents around."

The helicopter started to land.

I nodded and touched Rider's cheek, realizing that I might never see him again. "You'll look after him, right?"

"He's in good hands. Go make sure his partner stays that way as well."

Looking down at Rider, I knew I was doing the things I was supposed to do, but I didn't have the emotions to back up the actions. Rider didn't have to know that, though. In case he could hear me, I leaned down to Rider's ear. I wasn't sure what I wanted to say, so I stuck with the facts. "Logan is going to watch over you for me. I'm going to help your partner. When I get back to the office, I want to see you awake. Got me?"

It was unsettling when I didn't receive a response. I didn't realize I was expecting one until it didn't come.

"Bring Vincent around to the doctor first chance you get," Logan said, "he's looking pretty bad."

Gathering my strength, I nodded and stood. There were some feelings of fear and trepidation trying to make themselves heard inside me, but they felt far away. It was easy to thrust them away and focus on Vincent. The exhaustion weighed heavily on me and settled in by the time I reached him.

"You should go with Rider," Vincent said as I approached. He was crouched down next to Einar, but made no move to touch the clay man.

"Logan is with him. I'm where I should be. Do we know when the other team will get here?"

"Soon." Vincent still didn't reach for Einar.

Getting comfortable, I sat down cross-legged next to Vincent, staying well out of Einar's reach.

Not that Einar was paying much attention. The clay man was staring at the sky, looking lost in thought.

Those from other realms of existence have embraced those that have caused significant abuse. This is not my world.

"Your world has been gone for a long time," I said.

Were you telling me the truth when you said the Others had their own town?

"Yes, they run the whole town. There aren't any real roads into the town, so they live out in the open."

"There are a few other places throughout the world where the Lost can be themselves. There's even an island in the Pacific where they live in the open, although I think it's under British control." Vincent sounded like his mind had wandered far away from the words he was speaking.

It is time for this to be done. You will release them here? All of them?

Vincent looked at me before he answered and I silently pleaded with him.

"Yes," Vincent said.

The noise in the area increased as the helicopter took flight once again with Rider and Logan inside.

We are ready for the peace of home, even if it is far from our time.

"Is there..." I stopped and tried to reform the question in my mind. "Is it possible to get myself back?"

Einar looked at Vincent, studying him. *She is very much a part of you.*

Vincent glared. "That's not relevant."

I have seen no part of you, Walker, but I know her well. There are aspects she clings to more than others.

Vincent said nothing.

In some small way, I would try to redeem my tarnished soul. When you take us, ensure she stays in contact with you. I make no promises, but there is an intensity between you that will strive to keep you together.

"So," I said, "you're saying you don't know."

A very definite sigh came from Einar. *That is all I have to offer. As Einar, I am not sorry for the actions I have taken, but I would leave you with parting advice. The necromancer is no friend. Nor is your government. Neither of them are finished with the damage they intend to cause.* Einar turned his head and looked over the rolling hills.

We are ready.

"Please turn away." Vincent didn't look at me and he didn't demand, but his words left me with a chill.

A part of me wanted to say that I had seen this before, although I had been on the receiving end. When I looked at Vincent, his eyes had already started clouding over. I realized that it was because I had seen it before that he wanted me to turn around. Without standing, I turned away.

Using his good hand, Vincent took my arm and laid it on his own. "Don't let go," he said. Then Vincent gripped Einar's shoulder where the clay was unmarred from my destruction.

There was no noise. Einar was ready for this, although actually, it was probably Henry and the others that were truly ready for their nightmare to come to an end. Where I had fought with my every breath to save my soul from Walkers, Einar was still.

Beside me, Vincent started to breathe heavily. I could feel him strain under the weight of all those souls.

I realized that Vincent might keep a small piece of each of those souls. I gripped his arm tightly, knowing it was too late to say anything.

Maybe it was Einar that he would keep a piece of. I shivered at the thought.

Mentally, Einar gave a final gasp that sounded like relief. Then the clay man was only clay. Vincent lurched up, but fell back down again. I started to turn.

"Stop." His voice was steely and cold.

I froze in the act of twisting around. Instead, I gripped his good arm tighter to provide some sense of comfort. He didn't shake me away.

Power built around Vincent. I had felt the power of a Walker before, but this was different. Fierce, untamed energy radiated like the sun in a desert. It spread around me, rammed against me, and tried to drive me into the ground. When the strength started to dissipate, individual tightly knotted strands of power wove themselves around my core.

The Lost had been released. They were all familiar, although some stuck out in my memory more than others.

Slamming into me, a piece of myself embedded itself back in place. Intense sensations and flaring colors caused me to gasp. The dull edge of my emotions was sharpened to a point. After such a long day, it might have been better if they could hide in the background.

As the air became lighter, Vincent moved away. Not sure what to expect, I tensed, but when I looked behind me, he was laying on the ground and staring at the sky. This ratcheted up my anxiety since Einar had been doing the same thing before he left.

When I saw that Vincent's eyes were clear and he looked thoughtful, I tried to let myself relax. It wasn't working. "What's wrong?"

"That was..." He appeared to think it over. "Different." Vincent's voice was more serene than I had ever heard it.

Voices called out in the distance. We both ignored them, knowing that the other team would find their way to us soon enough.

Uncertainty started to creep over me. Not only did Vincent sound different, but his face also looked more relaxed. Did taking another Walker's soul change things? "How different-"

"We need to take care of the golem," Vincent interrupted.

"They're all out of there, right?" I eyed Vincent carefully, but I wasn't sure what I would do if any were still trapped inside.

Vincent sat up and looked at the inanimate clay. "It's empty, but I'm not confident we should leave it intact."

"You think someone will try to recreate it?" I didn't wait for a response. "We could smash it."

Our heads turned to the voices that were coming closer to our hilltop.

"I'm not sure we have time to destroy it." Vincent looked me over. "But it'll have to do. Look around for a rock, a tree branch, anything that might help."

My body felt weighed down and I didn't want to move, but I closed my eyes, knowing what needed to be done. The blackness that had barred my way was no longer an issue, but the memory of Einar still lingered. The jump to the Path took work, but I managed to get there. I grabbed Vincent's hand before he could stand up. A current jumped through us and tingling warmth stretched up my arm. When Vincent inhaled sharply, I knew that I wasn't the only one feeling our connection.

There was no time to analyze the feeling, even though I wanted to embrace it.

"I've got it." I broke our contact and turned my attention to the empty shell of Einar. Concentrating hard, I strengthened the Path around the clay, made it solid, and then squeezed it together. With Henry and all the others gone, there was little resistance. The hollow earth cracked and as I compressed it further, it shattered into a million pieces. When I pressed harder, ready to grind the remains into pieces as small as I could manage, something pressed back on the Path.

Startled, I pulled away.

Closing my eyes, I dropped away from the Path. "There's something still there." When I opened my eyes, the world looked dull again and I wavered.

Vincent moved over to the mound of clay. "I know I took everything."

My stomach clenched as Vincent brushed back some of the clay. That had been someone's body for over a hundred years. Moving it around like a pile of rubble didn't sit right. Then I thought about how easy it had been for me to create the debris and I suddenly felt sick.

Agents hollered at the edge of the woods on the hill. Thankfully, they had come into the open farther down the tree line. They were rushing in our direction, guns drawn, but not aimed, scanning the area intently as they moved.

"We've got company," I muttered.

"I've got it." Vincent stowed something in his pocket and looked strained when he stood. "Can you finish getting rid of the rest?"

It would take too much time and effort to respond, so I silently moved into the Path. Grinding the remaining clay to dust made my nose wrinkle up. When I was done, I let the Path fall away. Wavering, even while sitting, I wondered how long it would take to get home. My skin crawled and I wanted to scrub away any remembrances of the day.

Standing didn't seem like my best option. I was worn to the bone and didn't treasure the thought of the long walk to the car. Having agents standing around looking down at me, as though I couldn't handle myself in the field, seemed like a much worse option.

When Vincent offered me his good hand, I sagged, but took the help. He gripped my hand hard and didn't comment when it took me a while to steady myself.

A squeak from behind made us turn. The cage laid on the ground where I had dropped it.

CHAPTER 30

W E'RE CLEAR," VINCENT CALLED.
They were close enough that he didn't have to raise his voice, but I was still glad he did. You can never be too careful when people had guns drawn.

Vincent moved away from me and I somehow managed to stay on my feet. Before I could do more than blink, he thrust the cage into my hands.

"What happened here?" The agent put his gun away and pointed at the remains of Einar.

It took me a moment to put a name to his face. I really needed to get to know people outside my own team.

"Agent Paulson, we're glad your team got here when you did." I told myself that it wasn't a lie, only misleading. "That's our man."

"What's left of him." Vincent's voice had returned to flat tones. I wasn't sure if that was a good sign, or a bad one.

"And that?" Agent Paulson asked.

Clenching the cage in front of me, I wanted very much to hide the rabbit from everyone. "It's my rabbit. He took it, and..." I stopped, not knowing where to go from there.

Luckily, Paulson had more pressing things on his mind than a pet.

He nodded at Vincent's hand. "You need that looked at. I'll have someone get you back to the Farm. Agent Heidrich can take us through what happened here. We'll get a statement from you later."

"We can put it in our report," I said, anxious to get Vincent to the doctor.

Agent Paulson shook his head. "From this point on, it's our report."

"What? Why?" This was throwing me off balance. I had never had another team take over a case before.

"Standard procedure." Agent Paulson didn't look happy. "You can call it into Kyrian or your handler, Hank, but from what we understand at this point, our perpetrator picked you up and took you for a ride."

Took me for a ride? "It's not like I had a choice in the matter."

"Which makes you one of the victims. Add that to Agent Wolfe getting shot. The agency thought it best if this case shifted hands." Agent Paulson turned and barked out orders and his people broke apart and began to sweep the area. Once they were out of earshot, he continued. "From what Logan reported, and from what I've seen here, it's pretty clear you've already wrapped this case up." He nodded to the shards of clay. "Just think of us as putting on the final touches. Your team has had a rough go at it. Agent Pironius-"

"I'll wait for Agent Heidrich," Vincent said.

"That's your choice, but this could take a while." Agent Paulson scanned the hills.

"Excuse us a moment," I said.

Agent Paulson nodded and walked off to talk to his team.

Vincent looked at me, one eyebrow raised, waiting for me to argue.

When I knew everyone was out of earshot, he didn't have to wait long. "You need to go back to the Farm."

"I can wait."

I shook my head. "But you don't have to wait."

"Look, you're exhausted to the point that you can barely stand. I'm not going to leave you alone out here."

"I'm not alone. It's not going to take long to walk Paulson through what happened, and I really want someone to check on Rider."

The fragments of a worried look worked their way onto Vincent's blank face. "Logan's with him. We'll give them some time, and then call to check on both of them."

"You need…"

"Cass, today…" Vincent looked pained and took a deep breath. He couldn't manage to keep his voice or his face expressionless. "He was going to kill you. You were taken away from us. From me. When we got here, I wasn't sure what we would find."

My heart clenched. I hadn't thought about it from their point of view. I could barely comprehend the day from my perspective, much less that of my partners. And Vincent? It was always difficult to fathom what had gone through his head.

Vincent reined himself in. "I was afraid we would find you dead."

"But I'm not." I tried to smile. "You should go and get yourself taken care of. I won't be long."

"Right now, the best way to take care of myself, and everyone around us, is to keep you in sight."

Looking into his eyes, I knew he wasn't going to budge. If this had happened to him, instead of me, there was no way I would let him out of my sight until it really sank in that he was safe and would stay that way.

Instead of admitting that I would do the same, I changed the subject. "Did anyone talk with Gran?"

"Logan spoke with her and Susan is keeping her company at the house until we get back."

"Not Jonathan?" This came as a surprise since Jonathan was the oldest and most responsible of Logan's kids.

"He's out of town."

"Already?"

"For a few days. He'll be back before the move is permanent."

Nodding, I looked around for Agent Paulson. He must have been keeping an eye on us because he came right over.

"I've got the team sweeping the other hills. The cleanup crew is on its way to bag and tag the evidence. It looks like your pet was injured," Paulson said.

Looking down, I saw the dried blood still on the rabbit's fur.

"If you want I'll get someone to take it…"

"No." I latched onto the cage as though my life depended on it. Knowing it was a strange reaction, I tried to detract attention. "Do we have anything to numb Vincent's arm?" I asked.

Agent Paulson also noticed the arm. "Olsen is working on it. Want to walk me through what happened out here? We can try to make it quick."

Nodding, I jumped into the day, starting with Einar showing up at my house. I stuck with the facts that I saw, not what Einar had told me, and I didn't add in any of my assumptions. I never once used the word golem, but referred to Einar as a possible Lost that wasn't made of flesh.

Vincent stood nearby, giving a statement to another agent. Whenever I looked at him, he was watching me. I'm not sure he ever looked away.

We both pointed out where Rider was shot, where Einar's gun fell, and where Einar had crumbled. I downplayed the strength of the Path and hesitated before saying that Vincent took the soul. But Vincent had done his job. He took out the perpetrator before any more harm could be done.

I said nothing about Einar being already down before Vincent took his soul.

Agent Paulson looked uneasily at Vincent, but continued asking questions until he received a call.

It didn't take him long to get off the phone and wave Vincent over.

"The helicopter's on the way to take you back," Paulson said. "If you have anything else for me, let me know."

"Thank you, Agent Paulson," I said, "we'll do that."

"They'll be landing a little further away this time to try to keep the rest of the scene intact." Paulson looked at Vincent's arm. "But I can get them to land here if it's needed."

"Not necessary," Vincent said.

Paulson indicated where to go and Vincent and I walked away.

"How's the arm?" I asked, worried the helicopter wasn't moving fast enough.

"It's not as bad as it looks," Vincent said. "Let's stop here."

We weren't far away, but through my exhaustion, I wasn't going to argue. Sitting down the cage was a relief.

"Look at me for a minute," Vincent said. He was standing close and gave me a penetrating look.

"I'm in there," I said.

He didn't flinch away, appearing intent on making sure for himself.

I shook my head, but let him look.

"Any side effects?"

"Huh, I'm not sure I'd know the difference," I said. Seeing Vincent's anxiety start to rise, I shifted gears. "What I mean is, I can hardly stand. It was...I feel better than I did, but I need sleep before I can really know."

The answer I had given him had been real. My soul had already been a wreck, I'm not sure that one more round of abuse would have a noticeable effect.

"Of course," Vincent said.

I don't think he was buying that I was too tired to know, so I took his good hand in my own. When my fingers wrapped around his, a spark ignited in my veins and traveled through me.

Vincent's features became less strained as he felt our connection.

"The helicopter is getting close," I said.

We watched it approach and as it grew closer, Vincent let go of my hand.

The contact had been so natural that it felt wrong when he drew away.

Knowing the connection wasn't entirely welcome, I picked up the cage and shifted it between us so I wouldn't be tempted to reach out again.

As the helicopter landed, I was so relieved I shook. Vincent walked up to the aircraft as though he had done this a thousand times before. I gripped the cage tight and followed behind.

When an agent tried to take the cage, I resisted until he told me he could anchor it at my feet, but they didn't want me to hold the cage. Since I had no idea what to expect, I nodded and kept an eye on the rabbit until I was seated close to it.

Someone tried to give Vincent a shot, but he refused. When pressed, Vincent intimidated the man into silence with a look, but agreed to the sling the man held.

We had headsets in order to talk, but we sat silently, allowing the roaring noise of the helicopter to fill the void. Even through all the noise, it didn't take me long to fall asleep.

Bleary eyed, I woke up when Vincent nudged me. When I realized we were landing, my sluggish brain tried to wake up and my thoughts focused on Rider.

Vincent didn't look well, so once I had the zombie bunny back in my control, we went straight to the clinic.

With each step, my stomach grew tighter and tighter, afraid of what I'd see when we arrived. Seeing Logan slouched in a chair in the hallway didn't help.

"What's going on?" I asked. "Where's Dr. Yelton?"

"Rider's out of surgery, but he hasn't woken up yet." Logan nodded in Vincent's direction. "Go on in to see him and I'll go lasso the doc for your arm. Then, we need to do something to get that out of sight."

I looked glumly at my new pet, unsure of what to do with it. My mind wasn't able to think much beyond getting in to see Rider.

"I'll take care of it," Logan said. "Go see Rider." He took the cage before I could protest and disappeared down the hall.

Poking my head into the room that Logan indicated, I saw Rider laying alone. I never imagined my friend looking anything but healthy and vibrant. Hell, when I shot him, he laughed it off. Now, he looked lonely.

Vincent came in with me and the doctor arrived in short order. Before leaving, Vincent looked over his partner while I dragged a chair to the side of the bed.

"Cass, you need to get some sleep," Vincent said.

"I will." I didn't have the strength to make the lie sound convincing. "Go get your arm looked at."

He didn't argue and I settled into the chair as he left with Dr. Yelton.

Even through his brown skin, Rider looked pale. For a while, I watched the rise and fall of his chest, continuously confirming that he was breathing. My eyes grew heavy, so I got up and moved around the room. Machines beeped with Rider's pulse, blood pressure, and a number of other things that I couldn't name.

Logan showed up with coffee, to my great relief. When he assured me we were alone, I filled him in on everything that had happened, including what I said in our reports.

"Thank you for making sure someone looked in on Gran," I said and covered my mouth to yawn.

"She was pretty upset when she called me. She seems to be having trouble hearing as well," Logan said.

"Oh," I groaned. "I forgot about that." I covered my face with my hands. "Einar wouldn't promise her to bring me back, so Gran shot him."

"Margaret shot someone?"

"Point blank range."

"She had your gun?"

"No, she dug around in her purse and took one out."

Logan erupted in musical laughter. His voice trilled through the air, and I felt lighter.

I covered my mouth to try not to laugh, but it was like an infection that I easily caught.

"What is funny?"

My laughter died in a sharp intake of breath. Rider's eyes were open and he was looking at Logan.

Logan moved to Rider's bedside. "Never mind that. It's good to hear your voice."

My heart had leaped into my throat and caught there. Rider was awake. Awake and talking.

"The doc is going to want to see you. I'll go get him."

Rider nodded and closed his eyes. When Logan left, I took his place.

"He's right," I said. "You had us worried."

Rider's eyes flicked open to glance at me and then he closed them again.

I bit my lip. An uneasy feeling crept in.

"Is there anything I can get you? Anything I can do?" I asked.

"Is Vincent alive?" Rider asked.

"Yes," I rushed to reassure him. "His arm is broken, but Dr. Yelton is taking care of him."

Rider nodded, but said nothing.

"And Einar is gone," I said. "After-"

"Logan will fill me in," Rider said.

"Um. Yeah." I felt deflated, but tried to sound positive. "It's so good to see you awake."

"You do not need to stay here," Rider said.

"I may not need to, but…"

"You misunderstand," Rider said. "I would like for you to leave." He didn't sound angry. If anything, he sounded sad.

I swallowed hard and blinked back tears. "You don't want me to stay?"

"I do not."

He couldn't see me because his eyes were still closed, but I nodded because I couldn't trust my voice.

Confused and sniffing, I started to the door. I tried to run through what had happened. Things hadn't gone well that morning, but that had been a misunderstanding, right?

But then, Einar had picked me up and Rider, with the others, had followed me, and then Rider had been shot.

Because of me.

I sniffed again and turned. "I'm really sorry you got hurt." My voice cracked, but there was no helping that.

"I know," he said.

Tentatively, I moved closer.

"I am sure I will see you again in a few days," Rider said.

"Right," I said. "A few days."

Dr. Yelton came in, followed by Logan, who was grinning.

"A few days," I said, more to myself than to Rider, although I knew he could hear me.

I left the room without looking back. Trying to keep my mind blank, I kept my head down and took a seat in the hallway.

Once word got around that Rider was awake, he had a steady flow of visitors. At least until Dr. Yelton kicked everyone out. We were certain at that point that Rider would fully recover.

The exception to Dr. Yelton's banishment was Vincent. Once he was back on his feet, he visited Rider. Who was going to tell a cranky Walker high on pain meds that he couldn't visit his partner?

"Have you slept yet?" Vincent asked.

It took me a minute to pull out of my self-pitying reverie. "You saw me sleep on the ride here."

"Sleeping in the helicopter doesn't count. Let's get Logan to give us a ride home."

"Sure," I said.

"Do you want to stop by again before we leave? Rider's up."

"Um, I'm good. He needs his rest."

CHAPTER 31

W E FOUND LOGAN DOWNSTAIRS WITH Hank, who had the cage shoved under his desk. Seeing that I was too tired to drive, and Vincent was thoroughly drugged up, he agreed to give us a lift.

Logan made a few attempts at conversation on the drive, but I stared out the window and Vincent was unresponsive. I think the elf was happy to get us out of the car at my house, but he joined us inside.

"In the kitchen," Gran called when we walked in.

Hearing her voice made me rush through the room. She met me at the kitchen counter for a long hug.

"I'm alright, darlin'," Gran said. She patted my back and pointed at the rabbit. "What's this?"

"This is a long story, but he needs a home," I said.

"Well, he found a good one," Gran said.

When I let go, she smiled, looked me over, and brushed a strand of hair out of my face. "You probably haven't had a thing to eat." Gran bustled into the kitchen. "Logan, thank you for taking care of my granddaughter. Susan and I baked some lemon bars, but I'm pretty sure Gerald ate them, so I have some cookies here for you. I also made you some tea."

"Thank you, Margaret, but I really can't stay tonight," Logan said. "I wanted to stop in all the same."

"I know you're busy. That's why I have your cookies bagged up and your tea in a travel mug." She gave Logan a wink.

"Thank you kindly." Logan tipped an imaginary hat and took his leave.

"Where are you going, young man?" Gran called at Vincent who had turned to follow Logan out.

Vincent stopped and looked unsure of what to say.

Gran didn't give him a chance. "Take this," Gran thrust a plate into his hands, "and go to your room."

I smothered a chuckle.

"You too, young lady." Gran passed me another plate. "Upstairs. Both of you get cleaned up, eat, and get some rest."

"Thanks, Gran." I gave her a peck on the cheek.

"Take your bunny up. I think he'll be happier up there until the cat gets used to him."

After the day I had, the rabbit no longer scared me, but having it in my room was a bit of a stretch. I wasn't sure what to say, though.

"Go on now, the both of ya," Gran said.

I left the room, nudging Vincent on the way.

He looked up and I could see his drug glazed eyes. "I shouldn't be here."

It was a blow to hear him say that, but it had been such a rough day that it barely registered.

Gran tutted. "Eat down here with me. We can have a chat."

Vincent looked like he was trying to gain control of himself. "Yes. We should talk."

When I glanced at Gran, she winked and waved me away.

Vincent didn't stand a chance.

Looking at the sandwich, my stomach growled, remembering that it had been empty all day. There was no way I was touching food without showering, though.

I sat the plate on my dresser, settled the cage on my desk, and then I went to scrub myself clean in the hottest water I could stand.

The room steamed up around me and I didn't want to leave. We'd all been taken off a case the moment we were wrapping it up. The reasoning was sound. Agent Paulson had called me a victim. That grated my nerves, but he wasn't wrong.

My best friend said he didn't want to be around me. I couldn't blame him for that. Remembering the sound of the shot and Rider falling, I shivered despite the hot water.

Rider had every right to send me away.

Then there was Ethan. I wasn't sure how I felt about that. Nothing that happened today fit into his world. When we started to see each other, we each made it clear that work was going to get in the way and we had to be okay with that. Maybe that's what this was, only my entire job and life got in the way. Even worse, I wasn't sure how I felt about him anymore.

My stomach reminded me that it needed to be fed, so I took a couple of deep breaths and shut off the water. Even though my dinner was waiting, I took my time drying off and made a note of the new bruises that ringed their way around my neck. The memory of Rider and I sitting here, back to back with only the door between us slowed me down.

The heat and steam felt so good that I wanted to could curl up and go to sleep right there on the floor. Instead, I yawned and retreated to my room.

Snagging the plate, I went back to the cage and started trying to think of a name. Lettuce was hiding under the bread so I took it off and started shoving it through the gaps of the cage.

"I still can't believe you're feeding a dead rabbit."

A squeak that rivaled those of the rabbit escaped me and I jumped and turned at the same time, tripping over my feet in the process. It was only by grabbing the desk that I was able to stay standing.

Somewhere between the turn and the trip, I realized that it had been Vincent talking.

"Don't scare me like that," I said.

Vincent, looking unabashed, leaned against my doorframe and watched me.

"And of course I'm feeding him." I emphasized that fact by poking the lettuce the rest of the way through. "He's eating it, isn't he?"

Vincent came across the room and looked into the cage. As he approached, I realized he didn't have any shoes or socks on, and his hair was damp.

"I don't suppose he's actually alive," Vincent said.

Remembering the touch of fur and cold flesh when I first opened the box, I shivered. "No, he's really dead."

Vincent put his arm around me and rubbed my arm, which gave me chills for a whole other reason. When I looked at him, though, he was still paying attention to the rabbit and looked lost in thought.

"What are you going to do with it?" Vincent asked.

"Frank," I said, letting out a breath I hadn't realized I'd been holding. "Not it. Frank."

"Frank?" Vincent looked at me confused. "As in Frank the Rabbit?"

"Yes."

"From…"

"Yes, from the movie. It seemed fitting somehow."

Vincent grinned, but it was short lived. "Sorry," he said, stepping away. "I didn't mean…"

He's sorry he touched me. Exactly what a girl wants to hear.

"I know," I said, trying to keep the depression out of my voice. I took my plate and sat on the edge of my bed. "Did you and Gran have a nice talk?"

"She gave me some things to think about."

"She's good at that. Does she know anything about today?"

"Not much," Vincent said.

"That's good. And I'm glad you're staying the night."

He didn't say anything, but he didn't leave. I tore off a few pieces of my sandwich and ate them, waiting to see if he had more to say. My meal was almost gone before he got around to talking.

"Today was difficult," he said.

That was an understatement, but I only nodded.

"I never asked if you if you were alright."

"You asked if…"

"Being so intent on what he had done to you, what I watched him do, I asked about side effects. Between the time that I left this morning and when I found you on the hill, I have no idea what happened."

I shrugged and looked down. The last thing I wanted to do was relive the day, but I had a feeling he had gone through a worse hell than I had.

"What do you want to know?" I asked.

"That you're alright, and to see if there's anything else you need to tell me."

Need to tell him? He was giving me an out, or maybe himself. Either way, I would take it.

"I'm fine," I said.

I'm not sure if I felt the disappointment, or if I saw it across his face. Nevertheless, it didn't matter because I knew he needed more than that. The way his eyes darted to the bruises that ringed my neck weren't overlooked either.

"It wasn't an easy day, and it lasted longer than it should have, but Gran's safe and my partners are on the mend. Once I get some sleep, I'll be golden." I hesitated before deciding to nudge my honesty further. "It does make me feel better that you're down the hall tonight."

Vincent moved the chair closer to the bed and sat. He looked as if he was trying to choose his words carefully. "It's best if I only stay for one night."

I gave him a weak smile. "I know you can't stay down the hall forever, but I'm thankful to have you here now."

He nodded, but still looked like he still had something he wanted to say.

"It's been a rough day for everyone," I said, careful with my tone. "Are you okay? I mean," I gestured at his arm. "I know you're not okay, but is there anything else? Anything you want to tell me?"

"I need to take some time to figure out a few things."

"Time?" I asked, wondering if I had missed something. "You don't have to rush anything."

Vincent nodded as though I had said something important. "For now, I think we should get some rest."

The reminder was enough to make me yawn. "I can live with that."

Leveraging myself to my feet, I tossed back my covers.

"You know," Vincent said, standing up behind me, "Frank is a pretty great name for your rabbit."

I looked over to the cage, and then beamed at Vincent. "I thought so."

He stood close, and from the look he gave me, I thought he would close the distance. When he didn't, I was tempted to make that move. Instead, we stood there, frozen in the moment until it passed us by.

"Good night, Cass."

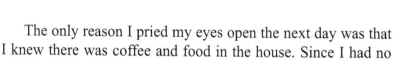

The only reason I pried my eyes open the next day was that I knew there was coffee and food in the house. Since I had no intention of going to the office, I stared at my closet. What do people wear when they're not working?

It's pretty sad when you don't have enough brain power to figure out what to wear. In the end, I threw on what I would be wearing if I was going to work. It made things easier. Figuring that Frank would be hungry or thirsty, I took his cage with me.

When I trudged down the stairs, I went straight to the coffee pot. Finding Ethan in my kitchen made me stop short.

He looked nervous, but I was surprised to find no butterflies flying in my stomach.

"Sorry," I said, "I didn't know you were here."

"Your grandmother asked me not to wake you. She said you had a long day yesterday."

"Yeah, it was definitely long. Where is everyone?"

"Margaret went out and Logan picked up Vincent."

He didn't sound upset or angry, so I nodded, set Frank's cage on the floor, and then went to the coffee pot.

"I tried to call yesterday."

"My cell phone is gone. I'm surprised you're not at work."

"No cases," Ethan said. "Yesterday's case was passed to another team because it wasn't a victim from my case. This morning, I was told that my case had been closed."

"That was fast," I said.

"Is that...?" Ethan bent over Frank's cage. "That's not...Is that possible?"

I shrugged and sat at the table. "Welcome to my world."

"That's one of the reasons I'm here actually," Ethan said, joining me. "I don't know your world."

"You know more than most."

"But to navigate your life, I need to know more."

The moment was laid out before me and there were so many avenues I could take from there. I could be sarcastic and condescending and end things right there, or I could try to make this work.

"Do you want to?" I asked.

Ethan took my hand. "Until I got here yesterday morning, it hadn't crossed my mind that someone you were investigating would come to your home. Then I saw Vincent here."

I nodded but wondered if that explained the odd look he gave me.

"I'm fascinated by some of the things that you have happening around you every day, but things like this," he traced a finger around the bruises on my neck, "they terrify me. I don't know what to do, or ask, or say."

I studied Ethan, trying to figure the man out. "Do you know what happened yesterday?"

"No, not after I left. I noticed Vincent's cast." His eyes landed again on the bruises. "But it looks like your day was harder than the others made it out to be. May I?" Ethan leaned forward, but waited for me to nod before he took a closer look at the bruises. "This looks bad."

I caught his eye. "This is my world. Not always, not even often, but we don't always know what to expect from one day to the next. And the bruises are nothing." He looked like he was going to say something, but I overrode him. "No, I think you need to hear this. Einar did come to my house the night before last. He came back yesterday and threatened Gran until I went with him. My partners followed me and together we made sure that he can't hurt anyone else."

Ethan swallowed hard and folded his hand around mine. "He kidnapped you?"

That made me think of the word victim again and my hand shook. "And Rider was shot. He almost died and he's still in the clinic. Vincent's arm was broken. We still worked to make sure Einar would never hurt anyone again."

I didn't realize that I had started to shiver from head to foot until Ethan gathered me into his arms. I held him and concentrated on stopping the shaking and avoiding crying.

Neither worked.

"Come with me." Ethan tugged me to my feet and led me to the living room. We sat on the couch and he held me, not saying anything until long after I had regained my composure.

I still didn't let go.

"I don't have any special skills," Ethan said. "I can't do what your partners do, but I can try to be here for you. I'll do what I can along the way, but I can try to be here after the dust settles."

I'm not sure what I wanted from Ethan, but right then I felt like I needed him.

But he also deserved the truth. "I'm not sure this is going to work." I sniffed. "And I feel like a giant mess right now. Are you sure you want to be around all of this?"

"It's not going to be perfect," Ethan said, "but I'd like to try."

The phone rang.

"Hold that thought." I wiped the last traces of dampness from my face and answered the phone.

"Cassie, this is Hank."

"Morning. Sorry I haven't called yet," I said.

"Don't worry about it," Hank said. "I wasn't expecting to hear from you today. There's some paperwork that I need you to look over."

"The reports? I can do that."

Hank cleared his throat. "The reports are in there, but there's also a form to sign off on for your leave."

"What leave?"

"It's standard in these cases. You take a few weeks off with pay. Rest and relax. Get yourself up to form and then when the doctor signs off, you come back to work."

"I'm not injured," I said.

"The company psychiatrist has to sign off."

"Who?"

"In a few weeks, they'll fly in, meet with you, and then you're back to work."

"That's it?" I asked, skeptical of the description. "What about the others?"

"Rider and Vincent have been stood down as well."

Stood down. That's not a term that went over well.

"Read the documents over," Hank said quickly. "I've emailed them. We'll get digital signatures and then you're on vacation."

"Got it," I said, not able to muster any enthusiasm.

I hung up the phone and stood in the kitchen thinking over the past week. Ethan must have noticed the call had ended because he joined me.

"Bad news?" Ethan asked.

"Um, I guess not," I said. An idea struck and I smiled. "Do you have any vacation time?"

He smiled. "I do. What did you have in mind?"

"I'm not sure yet, but let's get away from here for a while."

"How long do you have?"

"A few weeks."

"I know the perfect spot."

Hidden World Newsletter Sign-up

ACKNOWLEDGEMENTS

I'd like to make a special thank you to my parents, both of which supported me in their own ways while growing up. Today, they both continue to support and encourage me.

Thank you to JD Book Services and Frankie Sutton, my editors, for all of their assistance. Deranged Doctor Design has once again provided me with a wonderful cover design and formatting.

Special thanks to Erica and Oliver Jones for helping me iron out any wrinkles along the way. Many, many other family, friends, and acquaintances have been incredibly supportive. Thank you all.

Most of all I must thank my husband for his continued encouragement, patience, and assistance in all my writing endeavors.

ABOUT THE AUTHOR

Amanda Booloodian lives in Missouri with her loving, and often times peculiar, husband. In 2006, she took part in Great Beginnings and was awarded first place in the Mystery/ Thriller category. Amanda has been passionate about the written word throughout her life. Now, much of her spare time is spent at the computer, delving into worlds accessible only through vivid imagination. In warm weather, when she isn't pounding on the keyboard, she can often be found wandering through the wilderness. Occasionally she gets it into her head to SCUBA dive or to sit back at home and make wine, which can have interesting results and inspire her writing.

You can find out more about Amanda and her writing, including upcoming releases, on www.Booloodian.com. You can also find her on Facebook: Amanda Booloodian - Author, Twitter: @ajbooloodian, and Amazon: Amanda Booloodian.

Made in the USA
Lexington, KY
06 May 2017